the

portuguese

house

the

portuguese

house

pamela d holloway

Matador
9 Priory Business Park,
Wistow Road, Kibworth Beauchamp,
Leicestershire, LE8 0RX
Tel: 0116 279 2299
Email: books@troubador.co.uk
Web: www.troubador.co.uk/matador
Twitter: @matadorbooks

ISBN 978 1838591 199

British Library Cataloguing in Publication Data.
A catalogue record for this book is available from the British Library.

Printed and bound in the UK by TJ International, Padstow, Cornwall
Typeset in 11pt Sabon MT by Troubador Publishing Ltd, Leicester, UK

Matador is an imprint of Troubador Publishing Ltd

My wonderful grandchildren for all the joy they give me.
Alice, Rose, Sam, Dominic, Jacob and Rupert.

Acknowledgements

So many thanks to the supportive team at Matador/Troubador including Jonathan White and Joe Shillito. The Editor and Proofreader, Author Alfred Douglas. Dezi Dalton for, as ever her caring and enthusiastic support. Finally, Martin Wimbush (actor) for his kind and encouraging words.

chapter 1

Liz O'Malley stood on her balcony watching the sunset. It was like no sunset she had ever seen before, a great red ball sinking slowly into the sea. A boat silently moved over the water and for a moment its silhouette was like a black shadow picture against the orangey-red backdrop.

It was gone. With a sigh, she picked up the vodka and tonic from the glass-topped table and took a gulp. God, it was strong. Still, after that journey, it was exactly what was needed. For a few more moments she gazed out at the peaceful scene, the *caw-caw* of rooks sitting in the palm trees the only sound.

She sat in one of the two rattan chairs on the small balcony and leaned back, her head resting on the attached towelling-covered pillow. The last month had been difficult, no, she corrected herself, not difficult, a taste of hell. She closed her green-grey eyes in pain at her thoughts and buried her face in her hands, her thick, almost black hair falling over her face like a shield. For a moment she fought back the threatening tears. Then she could almost hear her father's voice, his lovely Irish brogue saying, "Now Elizabeth O'Malley, and what's my beautiful daughter got to cry about. Remember the O'Malleys are not quitters. Remember girl, never give in."

She smiled to herself, he had been dead almost three years now, but it was his words she always remembered in times of crisis. Padraig O'Malley had been both father and mother to his two girls when Sinead had died in the car accident that snowy Christmas. Breaking the news to his little girls, Elizabeth, aged seven, and Kathy, who was only four, had been as hard as losing Sinead all over again. He was grateful that Sinead had always said that if anything ever happened to her she would want the girls to attend her funeral and the mass. Elizabeth couldn't see the sense of it: "We won't see Mammy, she is in heaven now." Kathy had cried for her mammy. She missed the cuddles and little songs that Mammy would sing as she bathed them. So, Padraig, to his surprise, found himself singing them now, songs he didn't even know he knew, and he and his daughters bonded in a way that they never had before. It was as if Sinead was part of him now and he was able to display emotions he never knew he had.

In Derry, they all thought he was a fine father. The girls loved him and trusted his every judgement. Over the years, Liz, in particular, loved reading and writing short stories. Her father enjoyed reading the stories she wrote both at home and in school and she would write stories especially for her little sister. In time Liz became a writer and had four books published in fairly quick succession and was working on her fifth when she met Steve. He became her agent and she was swept off her feet from the moment she met him. He teased her later that from the moment he saw her "straight off the boat" he loved her too.

Her almost feline good looks and glossy black hair that hung below her shoulders like a cloak, and her pale, almost translucent skin ensnared him immediately. "My little cat," he called her in moments of affection.

Daddy, she recalled, had not been happy that she was marrying an Englishman, and a Protestant at that! But if Steve made Elizabeth happy then he accepted it and welcomed Steve into the family.

They had been so happy, she recalled. Her husband, Steve, was so proud of her achievements. Her second book had been shortlisted for the Whitbread Award and the film rights had been subsequently purchased. Oh yes, Steve was proud of her. She remembered their first serious row. They had only been married a few months when she began to talk about having a baby. Although a good Catholic girl, she had been on the pill and felt the time was right, at twenty-five, to start a family. They had talked before they married, of course, about children. "Oh dozens!" she had said carelessly when she expressed her feelings about a future family. She couldn't understand the change.

"Not yet, dear, your work is important, so is mine. We need a life together for a few more years," Steve said.

"A few years!" She had been scandalised. That night they lay as far apart as they were able. Her, up to the edge of the mattress on one side of the bed, and him up to the edge on the other side. He was cool, she remembered, in the morning, and every time she raised the subject he fobbed her off. By the time they had been married for four years she had, with deep sadness, accepted that he did not want children. Her writing became ever more her solace, and she poured out raw emotions that were not there before into her books. Her last book won the Booker Prize and Steve was proud to be at her side at all the many functions they attended. They were an A-list couple now. Young, good-looking, successful and, she in particular, talented.

Thinking back, she began to see where it had all gone wrong. She was wealthy now. Independent, while he just played the supporting role. He became withdrawn. At first, she had tried so hard to get close to him again but there seemed to be a wall between them. He went away to meet clients – and stayed overnight. She half wondered if he might be having an affair, but put it out of her mind because in bed at least life was good. He knew how to excite her and she knew she excited him. It was therefore totally out of the blue the evening he came home and instead of coming into the studio she heard him go straight to the bedroom. Intrigued, she had turned off the computer and wandered along the landing to their bedroom. He had collected one of the large holiday suitcases which was now open on the bed. "Goodness," she had said in surprise. "That looks like a long trip."

"I'm leaving," had been his response. She still hadn't grasped it. "Leaving when?" she had wondered. He had turned from the packing and looked at her, not, she noticed, quite meeting her eyes. "I'm leaving you," he had stated quite baldly. She remembered walking to the chair and almost collapsing on it. Had she heard correctly? He was leaving her…she felt a thrumming in her ears. She mustn't faint – she was made of sterner stuff, but she couldn't take it in, believe even what was happening in front of her eyes. He had closed the case and pulled it off the bed. "Just tell me why," she asked. Even now she could feel the physical pain his answer had given her. He was leaving her for Miranda. That had not been the worst. Miranda, his secretary. The secretary she had always thought so sweet, so caring, so efficient too she was always being told by Steve. The secretary who was now expecting a child. His. Steve's child. Once again, the pain seemed to cut into the very heart of her like a knife. She could hardly believe it, and he seemed happy, pleased even. She had wanted to shout and scream. Why Steve? Why her? Why not our baby? Something held her back, she managed somehow to keep her dignity, to remember she was an O'Malley. She could almost hear her father's voice in that soft brogue. "Remember Elizabeth, O'Malleys are not quitters."

She had stood up, walked back to the studio and quietly locked the door. It was only when she saw him from the window walking to his car that, knowing she was alone in the house, she could cry, but she didn't. Instead, she sat in front of the computer, turned it back on and started to write.

The divorce, uncontested of course, was going ahead with all speed. Steve didn't want his child born out of wedlock. It would be funny, she had thought over the past months, if it were not also so ironic.

She was glad her father was no longer alive to see her suffering. Her sister, Kathy, had been wonderful. They had always been close and Kathy, a successful fashion model, had come to live with her. She seemed to sense Liz's need for solitude though and never once came uninvited into the studio. She had let her flat and was planning to stay with Liz indefinitely. Her own life had been complicated enough.

The modelling world had its sleazy side and Liz had often been taken aback at some of the things she heard from her younger sister. Kathy was, as she put it, between affairs. Thank God, she was principled enough not to have affairs with married men. She swore she never wanted to marry. Miss Independence, she liked to call herself.

It had been her idea for Liz to come to India. A few months previously she had done a photo shoot on a beach in south Goa, staying at the stunning Taj Exotica Hotel. When she returned she had been full of excitement about India, longing to return and visit places other than Goa.

With Kathy's encouragement, Liz had emailed the Taj and reserved a room for a month. She had flown directly to Bombay and spent a few days sightseeing and a little desultory shopping, neither taking in the sights nor particularly interested in her purchases. Finally, she had arrived at her destination and it appeared to be all that Kathy had said.

Her arrival by air-conditioned taxi was through some of the worst housing she had seen or imagined. Shacks at the sides of the unmade-up roads, often with only plastic sheeting in the place of the walls or roofs. Women standing by water taps, ever graceful in their saris, and with the inevitable small child or children by their sides. Finally, thankfully, she had arrived at her sanctuary. The taxi had swept through the wrought-iron gates, a uniformed guard saluting as they passed. They drove through beautifully maintained gardens where bougainvillea grew in abundance and flocks of egrets pecked over the newly watered lawns.

They drove up to reception where a security guard opened her door. As she stepped out someone came forward to greet her and before she knew it, with minimal "check-in" fuss, she was whisked by buggy, her suitcases on the back, to her room.

Now, with her suitcase still packed, she was in the solitude of her room. Slowly, and with a certain reluctance, she searched in her bag for her keys and opened her main case. The thought of unpacking filled her with horror. On impulse, she delved around and found a bikini. Going to the bathroom to change she noticed a white robe hanging on a coat hanger on the back of the door. She undressed quickly, put on her bikini and the robe, and left her room following signs to the pool. The evening was dark, but the subtle lighting on palm trees or in tubs on either side of the path showed her the way.

The pool was, as Kathy had described, a wonderful oasis, particularly at night with no one around. It was like a lake with its curves edged with vegetation. The smell of frangipani and jasmine hung in the air and, as she slipped off the robe and walked down the broad steps, the water washed over her like velvet. She swam strongly, changing her stroke from breast to crawl as she turned to swim back the way she had come. She counted her strokes, it gave her an idea of how far she had swum.

Thirty-three breaststroke and sixty-seven crawl so far. Up and down she swam, at first her mind rushing from one thought to another, but gradually feeling the stress ebbing out of her.

She got out of the pool. The balmy air seemed to caress her wet skin and almost with reluctance she put the robe back on. She sat for a while taking in the scene, hardly noticed by couples crossing near her as they walked to dinner. Finally, she looked at her watch and found to her amazement it was nearly nine p.m. Taking a final look at the pool she headed back to her room realising for the first time in a while she felt hungry.

Deciding that she couldn't contemplate 'sorting out' something to wear for dinner and quite happy padding round in the robe and the towelling slippers they had provided she rang room service and ordered a light dinner. Whilst she was waiting she started to unpack and had almost finished when a knock at the door meant dinner had arrived.

Liz's days took on a regular pattern. She rose early, and at seven a.m. she was swimming in the pool. She only swam when there was nobody about and she hated the idea of lying on a sun-bed all day, so instead, she would swim early, shower and dress and have breakfast in the almost deserted open-air breakfast room. At first, she only ate fresh fruit and drank lemon tea, but after a while, she found her appetite was returning, and the chef would cook her a fresh omelette or scrambled egg and bring it to her. His smile, like that of nearly all the staff, was charming and friendly, helpful but not servile.

After breakfast she would set up her laptop on the balcony and, with an upright chair delivered to her from the dining room, she would work for up to three hours. Firstly, she would edit the previous day's work then she would continue with the plot. This book was different from previous ones as it was her first venture into the political scene and her characters were, as always, taking off in directions she had not foreseen.

Every day she read the *Times of India*, and she found it to be a revelation. Corruption seemed not only rife, but seemed to be the accepted norm in many quarters. Politicians equalled corruption in many eyes.

It began to change her own book and the research she had done before she began writing seemed almost a waste of time when here she had material she hadn't even dreamed of.

At lunch-time she walked down to the beach, wandering into one of the beach shacks where she generally ordered a litre of water, seldom wanting food. With a shudder she watched people tucking into curried eggs. Curried vegetables looked bearable, but she just wasn't hungry.

The water lasted her about an hour, and during that time she watched the walkers passing by on the beach, the dogs that, for the most part, roamed freely, generally somewhat mangy and the females frequently pregnant or obviously having had a recent litter. She felt sorry for them all. Their lives she believed must be hard and short-lived.

She noticed couples eating together and saw holiday friendships form as people met and re-met. Soon she was able to judge by their tans, whether their holidays were coming to an end or whether they had just arrived. Mostly coming from northern Europe people were, for the most part, very white when they arrived, by the end of the first week they were decidedly pink, by week two nicely tanned and those, like her she supposed, fortunate enough to stay longer were quite bronzed. Liz, despite not sitting in the sun, had turned a pale gold just from her lunch-time meanderings.

By around seven in the evening, the pool area was generally deserted and Liz would round off her day with a solitary swim in the pool. During her fourth week, she realised she was not ready to return home yet. There was, after all, nothing to go home for. She spoke to Kathy once or twice a week. Her new agent, Alex, telephoned her once and she asked him not to phone again. Apart from Kathy, she had no interest in being reminded of home.

One evening, on a sudden impulse she rang the front desk. "Liz O'Malley, room twenty-two," she announced firmly. "I would like to extend my stay for another month. To stay preferably in this room of course," she concluded. "May we call you back?" the disembodied voice answered. Liz put down the telephone, wondering as she did so if she was doing the right thing.

She noticed with a smile that the cookie jar had been restocked. Her eyes flew to the table in front of the small sofa. Yes, fresh flowers and fresh fruit. How she was enjoying these little treats. Even her towelling slippers were replaced weekly and a new pair in a new pack put neatly beside her nightdress on that enormous bed. The bed that was about a quarter slept in with only herself sleeping in it.

chapter 2

It was whilst reading *The Times* one afternoon that she saw the advertisement. Liz loved the ads, in their own way they were so informative of life in India. "Bahrain," she read. "Staff for the palace and v.i.p. families. Housemaids, house boys (under twenty-five), cooks, butlers." She envisaged the sort of households they must have to work in. She looked at the salaries with some horror, by English standards, a pittance.

Even graduates, she noticed, with several languages and skills were offered next to nothing to work in hotel receptions. Beach staff, sales staff. Mostly no prior appointments were made, just turn up on a certain day and hope you might be picked out of the hundreds of applicants.

It was on one of these days as she read through with a mixture of interest and despair about the lack of good opportunities for employment that she noticed in the "For sale" column under Property. Portuguese Villa in need of renovation. Away from the road near Benaulim Beach. There was, Liz saw, a contact number. On a sudden impulse, she pressed eight for an outside line and dialled the number. A man answered, and she didn't understand a word. He spoke quickly and although she realised it was English the dialect overtones were so strong she found it impossible to interpret!

He finally stopped talking long enough for her to speak. Very slowly and carefully she explained that she had seen the advertisement of the old Portuguese Villa for sale and she would like to see it. "Ah yes, Madame. That you can do. When would be convenient for you?" he too spoke slowly now and she understood perfectly. "Tomorrow," she began a shade hesitantly, wondering what she was getting into. "Of course, Madame. At what time, and where are you dwelling?" She smiled, glad he couldn't see her reaction to his charming English phraseology. *Early or late*, she thought, *cooler then.* "Is six o'clock alright?"

"Is that morning or evening Madame, may I enquire?"

"Six o'clock tomorrow evening." She gave her name which he solemnly repeated back as he did with the hotel name and the appointment time. She put down the telephone. "Well Liz O'Malley," she said aloud. "What have you done this time!" A sense of excitement took over. She nearly telephoned Kathy then thought better of it. Kathy might try to put her off, though knowing Kathy she probably wouldn't. Still, it was early days and probably nothing would come of it.

That evening she decided to try the beach barbecue. She knew there was one every evening and several other guests had said how good it was, but she had, up until now, found it easier to eat in her room. Tonight though, she showered and washed her hair, thankful for the dryer which at least made a stab at drying her hair. She put on a simple long white cotton dress and in case she needed it a soft pink pashmina Kathy had brought back for her after a photo shoot.

She had tried so hard not to think of Steve but dressed up ready to go out brought back memories of him eyeing her up and down before they went out. One of her favourite phrases of his was, "My little cat looks like a tiger tonight." She looked in the mirror again. "Well I don't feel like a tiger tonight," she muttered to her reflection. "I feel like a pussycat Steve, you kicked all the tiger out of me." She pulled a rueful face at herself in the mirror and, putting her room key in her evening purse, walked out into the balmy night air. It always surprised her that after the coolness of the room, even with the air-conditioning turned low, the softness of the evening air was liked being wrapped in the warmth and comfort of a lover's arms.

Liz meandered slowly along one of the paths that wove through the grounds and that would ultimately lead to the barbecue area. There was a direct route, but she found it pleasant to take in the evening like this. The stars so clear, so bright, untouched by the light pollution in London where it was seldom possible to even see the stars. The perfume of the flowers, night scented jasmine, oleander and the ever-pervading frangipani that was, she thought, as sensuous as any perfume she had worn.

By the time she reached the barbecue, it was nearly eight-thirty. The Maître d', anticipating her arrival as he saw her walking slowly in his direction, hastily checked the booking sheet. Not one single booking only twos and fours. Still, he always kept one table, the one nearest the beach. He beamed as she approached. "Good evening Madame, a table for one?" Liz nodded mutely, suddenly feeling alone and unnerved. It was times like this Steve's presence would have changed the way she felt. Arriving as a duo was so much easier.

She was shown to a table on the fringe of the beach. Two small spotlights shone in small arcs across the beach and just reached the sea. She watched in fascination as waves crashed down, the crests looking whiter under the spotlight. In moments the candle on her table, in its glass protection against the light breeze, was alight. Her waiter offered to show her around the buffet and she rose with alacrity, grateful for his help.

She followed him across the grass, which was dotted with occupied tables and lots of noisy chat. The waiter pointed out two huge copper pots of soup. One fish, he explained, the other mushroom. Then, on to a large selection of salads and terrines, both fish and chicken. Next, two chefs in their tall white hats cooked fish or steaks to one's personal preference. Then it was casseroles from lamb rogan josh to spicy curries, pasta and rice, and finally the most amazing desserts. The waiter turned to her proudly and with a flourish. Liz was alone, but suddenly she didn't feel a sense of aloneness that she had anticipated. The staff were diligently attentive. She was accompanied back to her table and her chair held out for her every time she returned after another foray to the "feast", as she mentally described it. Her wine glass was kept topped up and the music, from two very able musicians, was relaxing and not intrusive. She was glad she had taken the major step, for her, of eating out and by the time she returned to her room, she felt deliciously tired for the first time. She read for a few moments, then, putting down her book turned over with a contented sigh and fell into a dreamless sleep.

chapter 3

The next morning found her by the pool a shade later than usual. The guard and the garden boys smiled their greetings and she started her regular swimming up and down the pool, going from furthest point to furthest point of the irregularly shaped pool. Half an hour later, feeling refreshed, she slipped back into the towelling robe. She suddenly felt ravenous, despite dinner the previous evening.

After a quick shower, she put on a pair of cream shorts and a sleeveless pale blue top. Tying her hair back with a ribbon and putting on a mere touch of lipstick she found herself humming on her way to breakfast. For the first time since Steve, she felt happy and independent. She was coping – really coping – and she had an interesting appointment to look forward to later in the day.

Mr Chundra was exactly on time. Liz had arrived a few moments early and was enjoying the expansive marbled reception area with its easy chairs and sofas. She took the opportunity to change some English money and was served as usual by the beautiful Indian girl who looked smart as ever in her beige Taj uniform. Liz looked again at the lovely face and the most beautiful and darkest eyes she had ever seen.

"Madame O'Malley?" a voice beside her made her jump slightly, still bemused by the beauty and depth of those eyes. Somewhere, she decided, she must use them in a novel!

Mr Chundra, although at first overly obsequious, soon relaxed and chattered about the house he was about to show her, his neck moving from side to side as he spoke in the chatty way many of the people she had met in Goa did. The house, he explained, had belonged many years ago to a very important Portuguese government minister. When the Portuguese left Goa, he gave the house to his main "houseman" and his family. This was, Liz was informed, either the grandfather or great-grandfather of the present owner who, it transpired, was Mr Chundra himself. Liz found the whole history interesting although totally confusing, but the more he spoke the more she felt that it was what she was looking for.

The car drew up in front of a pair of finely wrought iron gates about eight feet in height Liz guessed. Mr Chundra opened the car door. "It is best we leave the car here," he said. Liz smiled, rather wishing they could drive through the gates. However, as the gate was opened, newly oiled she noticed, she understood why they couldn't drive in.

Vaguely, through the trees, she could pick out the house. The drive, or where a drive had been, was completely overgrown as were the gardens. Bushes ran into trees. Branches of trees were so intertwined it was difficult to find beginnings and endings. It was a completely overgrown and long-neglected garden.

A small path had been cleared by Mr Chundra and/or his family she correctly assumed as they made their way towards the house. At first sight, it was what she had expected. Graceful trellis balconies, wide steps up to an almost American-style porch, verandas, shutters some open, some not. That was the first glance. Then she saw broken trellis, shutters hanging by one hinge, broken steps and missing planks from the veranda.

"What a mess," she said involuntarily.

"Ah but Madame, you must see it with your soul, with your heart. Then you will know if it is right for you." Liz couldn't help smiling imagining an estate agent in England trying to sell a derelict property with such flowery language. Liz mounted the steps cautiously, feeling them move and hearing them creak as she did so. Mr Chundra produced a large key and with great solemnity tried to unlock the door. Either the lock was rusty or it was the wrong key. Whichever, Mr Chundra seemed to anticipate the problem and within moments he had opened a window and climbed inside, indicating, with his charming smile, that Liz should follow.

"That key," he said by way of explanation. "We have always had problems with it."

"Perhaps it is the wrong key?" Liz said gently, trying not to laugh at what she deemed a serious moment.

"You know Madame, I have said that very thing to my father when he was alive, and he too thought it could be the wrong key," responded Mr Chundra. Liz put her hand over her mouth to stop her laughter breaking out. He would be, she sensed, offended if she laughed.

The house was as good and as bad as Liz could have imagined. The rooms with their lovely proportions and high ceilings were in themselves perfect. The state of the rooms, of the whole house, was unbelievable. Rotten floorboards, peeling walls, limited plumbing and an archaic kitchen. Yet the more she saw, the more she wanted it. Even with the overgrown back garden, the view from the room that would be her bedroom was stunning. She caught glimpses of the sea and beach and knew opening up the vista would be inspirational for her.

She was surprised when she looked at her watch. They had been there almost two hours and Mr Chundra had lit the lamp he had brought with him. Now she needed answers to questions. "Yes," he assured her. "The house is registered, therefore it can be sold. No, you do not need a permit to renovate, unless you want to pull down the outside walls. Yes, here is water and electricity laid on to the house. No, there are no main drains, just a pit which is emptied as required. Yes, he would take an offer today and they could meet with the lawyer and the paperwork would be completed with all due speed in one week exactly."

Her questions answered, she felt she had an understanding and apart from pursuing a resident's permit and registering her tax details she was all set to move forward. "What are you expecting for this house?" she asked. He named a figure which she mentally converted to English pounds. By English standards, even for a ruin, it was low, but she knew that she must haggle a little or he would lose face! "Too much," she said firmly. Mr Chundra looked suitably downcast.

"Tell me your price," he said, his expression sufficiently forlorn to make Liz think he was either a very good actor or he was genuinely disappointed. She named a figure, he countered with a higher one, so they settled on a figure in the middle. Liz held out her hand. "You have sold your house."

*

The enormity of what she had done really hit Liz as she sat in the bar later that evening, drinking a Bloody Mary and eating marsala peanuts which she had come to adore. The trouble was, she thought a shade ruefully, that they were for her somewhat, if not totally, addictive. Still, they went well with her drink and she was as lean as a bean anyway. All her clothes hung on her these days, and although she hadn't bothered to weigh herself since Steve had left, she thought she had probably lost about fourteen pounds.

Thinking about clothes reminded her that she had noticed a tailor's sign in the village adjacent to the beach. On impulse, as she finished her drink she decided to visit the tailor and see what materials and ideas he might have. She walked quickly down the wide marble staircase and along the path to the village.

The first time she had seen the village she had been shocked by the poverty so close to the luxury and splendour of the Taj. Mud dwellings, some with corrugated roofs others with woven palm fronds and branches. Children ran around everywhere, the toddlers wearing just a short top. Nappies she realised were unheard of here. She had met several of the villagers. Pretty young girls selling sarongs and saris. Men, sometimes up to four of them, manning a small stall selling attractive papier-mâché boxes in varying sizes and shapes, and always, "Something special for you lady, we have gold, jewellery too." Liz always smiled and shook her head. The boxes, though attractive and beautifully decorated, didn't appeal to her at all.

She reached the tailor who surprisingly had brick-built premises, albeit very rough and ready. Like any tailor at home he had shelves filled with rolls of fabric and, to Liz's surprise, a number of fairly recent fashion catalogues and magazines.

Liz was looking for something long and cool with a jacket for back home. After measuring her carefully he pulled out silks and cotton for her to see. She finally chose a cream silk and arranged to have a loose shift dress and long matching jacket to go with it. The tailor tried hard to persuade her to have something else made, but she would not be persuaded. "Make this," she said, "and I will think about something else, perhaps," she added. The "perhaps" would be a necessary let-out clause if she was not happy with his workmanship. On impulse, Liz asked him if he knew anyone in the village who might be interested and capable of helping renovate a house.

She had two attempts before he completely understood. Konkani was his first language he told her. "You must find Ashok," he finally concluded. "Ashok with the bad leg."

Thanking him and following his directions, she wandered down the hard-baked track, noticing covertly curious glances coming her way. She turned right, following the directions she had been given. The track was narrower now and uneven. Large ditches were now on either side and she surmised were probably the only route for the monsoon rains. She felt a slight fear. No one knew she was here. Was she going the right way? Was she even doing the right thing? It would be so much easier to hire a firm of renovators. But, something stopped her doing that, perhaps the thought that she would be at the mercy of their foibles, delays and price increases.

About to retrace her steps she saw a young man step out of a narrow doorway. He took a step towards her and she noticed he limped very heavily. "Are you Ashok?" His smile lit up his face. His dark curly hair – his slight build. Liz judged he was only just over five feet in height which made her feel less daunted and it became clear he spoke English quite well. "Ashok," Liz said putting out her hand. "I think you may be able to help me." He indicated the narrow door he had stepped from.

"Please come into my home, lady." Just for a moment Liz hesitated, then, her heart pounding, she followed him. It was a few moments before her eyes adjusted to the gloom. Ashok was not alone. A beautiful young woman sat on the floor in a corner, suckling a baby at her breast. A little girl sat by her side, who hid her face against her mother's body when she saw Liz looking her way.

The mud hut, for that is what it was, was about seven feet by ten and as Liz stood there wondering what next, Ashok spread a rug on the floor and indicated she should sit. Her eyes were now totally adjusted to the gloom when it suddenly went even darker. The doorway was crammed with curious villagers wanting to know what this tall pale visitor wanted.

Ashok waved his hand. "Go away," he said in English. They melted away and Liz felt more comfortable. She began to talk about the house, how she wanted to live there. How much work needed to be done. "The tailor," she explained, "told me you might be able to help me." Ashok was silent for a few moments. Finally, when he spoke, he spoke slowly, carefully.

Afterwards, long afterwards, she realised he spoke as he did because he could not believe that someone was offering him work. So often because he was a cripple – that's what they called him – he was turned away because able-bodied men could do the work faster.

"I can do anything and everything, and because the people in my village need work they will do as I tell them. We have carpenters, builders – some who are good with gardens. Because we are a poor village and there is little work nearby we go from being poor to being poorer."

"I will pay you a fair wage." Liz countered, wondering if she was being totally stupid. Steve would have gone to Panaji, found a large company and given them the contract. Yet Liz felt, she had a gut feeling she was doing the right thing, not just for her – but for the house and for the people in this small community.

Ashok knew the house. "Sometimes we may sleep there if we do many hours?" he asked.

Liz nodded. "I haven't got the papers yet. I have all the legal things to see to before it is mine, but I will come back and see you and tell you more." Ashok smiled a smile that made him look so young that for a moment Liz wondered if she was making a mistake, but again, some gut feeling made her feel that this was somehow meant to be. Ashok stood. The meeting was over. His wife smiled shyly, and the little girl once again buried her head in the folds of her mother's sari.

The baby had stopped suckling and Ashok took the child. "My son," he said proudly laying the small child in a hammock made of sari-type fabric and attached by hooks or nails to the mud walls. He bent down and picked up the shy little girl and announced equally proudly: "And this is my daughter Maya." His wife stood and Liz shook her hand, then Ashok's, before going out through the narrow door and onto the now dark path.

"This way," a quiet voice said. It was Ashok's wife. She took Liz's hand and led her back to where the lights from the hotel grounds would light her way.

chapter 4

The next few weeks were wonderfully frantic. Once again Liz extended her stay at the hotel and, apart from a few hours writing every morning, the rest of her time was taken up with the house. She had found herself a lawyer and with a certain exchange of cash she now owned a residential permit and the house. She was aware that he would get as much money from her as possible and had asked him to present a monthly account. Sadly for him, all good things come to an end and with reluctance, he agreed with her that there was nothing else he could do for her. They parted on good terms both aware that one might need the other in the future!

Kathy and Liz talked regularly. Liz was happy that Kathy not only thought what Liz had done was a good idea, but was planning to visit as soon as her current commitments were completed. Liz stalled her as much as she could, she wanted her to see the house when all the work was completed and that was still a while off.

Ashok had become her right-hand man, her general factotum. He seemed to spend most of his time there at the house overseeing everything. There were now five men working full time on the gardens, front and rear. The drive had been cleared to reveal a well-laid surface and gradually the front garden was taking shape. In the far left corner near the front tumbledown wall they had found a dilapidated hut. Looking at it one evening as she walked around now more easily than before, Liz inspected it for the first time. It had a decent door, though the hinges needed replacing. The windows needed new glass and inside she discovered two rooms, one with a fireplace and chimney perfect for cooking. The other room, which was the same size, could be used as a bedroom. There was, she discovered, an area behind the back of the hut and the outside wall was large enough for a simple wash area and a lavatory could be fitted too. Liz looked thoughtful as she walked back to the house. The little hut had real possibilities.

The taxi was waiting for her and she carefully locked the front door which had now been fitted with a new lock and key by a locksmith from a nearby village, one of Ashok's contacts of course. Now the house was secure, work had begun seriously on the inside. The taxi driver stopped the car to close the gates firmly behind them and Liz began to feel that she would prefer to stay behind rather than go back to the hotel though she knew she was weeks away from that pleasure.

That evening she dressed in the new tailor-made dress. She put the jacket on too, feeling the light breeze on her bare arms. She put her hair up and small tendrils caused by the humidity formed little curls at her neck. The staff knew her so well now they all greeted her warmly. Not many guests stayed for so long and, despite her own discretion, word was getting around about the old house she was doing up.

Her favourite chef greeted her warmly. Liz chose roasted vegetables with a piquant sauce he had made especially for her. "You are such a wonderful chef," she murmured.

"Madame O'Mal" – they all called her that now, she thought perhaps it was easier for them to say – "Madame, when you look for a chef, my young brother is in training. He is even better than me," he added generously. Liz smiled in response, she hadn't got that far but living here in Goa anything was possible.

The next afternoon found her searching for Ashok. The gardeners were hard at work and in the house, the new marble floors looked wonderful. There was noise everywhere as men painted and hammered. The new wiring and plumbing had been completed and, in a week's time, the three new bathrooms would be installed.

She finally found Ashok in the back garden. His team had started to clear the last part of the garden that morning. Rajiv had called him and shown him what he had just found. A mother cat with three very newly born kittens. "Shall I kill them?" Rajiv wanted to know. Normally he wouldn't have asked, cats were a nuisance, like most of the dogs around.

"Better not," replied Ashok, thinking about Madame O'Mal. He had seen her sometimes stroking the stray cats around the hotel. He had even seen her take food to stray dogs on the beach. Ashok found her behaviour puzzling. He and Nina sometimes had barely enough to eat, before Madame's appearance anyway. "Leave them alone," he informed Rajiv. "I must ask Madame O'Mal." Rajiv nodded, he too understood that she was not like them with the animals.

Ashok found her by the brick hut. "Ah, Ashok I have been looking for you," she said.

"I too have been looking for you, Madame. I have something to show you."

"But—" Liz began then changed her mind. Her plan could wait. "Please follow," he said quaintly. His English was so good, even though he had left school at twelve. He had told her he was a clever student and she had no reason to doubt him.

24

Intrigued, she followed him around the house and into the back garden. Ducking under branches still waiting to be cut and weaving through shrubs in full flower, if not overgrown, she saw Rajiv eyeing her curiously and gave him a half smile. What was going on! Ashok stopped quite suddenly and pulled back some branches. He pointed. She leaned forward to look, wondering what she was supposed to be looking at. The eyes of the mother cat were frightened. She had thought she was safe, tucked away like this. The tiny mews made Liz look closer. There nestling close to their mother three tiny kittens. One wholly black, one black and white and the third the palest ginger. The mother, so protective, seemed to pull the kittens closer to her. "Leave the area alone," she said to Ashok, speaking as quietly as she could. "Leave plenty of space all around them."

The following morning, her writing was left as she took a taxi to Panaji. There, as she couldn't find cat food, she purchased tins of corned beef and sardines. At the last moment, she remembered a tin opener and a large tin of powdered milk. At the market she bought some small plastic dishes and then asked the driver to take her back to Benaulim and, once there, directed him to the house.

Liz couldn't wait to open one of the tins and chop up some sardines. The kittens were alright at present, being fed somehow by a hungry mother cat. Even the quick glance Liz had had showed the mother cat was pitifully thin. Soon she was walking back through the garden. As instructed the gardeners had left a big swathe of untouched overgrowth around the little family. She heard the mews before she reached them, three hungry kittens demanding to be fed. Easing the branches and undergrowth back she spoke softly to the mother cat, telling her that there was food and milk for her. The mother cat looked but didn't move so Liz moved away and stood silently, scarcely breathing. After a few moments, her patience was rewarded. The mother cat, thin, oh so thin – a tabby – crept stealthily out of cover, the lure of food too much. She put her nose in the milk. Uncertain, she left it and tried the sardines. This was more to her taste and every last morsel disappeared. She tried the milk now. The creamer had been mixed with water, and now thirsty, the cat started to lap.

Liz watched in fascination at the dainty *lap-lap*, until the small bowl was empty. To her surprise, the cat came slowly towards her and Liz heard purring as the cat circled her ankles a few times before returning to her babies.

It became a daily ritual and before long the mother cat seemed to trust Liz, even allowing her to stroke and then cuddle each kitten in turn. Ashok and Rajiv looked on in amazement at this strange behaviour, but they were learning Madame O'Mal had her own set of rules.

chapter 5

Returning to the hotel late one evening, Liz found an email from her agent wondering why she had stopped sending the latest chapters of her novel. It all seemed so far away. Agents, books, even writing. For the first time in years, Liz was having a real holiday and loving every moment of her busy, fulfilling life. She emailed Alex saying she was catching up with other things at the moment and was giving herself at least a month off. If he was dismayed he didn't let her know, just sent a brief and totally satisfactory response: "Message received and understood. Alex."

Liz had been full of plans for the small building in the grounds. Feeling rather guilty that she had not done anything about it yet, she sought Ashok out one morning. He was watching two men from Panaji tiling the bathrooms. He had never seen walls tiled before and was full of astonishment. Liz forgot sometimes he still lived in a mud hut. He looked guilty when he saw her, expecting her to be cross that he was wasting time. As far as Liz was concerned, everything he saw broadened his knowledge and he would be even more useful.

"Ashok—" she began.

"Madame O'Mal, I shouldn't be here. I should be seeing the carpenters in the bedrooms."

She smiled. Yes, he should, but she liked him to learn new things all the time. "Ashok please come with me." Ashok felt worried. What if she sent him away? His whole life had changed, now every week she paid him and the men he had found to do the gardens, the woodwork, the painting. Now perhaps she had no further use for him and Nina would cry. For the first time in their three-year marriage, they could eat less meagrely. Ashok wouldn't let Nina have all the money for food. He hid some in the crack he had made in the wall. One day, soon perhaps, Madame would no longer need him.

Thinking doleful thoughts, he followed her down the stairs, being careful with his bad leg not to slip on the marble stairs. She continued to walk through the front door and down the drive. Ashok followed as quickly as he could, his leg aching at the knee with the effort. He put his right hand down to assist the movement in his leg when Madame suddenly stopped and pointed to a corner of the front garden, where the little house stood, an area she had told him to leave alone.

Smiling in anticipation of what she was about to tell him, she was suddenly concerned. In her eagerness to share her plan she had made him hurry, which she knew hurt his leg. She knew better now than to apologise, it drew attention to his disability which he didn't like. She stood patiently for a few seconds until he was by her side.

"Ashok," she began. "How would you, Nina and the children like to live there? It needs a lot doing to it, of course, running water, washing facilities, lavatory, cooking area—" She was allowed to go no further. Ashok took her hand and kissed it. He drew himself to his full height and looked her straight in the eyes. He seemed, unusually, incapable of speech. Then the words tumbled out one after another, so fast she could barely understand. She smiled and waited for him to become calmer. "Oh, Madame O'Mal, a brick house, a proper roof, but I cannot pay."

"Ashok, let's go and look inside." Secretly, when everyone had left the site, she had swept through and realised it was bigger than her first impression. It must have been a workshop and the ceiling was high enough for a platform to have been erected. With a modest stair it could be a mezzanine sleeping area for Ashok and Nina and, with the addition of a window cut into the roof, they would have light and air.

"I shall pay you Ashok. You and Nina to live here. Nina can help in my house and you will keep the gardens in good order and do any maintenance and repair work." Ashok looked puzzled. "Then when I am away in England I will know that my home here is well looked after. Tomorrow, I want you to bring Nina here so we can plan how things will be. I will arrange for the water and electricity." Ashok kept shaking his head. He could hardly believe what he was hearing. A proper house, work for him and Nina. All he wanted was to go home and tell her the news.

His face mirrored his thoughts. "Would you like to go and tell Nina?" Liz asked. His smile, a wonderfully happy smile that said more than words ever could, lit his face. He could hardly speak, he was so full of emotion. "You go, Ashok, please." Liz watched him limping away as fast as he could without even a backward glance. He didn't want her to see the tears running unchecked down his cheeks. It was a long walk home for him and she hoped he would manage to hitch a ride from one of the many two-wheelers that passed that way searching for business.

Two hours later Ashok arrived with Nina and the baby. They had left Maya, their daughter, with a neighbour. Nina was so shy. Her English was much more limited than Ashok's and she seemed somewhat dazed by the news. Liz saw them arrive and saw Ashok paying a taxi driver – one hundred rupees. She knew he and Nina had never been in a taxi before, and to hire one and pay for it out of their precious earnings was a huge step.

Liz watched as Ashok pointed to the "house" and led the way. They disappeared through the door and Liz could not imagine what was going on in their minds.

"It's a palace," Nina said, inside the small house. "Are you sure we can live here? What happens if she sends us away and someone else has our home?"

"There will be water and electricity, and look, Nina, look up there. Madame O'Mal says we could put steps up and we could sleep up there."

"We might roll off in the night." Nina sounded anxious.

"I shall put boards along, like a fence," Ashok responded. Nina was silent.

"I don't believe it," she said finally.

"Wait, wait here." As quickly as his legs would allow, Ashok walked through the garden to the main house. Before the renovations had been done, he used to just walk in the main door. Now, with marble floors everywhere and lights hanging from the ceilings, it seemed so important a place that he knocked. Liz had seen him coming but decided to wait. She noticed he knocked now and realised they would soon have to talk about his comings and goings, but for now, she was sure he wanted to talk about the hut.

"She doesn't believe me," he began. "Madame O'Mal, please tell her it is all true." He sounded so upset that Liz knew she must take this conversation very seriously.

"I will talk to her straight away," she said, walking out of the house and keeping pace with the anxious young man at her side.

Nina was finally convinced. Liz couldn't help it, she felt so happy at their happiness that she felt warm inside. When the idea had first occurred to her she had thought how good it would be to have someone living nearby, but seeing the couple's reaction she recognised that she benefitted from their happiness, because she felt happy too.

chapter 6

The flight to Mumbai was quite straightforward. To Liz's relief, she found internal flights considerably easier than arriving or leaving the country, which was a hideously long drawn out procedure.

Although she was only flying internally she had heard gruesome tales of bureaucracy in the extreme. Pleasantly surprised she arrived in Mumbai and took a taxi to the Taj hotel, Mumbai. She had arranged to stay for three nights as she was sure she could choose furniture for her bedroom, two guest rooms, dining room and sitting room within that time.

The hotel was as expected. The staff were extremely helpful and the following morning she was whisked in an air-conditioned taxi from major store to major store. Finally, she had chosen everything she needed including fabrics for Nargis, the tailor's wife who was going to make her curtains.

Liz enjoyed the bustle of the city, trying not to become too disturbed by the poverty, but being very aware of it. It seemed somehow worse in the general melee of Mumbai than in the more rural Benaulim. The poverty was the same she supposed but it felt harder to cope with.

On the return flight, she closed her eyes and visualised her new home with all the things she had purchased. Her mind wandered over the newly completed bathrooms and her splendid kitchen, her laundry area with the staff dining area off it. In one week she surmised, when the furniture arrived, she could move in. The curtains would not be made but she could close the newly repaired and painted shutters, sparkling white with a soft green trim.

The intricate iron trellis balconies upstairs and around the veranda downstairs had now been completely repaired and painted. She had tried to match the paint to the original, which she described as a "quiet green" to Kathy in one of their many chats.

The linen had arrived safely from Peter Jones in England, all now stored away in the huge linen cupboard one of Ashok's carpenters had made. Ashok had come up trumps, she thought, with painters, carpenters, gardeners and builders to rebuild the adobe-style outside walls around the grounds that had been tumbling down all over the place.

Electricians and plumbers had come from Panaji, the capital of Goa, along with the bathroom suites and kitchen. Liz longed to check out of the hotel. It had been wonderful, they had looked after her so well. She was now a "gold" guest because of the money she had spent with them and had been very spoiled and pampered. But now, quite suddenly, with the end in sight, she longed to move "home". The cats would enjoy it too. Gradually, she had gained the mother cat's trust and had decided she wanted to adopt this little family. First of all, Liz decided she needed a proper bed for them. The baskets that the hotel returned clean laundry in would be perfect. On impulse she requested the housekeeper to come to her room. The poor woman arrived looking very anxious and she was so relieved at the request, having expected a complaint, she immediately offered two! At first, Liz demurred, then realising that kittens grow, changed her mind and accepted, insisting she must pay for them. Despite her pleas, the housekeeper refused to accept any payment. Liz thanked her warmly and mentally added something extra to the tip she had planned to give her when she checked out.

Armed with the dimensions of the baskets, Liz asked the tailor's wife to make her some flat covered padding and covers that were washable. She chose a bright fabric and finished up with zippered covers that would be easy to remove from the pads for washing two quite upmarket cat beds!

Sanjay, one of the carpenters, was prevailed upon to make a cat flap from the garden into the laundry room. Though why Madame wanted cats in the house no one could understand. "Do you think she might be a bit mad in the head?" Sanjay asked Ashok in all seriousness.

"No, it is just that Madame O'Mal is not like us."

"Mad," concluded Sanjay.

Liz arrived back at the hotel, showered and changed, and then went to see the general manager who had become a friend. "I am leaving in one week," Liz informed Vihaan de Sousa. "I just wanted you to know before I told the front desk."

"The villa is ready?" he asked. She nodded. "Do you know what it is called by the locals?"

Liz shook her head in surprise, she hadn't even thought of a name for her new home yet. "What have they come up with?" she asked.

"Villa O'Mal," he grinned as he spoke. "I think it is quite good."

"Well," she answered thoughtfully. "They call me Madame O'Mal, so why not Villa O'Mal." It seemed as if the last piece of the jigsaw puzzle had slotted into place. She was going home next week. Going home to Villa O'Mal.

chapter 7

The furniture had arrived as promised from Mumbai. Liz was so excited, she felt as if she was having all her Christmases at once. The furniture, which she had chosen with such care, in her opinion, looked better in the Villa than in the shops where she had first viewed it! Her bedroom with its king-sized bed and the built-in cupboards, built to her design by Sanjay, plus a dressing table and padded stool.

The marble floor now had rugs on either side of the bed and another rug by a low table placed near the veranda windows, with a comfortable chair so she could sit and enjoy the view of the gardens. Feeling incredibly contented she sat for the very first time in the chair she had carefully selected. A deep sigh escaped from her as she leaned back, marvelling in the transformation that had been wrought in the garden.

Now, she could see the beach between the palm fronds – and the glitter of the sea in the bright afternoon sunlight. Standing up, she realised that apart from Nina who needed training, she had not organised the household staff she needed. The hotel chef's brother had not yet been for an interview and, even if he had, the top floor needed work done to redesign it into more suitable staff quarters than the Portuguese had provided for their staff.

Liz walked into the huge bathroom with its built-in linen cupboard. She had decided it would be practical if each of the bathrooms had storage for bed and bathroom linen, so that when beds were stripped and towels removed for laundry the replacements would be to hand. She also felt it would be an easier way of controlling her purchases. It also provided space for cleaning materials and spare toiletries which were not needed immediately.

Her bathroom, with its sunken bath, had a generous shower corner fully glassed-in. A small design on the marble there and the touch of peach was picked up by the towels. A generous bath sheet and two hand towels awaited use. Liz couldn't help but feel proud of all she had achieved and tonight she and Nina would make up the bed. It would give the young woman her first experience of working in the house.

Later that evening Liz telephoned the number she had been given for Aarav, the potential cook. At first, there seemed confusion at the number she rang, but after repeating her request to speak to Aarav several times to a variety of voices, she was finally understood. "Madame?" a clear voice said down the line.

"Aarav?" Liv asked.

"Yes, is that Madame O'Mal?" Liz grinned, the name was obviously a fixture now. After several minutes they arranged for Aarav to come and see her the next afternoon. He suggested, and Liz thought it a brilliant idea, that he bring ingredients with him and cook her a meal. "What do you prefer?" he wanted to know.

"Indian, Chinese or International." Liz was charmed. If he was as good as he sounded she may well have found the perfect cook. Chef, she corrected herself mentally, they did prefer that title and if he was good, why not!

The following day Aarav arrived promptly on his bicycle. The ingredients carefully strapped in a box on the pillion. As soon as she met him Liz was taken by his infectious enthusiasm and his longing to cook something she would enjoy. She had decided for tonight she would eat Indian food. Goan she found didn't really appeal to her and Goan rice she found chewy and unpalatable. No, tonight Indian, and yes, she had told Aarav, she liked it moderately spicy.

Once or twice she wandered into the kitchen. First, he was chopping and preparing. Then, wonderfully aromatic smells emanated from that direction. He was scandalised when she came back into the kitchen for the third time. She realised he didn't want her there – he was, she felt – a genius at work! She showed him the extractor fan she had installed, otherwise, despite closed doors, her entire house would smell of curry!

At exactly seven p.m. the pre-arranged time, she went into the dining room. Nina, having been shown the intricacies of bed-making, had also been shown how to set the table. Talking about it later to Ashok she confessed to finding it all very strange. They had already moved in to their little home with its new simple wood floors and cotton rugs given to them by Liz. She had also bought mattresses – one larger one for Ashok and Nina, and a smaller one for their daughter. She had also bought a cot for the baby but they were not sure they wanted to use it as the baby usually slept with them. Nina and Ashok were trying to get used to the comfort of the mattress which rested on a low frame that Ashok had made. More often than not though, they slept on their old familiar rug on the floor!

The couple ate their food with their fingers, scooping up their rice more easily than Liz did with a fork. Nina found the array of cutlery on the table excessive for just one person. "It all has to be washed and polished as well Ashok."

Ashok put his arm around his pretty wife. "She has taken good care of us and of our children. Now we must take care of Madame O'Mal as long as she needs us, maybe our whole life." Nina was silent. It was true. They had more than they ever dreamed possible; for now, though, she felt confused by the big villa and all the things she had to learn. Even Ashok had changed because of Madame. He now wore leather sandals on his feet and smart navy shorts and loose tee shirts in the same colour, and Madame had even bought him a hat to protect his head as he worked in the gardens.

Liz sat patiently waiting for her dinner to appear. Aarav, looking taller than ever in his chef's hat, came into the dining room carrying, no bearing, she smiled inwardly thinking, as he walked towards her with the first course. "I have made chaat dahi batata puri Madame O'Malley, for your starter tonight. I hope you will enjoy this." He put it solemnly in front of her and the delicious aroma of the sauce was as tasty to eat as to breathe in.

The main course was a simple chicken jalfrezi and it was one of the best she had ever tasted. For dessert, he produced mango ice-cream with green coloured halwa – feather light and a sufficiently small portion that despite having eaten so well she managed to eat and enjoy. She sat back feeling relaxed. This decision was one of the easiest she had made.

Aarav came in to inquire if she would like coffee. Liz shook her head, she could tell he was on tenterhooks. "Aarav that was one of the most delicious dinners I have ever had." Aarav beamed. He waited, thinking this was a good sign. Madame took a small sip of white wine. Aarav felt his heart beating faster. "The flavours you created tonight were amazing, strong, yet subtle. The meat was so tender and the rice the lightest, fluffiest, I think I have ever tasted." She stood up. "Come with me Aarav." She led the way to the sitting room with its cream sofas and bright silk scatter cushions in deep pinks, blues and yellows. They would have looked garish in England but here their splashes of colour only seemed to emphasise the restful room they were in. "Please sit Aarav," Liz indicated a chair. Aarav sat feeling somewhat overawed. Madame O'Mal seemed pleased but this was the moment of truth.

"Aarav, what can I say? The dinner tonight was superb. Is your International, Chinese and Goan cooking as good?" For a moment Aarav looked modestly at the floor. Then, squaring his shoulders, he looked Liz steadily in the eyes.

"I shall make occasional mistakes Madame, or cuisine that may not appeal to you, but I can say I am a good chef." Liz smiled. She loved the directness of these Goans. She stood up and walked towards him holding out her hand. He stood immediately.

"If you are happy to take the job, then I am happy to employ you." She named a figure that was beyond his dreams.

"The top floor of this house will be for staff. The work there has not really started yet, but if you don't mind it being a bit basic you are welcome to move in straight away. I will go to Panaji tomorrow to buy furniture for your room." Aarav almost danced. He could hardly wait to thank his older brother for the recommendation – and his mother, father and sisters would be so proud of him. He would be able to give them money every week and make a real contribution to the family. It was what was expected and what he wanted to do.

"I shall arrive tomorrow Madame in time for me to cook your dinner."

chapter 8

Liz felt lonely. The house felt big and empty now Aarav had left. He had cleaned the kitchen until it gleamed, she would have no worries on that score. The huge extractor fan had done its work and the room smelt only sweet with the faint fragrance of herbs.

The following morning, before leaving for Panaji, Liz telephoned the *Navhind Times* to place an advertisement for a housekeeper. She made it clear that the person must be fully trained. After all, she thought, this person must train Nina too. Nina, she quickly realised, was willing, but a little confused and frightened by the size, and to her, the luxury of the Villa O'Mal. Even Liz thought of it by that name now, and Vihaan de Sousa, the hotel manager and now her friend, had even had the name carved in stone as a house-warming gift. It stood like a sentinel, at the left side of the wrought-iron entrance gates for all to see and admire.

Kathy was coming to stay. At last Liz was ready for her. She had started writing again and the smallest room on the ground floor overlooking the back garden had become her study. Aarav had moved in, sleeping at first on a simple rug, but within a week the furniture for his room on the top floor had arrived along with furniture for the other two bedrooms. The two lavatories on that floor had been fitted earlier and the one bathroom was almost completed. Liz felt a great sense of satisfaction that her new home was so nearly ready from top to bottom.

Kathy was bringing a male friend. She had told Liz that he was a really good friend but nothing more. Kathy had been so insistent that Liz thought the reverse was probably true, but nevertheless Nina and she had made the beds up in both guest rooms. Nargis continued to make good progress with the curtains. Sumptuous curtains now hung from the rails, the windows in the sitting room and one pair were up in Liz's bedroom. Nargis was making them far better than Liz could have hoped and by using pictures from English magazines Nargis had quickly understood what Liz required.

Ashok was having driving lessons. Liz had bought a Hyundai, she didn't want or need anything pretentious, preferring for the most part to use taxis. Today, however, when meeting Kathy and Ronnie a taxi might not have the capacity. She found driving a total nightmare. Officially the driving was on the left, but of course, if there happened to be a large pothole, of which there were plenty, then quite calmly the drivers would drive happily on the right whether heavily laden lorries or a myriad of two-wheelers were coming directly towards them or not.

So, Ashok was learning to drive. At Liz's insistence, he inched slowly up and down the drive practising clutch control. He had driven her once and she had to keep her eyes closed for most of the journey. Not yet confident enough of driving her to the airport, Liz made the major decision to drive herself. Allowing plenty of time to get lost, she actually drove straight there, but the drive was not without its hairy moments. Stray dogs, blaring horns, potholes that in trying to avoid pushed her into oncoming traffic. "The sooner Ashok learns to drive the better," she muttered to herself along with a number of expletives she had never verbalised before!

Having parked the car Liz walked into the airport and straightaway saw her sister, Kathy, and a tall lanky chap that must be Ronnie. His hair, blonde, hung over his face half hiding it and she could see, even from a distance, the warmth between the two of them. For a moment she felt excluded from the magic circle, but soon Kathy was hugging her and the sisters clung to each other, equally happy to be together. "This is Ronnie," Kathy said, finally extricating herself from Liz's arms. He was tall, at least six feet something, and so thin Liz felt a puff of wind would blow him over.

"You can call me Ronnie if you like, though it isn't my real name," he said as he shook Liz's hand. Kathy laughed. "Darling, you are Ronnie to everyone, you know you are." There was a certain intimate banter between the pair that Liz found confusing. Kathy had been so definite that they were "really good mates", nothing more.

Whilst Liz tried to keep her entire attention on the road with its many hazards, Kathy talked non-stop with Ronnie chipping in a word here and there. Kathy had of course been to Goa before for the photo shoot, but Ronnie oohed and aahed as he saw the abject poverty, with mean huts adjacent to the road, to run-down old villas that had once seen grander days.

"I'm longing to see your villa," Kathy said excitedly.

"Well, here we are Kathy darling!" Ashok was at the gates and opened them as they turned off the road. Kathy saw the huge stone with Villa O'Mal carved into its surface. Before she could ask why the strange name she had her first sighting of the villa and she and Ronnie said, almost together, "Why, it's stunning. It's heavenly." Liz felt a warm glow. In a way, she was used to its gentle beauty now, almost finding it hard to remember how it used to be.

The new housekeeper opened the door, wearing the simple grey and yellow sari that she had chosen as her "uniform". Anjali, as she liked to be called, had been one of six interviewees, and in Liz's opinion, she had all the qualities that had been required. For the past four years, she had worked for a diplomatic family in Panaji, who now no longer needed her as they were moving to Delhi and fully staffed accommodation. She had been taken on as a housemaid, but soon outshone the housekeeper and the family had promoted her, getting rid of her lackadaisical predecessor. Anjali had quickly built a rapport with Nina and together they spoke Hindi and Konkani and some English. Ashok was teaching Nina English too and the girl was gaining in confidence.

Anjali welcomed the guests and hoped Madame O'Malley's journey had not been too hazardous. Anjali was the only member of Liz's staff who called her by her correct name, and it distinguished her from the rest of the staff as if she was the most senior, which in fact she was.

"Aarav has put tea and cookies in the sitting room, or would you prefer to go straight to your rooms?" Anjali asked.

"Tea and cookies sound wonderful." Kathy winked at Liz in response. Liz read volumes into it. "Darling Liz this is bliss. How have you done it? And last but not least I am glad to see you looking so happy."

Liz didn't return to work, it was so lovely having Kathy staying with her, and she smiled as she thought of the wink, interpreting it as connected to her relationship with Ronnie. Kathy's presence was really the icing on the cake at the end of her project.

Ronnie had exclaimed when he saw the cool comfort of the sitting room with its restful outlook on the gardens. "Can I see the sea?" Kathy spoke excitedly.

"You wait until you see the view from your bedrooms." The main bedrooms all overlooked the back gardens with the view that Liz so adored. She hoped her first house guests would feel the same.

The lemon tea drunk and enjoyed, and the freshly baked cookies consumed, Liz then accompanied her guests up the curved marble staircase. She showed Ronnie his room first. She had made one of the rooms less feminine with shades of soft blue and green. She showed him the bathroom too, with its restful colours being picked out by the softly luxurious towels. "This is a taste of heaven," Ronnie exclaimed, as the sisters left him to unpack his belongings and shower and change.

"Dinner at seven p.m.," Liz informed him, rather hoping he would keep to his room until then, leaving her with an opportunity to catch up with her sister.

Kathy's room displayed its yellow tones with the curtains and bedspread finished just before they arrived from the airport. Nargis had been putting in overtime in order to complete the sewing before Madame's important guest arrived.

Once alone, the sisters sat on the sofa by the open French doors in Kathy's bedroom. "Will you ever be able to tear yourself away from all this?" Kathy wanted to know.

"I'm not sure," Liz said thoughtfully. "I think it will get harder, not easier, but I think it is important I do come home to England from time to time." The girls were silent, each wrapped in their own thoughts. Kathy, observing Liz, realised she had not seen her look this happy for several years, and Liz was so happy to see her younger sister but full of questions about Ronnie.

"Tell me about Ronnie," she began tentatively. "What on earth is his proper name?"

Kathy smiled. "You do realise he is as gay as the poofiest poof." Liz swallowed hard. How stupid of her, she should have realised. "Why 'Ronnie'?"

"Veronica Lake hairstyle, blonde and over one side of the face. His real name is Walter, Walter Lake. Then people started saying he had a real Veronica Lake hairstyle and before he knew it, it was shortened to Ronnie. He is a dear, Liz, and such a good friend." Liz wanted to know what he did for a living. "He is an artist, not at all bad actually. One or two exhibitions, he just about survives off his work, but as things so often go. He has had an unhappy time lately. His partner died, and when he heard I was coming to see you he asked if he could come too. You don't mind do you, Liz?"

"Sweetie, of course, I don't mind – the more the merrier. I have so many staff looking after me it will be good for them all to work a little harder! I have invited friends to join us for dinner tonight. The general manager of the Taj Hotel and his wife. They have become very dear friends."

The girls talked for a while longer and then noticing her sister trying to stifle a yawn she stood up, kissed her sister on the forehead and suggested she had a rest and later she could shower and dress and come down around seven p.m. "I will ask Aarav to make dinner for seven-thirty giving us time to have a cocktail first."

Liz phoned the hotel and told Vihaan to arrive at seven rather than six-thirty which had been the original plan. Feeling everything was now in place, Liz went to her bedroom and sat at her favourite spot, breathing in the cooling evening air. The sun had started its journey towards the sea and despite the mosquito screen she revelled in the ever spectacular beauty of the sunset. Life felt good. She had her household. She had Ashok and Nina. She had her sister and Ronnie staying with her, and dear friends coming to dinner. All seemed right with the world…

chapter 9

It was while Kathy was staying with her that Liz thought she had another family of kittens in the garden. The original quartet now acted as if they owned the place. Mother Cat, as she was known, had been spayed and as soon as they were old enough Liz planned to have the kittens spayed too. She didn't want to part with them, but equally, she had no desire to be over-run with cats. The black kitten, who had surprisingly blue eyes, was unsurprisingly called Blue. The black and white one, a female, was named Dotty, and the smallest, and Liz's personal favourite, the pale ginger who had incredible rings of deeper ginger going up its legs like bangles. She called him Little Kat and he followed her everywhere. He seemed to sense her moods and when to play and when to lie still on her lap, lifting his head at intervals to look at her with his tiger eyes.

"My little tiger," she would say caressingly, and he would purr profusely. Kathy was amazed.

"You don't even like cats, Liz." Liz laughed. She didn't "before", and she didn't like cats in general, but these, her cat family, were like her children.

The first dinner party had gone well. Ronnie in his languid way had a knack of saying the most priceless things. Liz was already growing extremely fond of him and could quite see why Kathy valued his friendship.

It would soon be time for Kathy to return to England. She had been booked for a catalogue shoot for an Italian company based on Lake Como, which she thought would be quite fun as well as lucrative. Ronnie, on the other hand, seemed to have quite settled in.

Every morning Liz wrote, Ronnie painted and Kathy went out with Ashok in the car. She was, Liz told her, very brave. Kathy enjoyed the experience though, heart-stopping though it was at times. Ashok seemed to gain in confidence and, at Kathy's importuning, he applied to take his test. Indian tradition allowed for family and friends to be in the car during the test and Ashok asked Kathy to sit in the back. Nina had said she would scream all the time, so Kathy, with some misgivings, agreed.

To Liz's amazement, Ashok passed his test and was now a fully accredited driver! Liz was nothing like as confident as Kathy about his driving ability, though Kathy assured her sister that Ashok had improved radically.

Ronnie sought his hostess out, three days before they were due to leave. "Liz, dear Liz," he began. "Can I ask the most enormous favour? Can I possibly stay on for a little while longer? I feel inspired here, the light is so wonderful, I am painting better than ever," he paused. Liz smiled happily. She had been dreading the thought of them both leaving, now, although she would miss Kathy dreadfully, she would enjoy having Ronnie around. He was such good company.

So, with Ashok driving, Liz and Ronnie went to see Kathy off. There were tears from both sisters and Kathy promised she would phone as soon as she was home. She had agreed to put Liz's house up for rent through Savills and arrange for certain items to be stored.

It was good to have Ronnie with her on the homeward journey and, while Ashok was putting the car in the refurbished garage at the end of the drive, Ronnie disappeared to walk on the beach and Liz wandered aimlessly around the garden, snapping off dead flower heads as she saw new shoots where major cutbacks had taken place. It was then she heard the mew. *Drat*, she thought. *I really do not want more cats.* She followed the sound and saw a small bundle of something tucked under a branch. *Not much protection against the sun*, she thought. *Silly cat.* She pulled away a scrap of material, and there, naked to the world, was a tiny baby girl, her face screwed up with crying. Liz ran to the gate and looked up and down the road. No one, nothing. She went back to the baby and gingerly picked her up, scared she might hurt her. The baby stopped crying and opened its eyes in surprise. Liz felt her heart miss a beat, she had never seen so young a child perhaps almost a newborn she wondered.

She kicked the front door with her foot, not having a free hand to open it. Anjali opened it almost immediately. "Oh, Madame O'Malley what have you got there?"

"A baby," Liz answered simply. "Do you think it has been abandoned? I found it, her," she corrected herself. "In the front garden by the tree near the gate."

"I will ring the police," Anjali said. "Not," she added darkly, "as if they will do anything. "We could ring the orphanage in Panaji too, they are quite good."

"What will happen to her?" Liz asked.

"They are quite good. The children are cared for and educated." Liz held the baby closer.

"She can't go to an orphanage."

"But you can't look after her." As Anjali spoke, Liz knew, for sure, that she could, and she would. For now though, they must notify the police, borrow some clothes and things from Nina and Ashok and work out a place for the baby to sleep.

The police came and were surprisingly helpful, delighted that Madame was happy to keep an unwanted baby, particularly as it was a girl. They promised to make enquiries and contact the local hospital. Anjali made it clear that she did not hold out much hope. "Please Madame O'Malley, please take her to the orphanage. Really, she will be fine there."

Looking at Liz's determined expression, she shrugged and went away, muttering as she did, that the British were a strange race. Liz was left holding a rather damp baby and was wondering what now, when Nina arrived and, as far as Liz was concerned, "saved the day". She rigged up a sari hammock and fetched a couple of cotton tops. She looked askance at Liz at the mention of nappies and suggested that Liz could lie the baby on towels in the sari hammock.

That night Liz hardly dared to close her eyes. The constant little snuffling noises from her dressing room where Nina had managed to hang the hammock between a cupboard handle and a chair, necessitated her making frequent forays to see if everything was alright with her new charge. She had sent Ashok to the market to buy baby milk and nappies, so at least temporarily the baby was fed and dry.

Nina could hardly believe the nappies when she saw them. She'd heard of them, but not one person she knew had ever used them. By the next morning, Liz realised she needed help. Leaving the baby sleeping blissfully after her early morning bottle, she made her way to the kitchen.

Anjali was having her breakfast of fresh fruit and yoghurt. She stood the moment Liz walked in. "Please sit down, Anjali. I need your advice." For a few moments, the two women faced each other across the table.

Gradually the stony-faced Anjali mellowed. "Of course, I'll try and find someone to help with the girl, but – and I know it is none of my business – I think you are being very foolish. Wait and see," she warned. "Wait and see. Babies will be dropped here all the time once they know you are a soft touch."

Liz felt a moment's panic – then her heart beat faster. She knew, calmly and for certain, that this was what was to happen. She wanted to look after abandoned babies. There was still plenty of space on the top floor for a nursery. Then when they got bigger she would build a school, just a small one, in the garden. It would not be an orphanage, it would be a home, a real home for children who nobody wanted.

chapter 10

Kathy was horrified. Liz had telephoned and told her the bizarre plan. She telephoned Ronnie. "I'm desperate Ronnie," she wailed, repeating what Liz had told her. "Please Ronnie, will you try and knock some sense into my sister's head? You know I can't come over, I'm off for the Milan fashion week, then Paris." The silence unnerved her. "Ronnie, are you there?"

"Just thinking, darling. Just thinking." Ronnie had been so caught up in a painting project for one of the clients at the Taj Hotel that he had not really been fully aware of what had taken place in the Villa O'Mal in the last twenty-four hours. "I will offer my moral support."

Kathy gave a frustrated groan. "Just stop her, stop the whole thing," she said urgently. Ronnie said a few placatory things and hung up, feeling worried about what he was getting drawn in to. For the first time, he rather regretted not returning to England with Kathy.

Liz was glad to see Ronnie. He would, she felt sure, be supportive. Apart from Nina, everyone else seemed against her at the moment. She now had a cot, and her dressing room had become the temporary nursery. Bernadette, an eighteen-year-old Christian girl who had spent most of her life in an orphanage, was due to start caring for the baby the following day.

Anjali, as good as her word, had been to see the Roman Catholic priest who had contacted the nuns for a recommendation for a nursery nurse. Bernadette had been helping with the babies and smaller children for some time now and Liz was impressed with her quiet presence and the way she had held the baby when she met her. Not officially trained, she was, in Liz's opinion, a real "find".

Ronnie was happy that the atmosphere was calm again with a gurgling baby holding court and the pretty Indian girl doing a great job as a nursery maid. He immediately ordered a pram from Mumbai and arranged for it to be delivered.

Life settled into a new pattern, with Ronnie continuing to paint local scenes around the villa and the beach. Concerned that he might be overstaying his welcome, he invited Liz out to dinner. "Ronnie," she replied in response to his query. "I love having you here, we all do, please stay as long as you want. The chef loves having another mouth to feed. The staff are fascinated by your paintings of scenes they know so well but hadn't really noticed until they looked at pictures you painted of them. And I, well, enjoy your company and I can continue to spend several hours a day writing."

Ronnie tipped his head back and laughed. "Darling Liz, what a compatible pair we are. What a pity I'm gay!"

"I agree," Liz said, smiling broadly. He was indeed a great friend to have. "Please stay as long as you want Ronnie."

"Thanks, Liz – but kick me out if I become a bore or a nuisance." She inclined her head slightly as if to acquiesce, smiling as she did.

Little Marie, the baby, was thriving, and before long, and inevitably, baby number two appeared on the scene. Anjali was horrified, Nina was delighted. Liz was constantly surprised by Nina, she had changed almost beyond recognition. The shy young woman was now confident and assured. She was a quick learner and, under Anjali's tutelage, had learned how the villa ran on such well-oiled wheels. She had also persuaded Aarav to show her the mysteries of a modern kitchen and her days of squatting over a small fire whilst cooking were becoming a distant memory.

Nina had also developed a flair for desserts. Aarav enjoyed having a pupil and, rather than guard his chef's secrets, he generously shared them with Nina.

Bernadette looked after the two little girls Marie and Therese and Liz found she was able to maintain her writing schedule of three to four hours every morning.

The big, square envelope addressed to Ronnie arrived some weeks later. Liz handed it to him as they ate their lunch on the terrace overlooking the gardens and sea. Mystified, Ronnie turned it over. "I wonder who is writing to me?" he said curiously. Liz was equally curious.

"Don't keep us both in suspense!" she laughed. "I want to know too." He opened the envelope and took out a square card. Liz saw the gold crest. "Goodness Ronnie, that looks impressive."

Ronnie was reading a short letter that accompanied the card. He was smiling and a slight flush covered his face. He folded the letter and slipped it into his pocket. "I met this chap," he began. As Liz grinned he shook his head in mock reproval. "I met this chap on the flight over," he repeated. "It transpires he is in the diplomatic service and we have been invited to attend a reception in Delhi at the embassy."

"We?" queried Liz.

He nodded. "I had mentioned I was visiting you and he has asked us both. Shall we go?"

Liz stood up and fetched her diary. The date was clear. "What fun," she said. "But whatever shall I wear?" Ronnie burst out laughing. "Just like a woman! Much more important, my dear Liz. Is what shall I wear? I didn't bring a tuxedo with me!"

That problem was soon resolved and within a week Nargis's husband, the tailor, had made him a white dinner jacket, black trousers and even a black bow tie. Ronnie was delighted. "Whoever would have thought of a handmade bow tie?" he marvelled.

Liz scoured her wardrobe and finally concluded that the scarlet Frank Usher that she had worn for the Whitbread Award ceremony would be perfect. Ronnie approved when she showed it to him.

"Um Liz with your light tan as a foil, you will look stunning," was his comforting comment.

She kept the thought to herself but concluded all women should have a gay houseguest – very good for the morale and generally excellent company.

There was no problem leaving the villa. Anjali ran the whole place on oiled wheels. The baby girls kept each other amused and Bernadette made sure they were properly cared for. With the future of the girls in mind, Liz had recently been in conversation with Father Joseph, the local priest who also oversaw the church school. Liz had been scandalised when she first saw it. Mean, was a complimentary description. With this in mind, and with the blessing of Father Joseph, she had acquired a piece of land about a ten-minute walk from Villa O'Mal and was in the process of working on plans with a local architect for a primary school. It would be private, but Liz had already decided she would subsidise it heavily. Even to the extent of supplying bursaries.

Liz believed Marie and Therese should be educated close to home but with excellent teachers in an excellent school. "Another of your projects," Ronnie had teased, secretly impressed with his new and increasingly dear friend.

He had of course seen the dress she would be wearing in Delhi and was sure she would look lovely in it. Trying on his new silk tuxedo he was pretty impressed with himself. He had a light tan now, and with his blonde hair with its few streaks of white, he felt he looked rather distinguished.

They had agreed to meet in the foyer at the Delhi Taj Hotel. The hotel was as impressive as the other two Taj hotels Liz had visited with its broad flight of marble stairs leading to a grand foyer, where attractive, turquoise sari-clad young women plied trays of tea.

Ronnie was standing looking out at the pool area when he felt a light tap on his arm. He turned to see a vision in red beside him. Liz, with her freshly washed gleaming black hair, her beautiful skin with its light tan, and her red sheath dress that showed her sylph-like figure to perfection.

He indicated by a movement of his hand that she should twirl, and twirl she did. "Stunning from all angles Liz – you'll wow them all." Liz was not displeased with her escort either. "You do up nicely yourself," she said, kissing him lightly on the cheek. Satisfied and happy they went out to the waiting taxi, pre-booked by Ronnie.

"You shall go to the ball, Cinderella," Ronnie said apropos of nothing.

Liz smiled happily. "I must say, I do feel a bit like that tonight."

chapter 11

The Ambassador's residence was all it should be. Grand without being over the top. The Ambassador greeted his guests warmly, introducing the rather dumpy woman by his side as his sister-in-law, Imogen Reeves. Liz had done her homework. Philip Broderick was a widower of about two years. He was considered an outstanding ambassador by the Indian Government, slightly less so by their neighbours in Pakistan. Nevertheless, he was credited with improving relations between the two countries.

Liz had been looking forward to meeting him as she had equally looked forward to meeting the consul who had struck up a friendship with Ronnie during their shared flight.

If Liz thought she had to write a job description for an ambassador, Philip Broderick would have fitted every detail. About six foot two, she surmised. Thick, slightly wavy, silver hair. Like everyone she met, he had a slight tan just from going about his duties and, she acknowledged, in his ambassadorial uniform he cut a dashing figure.

Imogen, though, at five-foot-two and almost as square as she was tall, cut a somewhat different figure, but her friendly charm made her instantly likeable and later in the evening, the two women had an animated and friendly conversation.

The reception was scheduled for two hours from six-thirty until eight-thirty, and by eight-thirty the only remaining guests were the honoured few who had been invited to dine. Liz found herself sitting next to Tim Barnes, the consul, and on her right, the chairman of one of India's largest companies. He was unfortunately rather pompous and full of self-importance and Liz was glad that Tim provided light relief on her left.

It was not long before she realised he was subtly getting her to talk about Ronnie – perhaps not quite subtly enough, for she quickly suspected he was interested to find out all he could in order to further the relationship. Without letting him suspect that she had twigged, she let him know that Ronnie's friendship with her and with her sister was a warm caring one but no more. His relief was almost tangible and she saw him glancing down to where Ronnie sat entertaining the two ladies who sat either side of him, but returning Tim's glances in his direction with a broad smile.

It was proving to be a lovely dinner and she mentally noted all the details so that she could tell Aarav. He was always enthusiastic for new and fresh ideas, and would also want to know about the presentation of the dishes too. Really, he was wasted cooking for her, Liz thought, although he didn't seem to think so and always enjoyed presenting her with some new and original culinary ideas.

Imogen gave her a hug when they finally left at almost one a.m. Philip shook her gravely by the hand. Their eyes held as he wished her goodnight. "What a pity you live so far from Delhi." He spoke quietly almost as if it was something very personal between them, whereas Liz knew that it was undoubtedly something he said to all his guests visiting from outside Delhi.

They were silent on the drive back to the Taj Hotel, both wrapped in thought. Ronnie hugged her as he deposited her outside her door. "A night-cap?" she suggested tentatively, hoping he would say no.

He smiled. "I'm tired and I am sure you are too – though you don't look it," he added hastily. "Quite the bell of the ball Cinderella. Mr Ambassador couldn't keep his eyes off you."

Liz felt the colour rush to her cheeks. "What nonsense," she said, slightly more tartly than she meant to. "Anyway, what about you and Tim?" Before he could answer she had let herself into her room and now leaned against the door glad of its support.

Undressing, with only moonlight shining through the windows, she pushed open the balcony door. The warmth of the air hit her after the air-conditioned coolness of the room. Below her there was a light hum of traffic but, looking up at the dark sky, it was a myriad of stars. Suddenly, unexpectedly, she saw a shooting star. She knew it wasn't a spacecraft making its lonely journey around the earth, but a meteor, a once-in-a-lifetime experience for this portion of the celestial sky. "Are you my lucky star?" she whispered to herself, watching it carefully, still now, in its new position in the heavens.

Once in bed she lay unable to sleep, feeling somewhat unsettled. She finally drifted into a dreamless sleep and woke when Ronnie rang at eight a.m. wanting to know if she was ready for breakfast. She laughed, nothing and nobody, late night or not, would allow Ronnie to miss his deadline of breakfast at eight!

Back at the villa, they seemed to have managed perfectly adequately without her. The babies cooed and gurgled and Liz found herself, to her surprise, feeling a shade jealous of their relationship with Bernadette, but she quickly recovered, realising how right it was for them to identify with the girl.

Bernadette loved them as if they were her own and Liz prayed she would stay indefinitely in the household and as part of their lives.

She threw herself into the proofreading of her most recent book. Already having begun her next novel, she always found the edited version slightly irritating. A word changed here or there by her editor was usually acceptable, but for some reason today she found herself getting annoyed. She missed Ronnie's company too as he had decided to stay on in Delhi for a few days.

Somehow, Ronnie had become part of her life and she missed his companionship at mealtimes and the evening drinks they shared before dinner. On impulse, she rang her friend Vihaan de Sousa and invited he and his wife over for dinner. Aarav was delighted. He had listened with interest to Liz's description of the embassy menu and determined to make at least one of the courses to surprise Madame O'Mal.

Equally, on impulse, she wandered through the garden to visit Ashok and Nina. They both worked for her, yet she only saw flashes of them as they went about their work, always working so hard and diligently.

Their two children were sitting outside making mud pies and looked deliriously happy and totally filthy! Laughing out loud she called to their parents. They came to the door together. It was seldom Madame O'Mal called on them and their anxious faces made her realise she should do this more often so they didn't assume it was bad news when she did turn up.

Nina put the kettle on and Liz found herself looking around in wonderment, from a mean dwelling, they had created a home. Nina had watched and learned. Simple rugs adorned the floor and walls. On the left, a small kitchen had been fashioned and a modest wood-burning stove with its chimney going up through a specially made aperture in the roof provided the heat for the kettle. "I still cook outside as well," Nina said a shade defensively. "It keeps the house cooler."

"Of course," responded Liz, wondering if it would be at all possible to lay on air-conditioning for them. They had electric lights now the electricity had been laid on, so why not, and it might make a real difference to their comfort, particularly on the raised area that was their bedroom. She filed away the thought and determined to discuss it with Ashok later.

They wanted to hear about Delhi. She talked of the broad streets of New Delhi and the Ambassador's garden which she could see interested Ashok. "But it is old Delhi I really like," she continued. "The Red Fort and the amazing market Chandni Chowk. You can find everything you need or want with more spices than I knew existed and wonderful street food, jewellery and clothes, and of course everyone barters." The couple listened, fascinated, but were taken aback that Madame O'Mal was surprised about the bartering. Of course, in India everyone barters, but foreigners don't understand they thought, giving each other meaningful little looks.

"The British Ambassador," Nina wanted to know. "He is a very powerful man."

"He is just a very nice man, and so is his sister," Liz responded.

"He is not married?" Nina asked curiously.

Liz laughed. "No Nina, he is not married, he is a widower." Nina looked puzzled.

"That means his wife is no longer alive," Ashok explained helpfully to his wife.

"Oh," said Nina. Then a look passed over her face and she smiled happily. "He could marry you Madame O'Mal. You are a widower!"

Liz laughed again. "Dear Nina, I am divorced, not widowed, and life is not as simple as that I'm afraid." Nina lapsed into silence until the sound of crying outside had her on her feet and out of the door. She returned carrying one crying, very muddy child with another following, equally muddy and looking rather solemn. He looked at his father, knowing he would be told off. "I think that is my cue to leave," said Liz, not particularly wanting the mud transferred to her!

She walked away from the little household feeling perhaps, for the first time, that she didn't know love like that of the little quartet she had just left. Being Liz, she wanted to do something about the air-conditioning straight away, and decided not to consult Ashok until she knew how feasible it would be. She rang Vihaan for the name of an installer, and before the day was out, arrangements had been made for an air-conditioning engineer to visit her to discuss the practicalities.

chapter 12

The telephone rang in her bedroom as she was showering for dinner. Throwing a towelling robe over her dripping body, she walked into the bedroom hoping whoever it was would wait for her to answer the phone. Drying her hands on the body of the robe as she tied the belt, she picked up the phone. "Liz O'Malley," she gave her name as always.

"Philip Broderick. Hello Elizabeth." It gave her a jolt. True, Ronnie had introduced her as Elizabeth, but for as long as she could remember the only person who ever addressed her by her full name had been her father. For a moment she was taken aback. "Are you there Elizabeth?" asked a slightly anxious voice.

"Yes," she responded quietly. "I'm here. Just surprised to hear your voice."

"A pleasant surprise I hope?"

"Of course," she replied, not quite sure what she felt.

"Look Elizabeth, I'll come straight to the point. As you know Imogen acted as my hostess recently. I don't actually like commandeering the wives of staff."

"I'm sure they don't mind," she replied.

"Mind or not, I'm ringing to ask you an enormous favour. Would you be prepared to act as hostess next month?

Imogen has returned to England. I wouldn't ask you to come all this way, but it really is a big occasion. I am not at liberty to tell you who our international guest is – particularly over the telephone if you get my meaning – but it really would be marvellous if you could co-host the occasion with me. I hate to bring money into the conversation but, of course, we will send you the air ticket. The last thing I want is for you to be out of pocket."

She supposed he didn't really know her circumstances so she should not feel offended by his thoughtfulness. "When is it?" she said, reaching for her diary as she spoke. "I am flying to England next month." He gave her the date. It was in three weeks. Her diary showed she had a dinner engagement that week which could be postponed and a speaking engagement with the mothers of the children at Father Joseph's school which could not. "I have to be back here on Friday evening," she said. She almost felt him breathe a sigh of relief.

"If you could arrive on Tuesday, we expect our guest on Wednesday. The major event is on Thursday and I guarantee you will be back in Goa by lunch-time on Friday. Is that alright?"

"That's fine, what do I wear?" she enquired. She didn't see his lovely smile but his tone when he spoke sounded as if he enjoyed the question. "I thought you looked gorgeous in that red dress, that or something similar would be perfect. And perhaps something long for the dinner – is that alright?"

"Of course," she murmured, panicking as she spoke. She thought longingly of her wardrobe in England and of the long dresses she had hanging there, so little used during the past few years.

"I'll write and confirm the details and enclose the plane ticket," he said. She started to protest, then realised she would only sound churlish if she did.

"I look forward to hearing from you," she said sincerely, before putting the phone down rather more hastily than usual.

She found she was trembling and sat down rather hurriedly on the edge of the chaise longue. There was a knock at the door. "Come in," she said automatically. Anjali came in.

"Madame O'Malley are you alright? Aarav has dinner ready." There had been great concern downstairs for Madame O'Mal was never late.

"I'm sorry, my apologies to Aarav. I had rather a long telephone conversation. Tell him five minutes please."

"Yes, Madame O'Malley," said Anjali, wondering at the flushed face before her.

Liz brushed her hair, put on a neat pair of bikini briefs and, without bothering to put on a bra, pulled on a cream caftan trimmed with gold over her head. Slipping her feet into soft gold mules and having put on a touch of lipstick, she made her way downstairs to the dining room.

The following morning her normal writing routine changed. She had woken in the early hours thinking, of all things, about clothes. The red dress would be fine for the reception on Wednesday, but during the night she had mentally gone through her wardrobe and decided she had nothing suitable for the "important" dinner on the Thursday evening. In other words, she hadn't got a thing to wear!

It was definitely a job for the tailor. She rang him straight away and he agreed he would see her in the hour. He convinced her he would have exactly the fabric she sought for a very special dress made in record time.

A little while later she noticed the engineer's van driving along the drive. She clapped her hand to her head, she had forgotten to alert either Ashok or Nina – she had really hoped to get them out of the way on some pretext or another. She ran down the stairs and was by the side of the van before the driver had even opened the door. "Please go to the kitchen," she said, directing him to the side of the house. "Aarav my chef will give you a cup of tea. I need to talk to my staff in the bungalow."

Some weeks ago Liz had started referring to Ashok and Nina's home as the bungalow rather than the hut, which it had originally been called. Walking quickly she arrived outside Ashok's home. With its running water and a brick-built bathroom and toilet directly behind it, it was gradually taking on all the things she wanted them to have. She had even had Nargis make curtains for the small windows and Nina had had the fun of choosing the fabric.

Now this was the next surprise for them and she felt excited at the prospect of their pleasure. But how to get them out of the way? Ashok saw her coming and was already in the doorway waiting to greet her. "Two visits in two days Madame O'Mal – what a nice surprise."

"It's not exactly a visit Ashok. I need you to take me to the tailors, and I would like Nina to come too. She has such a good eye for colour and I need her help. Bernadette will look after the children." Nina had by now joined Ashok and she was beaming with delight. To be told by Madame herself that she had a good eye, what a compliment and to be invited to accompany Madame was so exciting.

"Please take the children to Bernadette now and she can take them to nursery school. Ashok I need to leave in ten minutes, please," Liz said.

She left them scurrying around and walked quickly back to the house. Liz found the engineer sitting at the kitchen table enjoying his tea. She explained that she did not want him to go down to the bungalow until he saw her leaving in the car. "Of course Madame O'Mal, if that is what you want."

She wanted to know how long the work would take to

complete and was disappointed to learn that it would take at least two full days.

Running upstairs to the nursery Liz quickly explained what she needed of Bernadette, and as unfazed as always, she smiled and said, "How nice."

chapter 13

Ashok was already in the car which was now parked outside the front door. Nina stood waiting not sure where Madame O'Mal would require her to sit. As if reading her thoughts, Liz suggested that Nina sit in the front beside her husband. She preferred the rear seat anyway as she found Ashok's driving, along with most of his fellow countrymen's, somewhat unnerving.

True to his word the tailor was waiting for her. As ever, Liz felt almost overwhelmed by roll after roll of fabulous silk and cotton. Nina seemed to have fallen for a red and gold fabric (very traditional). She fingered it, sighed over it and then tried to pretend, when Liz looked in her direction, that she didn't like it at all!

Suddenly Liz saw what she was looking for – beautiful yellow silk. Not garishly overly bright but not too subdued either. She had brought her red Frank Usher dress with her and, carefully unwrapping it, she laid it on the table. "Can you copy this dress but make it full-length?" she asked. The tailor looked at the dress, examined the seams, exclaimed over the workmanship and he almost reverently fingered the fabric. Finally, he looked up and smiled happily at Liz.

"Madame O'Malley," he said formally. "It will be an honour to copy such a garment."

"With this?" she asked tentatively, touching the delicate silk carefully.

"Madame, the silk is so fine, but once it is lined it will hang like the red," the tailor said. Liz explained that she needed it quickly for an important function at the British Embassy. Normally she would not have mentioned the venue, but she knew, in this case, it would encourage the impetus needed!

"I will cut and tack today. I will do the first fitting in your home tomorrow and you will have it for the day after." The tailor smiled confidently. Liz had such a sense of relief, if it looked like the red it would be perfect. "A suggestion Madame O'Mal. This," he said, touching the red dress which had no sleeves. "It would be different, yet the same, if we put a sleeve just to here." He touched just above his elbow.

Liz didn't hesitate, it was after all a formal dinner. The dress was changing anyway from mid-calf to full length. She nodded. "I am sure you are right – with the longer length the sleeves will balance it."

"Exactly so," he replied with a smile. Nina had been exclaiming over the red dress and approved of the yellow, but Liz knew where her heart lay. "How much fabric do I need for a sari?" she asked, casually pointing to the red and gold fabric that Nina had sighed over. He told her the metres she would require. Whilst the tailor started cutting Liz asked Nina to find Ashok who had parked in a shady spot and ask him to bring the car around. As soon as she had left, Liz explained to the tailor that the red and gold fabric was for Nina. "She is fortunate," he commented. "She will look very beautiful."

"I know," answered Liz, watching as the man deftly cut, folded and packed the fabric.

Once back in the car and driving home Liz knew this was the time to tell them that their home was, in their absence, being disrupted. Ashok almost ran down one of the many stray dogs that sit or lie in the shade of the trees that line the roadsides. Nina clapped her hands in nervous disbelief, as Liz explained she wanted to give them air-conditioning. They were almost speechless, falling over their words in excitement.

"Anyway," Liz continued, delighted with their response. "Just to help you get over the disruption over the next few days, this is for you Nina." She handed the carefully wrapped package to Nina who hugged it to her, not daring to believe it might possibly be the fabric she had so coveted.

Nina started crying, she realised now why she had been sent out of the shop to find Ashok. He stopped the car, causing the squealing of brakes and horn blowing from behind. She cried because their life was so different since Madame had come into their lives. She cried because she was happy and she cried because, in a package on her lap, was the most beautiful fabric she had ever dreamed of. Ashok turned in his seat and flashed Liz a smile of pleasure. His white teeth gleamed against his brown skin. "Madame O'Mal," Nina said between sobs. "You are so good to us. We don't deserve such kindness."

"You most certainly do," Liz responded. "You help me so much Nina, I don't know what I would do without you and Ashok. Particularly driving me about and stopping all the traffic behind us." Nina laughed, an understanding laugh.

"His driving, oh Madame," she giggled whilst Ashok, pretending to be affronted, restarted the car and it was a merry trio that arrived back at the villa, where Nina handed her precious package to Ashok before rushing to see if Bernadette had managed alright with Maya and Samir. Ashok carefully parked the car, trying to contain his excitement about the air-conditioning. Who would have believed that only a short while ago he and his family were living in a mud hut, and now they were having air-conditioning…

As good as his word, the tailor arrived the next afternoon having tacked the cut silk pieces together. Liz stood as still as she could whilst he tightened here, and let out a little there, until both he and Liz were equally satisfied. He had done a splendid job. The cut was as good as the red dress and the additional length, plus the addition of elbow-length sleeves, made it sufficiently different and equally good. She mused inwardly that the designer Frank Usher would be amazed.

Having professed her satisfaction, the tailor left and Liz decided now was as good a time as any to decide what she would travel in and what other things she needed to take with her. Fortunately, it was not a difficult decision. She decided to travel in a white trouser-suit, worn with a simple pale pink tee shirt and a flowing silk scarf in exactly the same shade to soften the outline.

She had a well-cut blue denim skirt which she would wear with a smart blouse during the day on Thursday, but for good measure decided to take her stone-coloured shirt-waister in case she needed to change during the day or felt it more appropriate apparel!

Shoes, undies, etcetera, were easy and a small pearl-beaded evening bag would work with the yellow silk. She felt an innate sense of relief when all the decisions had been made. For some reason, and unusually for her, she felt surprisingly nervous and was not sorry that Ronnie was due back that evening in time for dinner.

chapter 14

It was good not to be sitting in a solitary state. Ronnie seemed in the best of spirits full of what he and Tim had been up to, culture-wise at least. Having let him chatter on for most of the dinner she finally asked him if he wanted to hear her news.

"How thoughtless, Liz. I am so sorry!" He was full of contrition and sat back, dessert finished, waiting for her to speak. She told him about the telephone call – the mysterious "high-powered" guest. "Ah," said Ronnie finally. "That explains it." Liz raised her eyebrows questioningly.

"Tim packed me off – I thought in a rather an abrupt way after all our lovely intense moments."

"Don't tell me." Liz grinned.

"I wouldn't dare my darling! Tim said he was going to be very tied up for the next week or two. I offered to be tied up with him." Liz smiled at the mix of disappointment and innuendo in his voice.

"Ronnie," she remonstrated. He tried to look apologetic, somewhat unsuccessfully she thought.

"What are you going to wear, darling?" Liz loved him for the question, only a gay man bothered about women's choice of clothes, so comforting at times like this. She told him every detail, which she knew he wanted, of her planned wardrobe including The Dress.

"When can I see it?" he wanted to know. Liz smiled, explaining that the tailor was arriving the following morning for a second and hopefully final fitting. "I hope he won't let you down." Ronnie sounded a little concerned.

"He won't," replied Liz, with more confidence than she felt.

They chatted on in a desultory fashion, though Ronnie sat up when she talked about the air-conditioning for Ashok and Nina. "You are so good to them Liz. No wonder all the staff here love you."

"Do they?"

"Of course darling! Of course they do." He repeated emphasising the point with one of his expansive gestures.

She had been expecting the airline ticket to arrive in the post and was somewhat concerned at its non-appearance. Just before lunch on the day before she was due to leave she received a telephone call from Tim. "Just to let you know Liz, the ticket will be waiting for you at the Air India check-in. The Ambassador asked if you needed transport to the airport?" She assured him not. He continued by telling her that there would be a car waiting for her in Delhi. They chatted for a few moments more, Liz longing to ask who the important guest was, but carefully refraining. "Well I'll see you soon," Liz said just about to finish the conversation.

"Could I have a quick word with Ronnie?"

"Of course," Liz replied handing the 'phone directly to a hovering Ronnie who had quickly realised who was on the other end of the line.

Liz felt slightly disappointed that Philip hadn't telephoned her himself with the details, but she rationalised that Mr Ambassador was probably far too busy and important to worry about travel arrangements for a guest – a fairly lowly one at that, at least compared to whoever she was to meet. Still, she couldn't stop herself feeling a little piqued!

chapter 15

On the plane flying to Delhi, enjoying the unexpected luxury of First Class, Liz realised she was excited. Her dress completed just in time was all she had hoped it would be. Ronnie's ecstatic approval confirmed that she had made the right choices in the colour, silk and more or less copying the red dress which he loved. She had, at Ronnie's insistence, tried it on for his benefit, he had made her walk and turn around. "Very, very special Liz. Your tailor-man has outdone himself!"

Now, enjoying a glass of champagne and a canape or two, Liz felt comfortable about the clothes she had organised, now she could relax and enjoy herself. It was a short flight of little more than two and a half hours and before long she was walking through Customs. A liveried chauffeur carrying a large card with her name on was standing in a prominent position, and she gladly handed over her case, holding on to her leather vanity case and small shoulder bag.

It was not long before they were driving through the gates of the Embassy. The car drew to a stop outside the main door of the residence and the chauffeur was out of the car and opening her door before she knew it. The double doors opened and the butler welcomed her in, whilst a maid appeared, as if from nowhere, and took her case from the chauffeur. The whole place, perhaps unsurprisingly, seemed to run on extremely well-oiled wheels.

"I am afraid Madam the Ambassador is in a meeting, he sends his apologies and will meet you for a late lunch at one-thirty p.m. Would you like something in your suite in the meantime?" Liz looked at her watch, it was noon and she realised she was starving – still, she would have to wait of course.

"Tea would be pleasant," she answered. "Earl Grey with lemon, please, and perhaps some fruit."

"You will find some fruit in your sitting room," the butler replied, indicating to the maid waiting patiently with her case that she should show the way. "I will attend to your tea personally Madam."

Liz followed the smartly dressed maid up the broad curved stairway. Liz felt as if she was on the set of an old Hollywood movie and almost expected to hear an orchestra playing softly in the background.

The suite was delightful. A moderately sized sitting room overlooking the manicured gardens and a bedroom with a king-sized bed – a light and airy room with a marble floor that was partially covered with an Aubusson-style – or maybe the real thing, she smiled to herself, probably was – rug.

The maid unpacked her case and she was relieved to find that, with the many layers of tissue paper, the dress had travelled as well as the red one had. Liz took off her jacket and relaxed on one of the comfortable sofas, kicked off her shoes and curled her legs up under her. A light knock at the door indicated her tea had arrived and, as she poured herself a cup of tea, she looked at the headlines of *The Times* and the *Telegraph* that had been neatly folded on the tray.

She must have dozed off. When she woke she looked at her watch. With a jolt, she found it was one-fifteen. Hastily getting up, she went to the bathroom, splashed some water on her face and dabbed it dry with one of the incredibly soft towels, brushed her hair, put on a touch of moisturiser and blusher, a swipe of lipstick, replaced her jacket and made her way towards the stairs.

As if on cue, the maid she had seen earlier came towards her. "This way Madam," she indicated. They walked along the wide corridor and came to another set of double doors. "Please Madam," she indicated again opening the door. It was not a large room. A round table that would seat about eight, she imagined, was set for two – she was one, but of Philip, or whoever she was to have lunch with, there was no sign

With a sigh and feeling hungrier by the minute, she wondered what next. The door opened just as she was about to sneak a piece of a bread roll. The smell of the freshly baked bread was tantalisingly tempting. Her hand hovered over the bread basket as the door was flung open. "Ah, caught you," were Philip's first words to her. Liz felt herself blushing and started to mumble some excuse.

"You must be starving. I am. Breakfast was at six-thirty and apart from coffee I haven't had a thing since." He rang the bell on the wall, then indicated she should sit while he sat further around the table where the place was set. "Look Elizabeth—" he began as she started, "Are you going—" They broke off and laughed and the tension eased. "Ladies first," he said.

"I was just going to ask if you were able to tell me yet about the special guest?" Liz asked. Philip smiled.

"Now I have you locked in my embassy – with no mode of escape – I can certainly tell you. It's our Prime Minister."

"How interesting and exciting," said Liz. "I've been longing to meet her. I think it's good to have a woman again and she is so different to Mrs Thatcher – or she certainly appears to be!"

Lunch arrived. A cold cream of avocado soup, followed by slices of chicken breast and salad. Dessert was pomegranate seeds and oranges in Curacao. "I chose a light lunch, I hope that is alright. I know you were hungry, as was I."

"It was perfect." Liz meant it. The soup, plus the delicious bread, would probably have been sufficient, as it was the chicken and salad had filled any remaining gaps. She couldn't be fiddled with pomegranates and after two glasses of wine felt the oranges in liquor were best left alone.

They had coffee on the balcony, which, despite being outside, was pleasantly cool being on the north-facing side of the building.

Philip stood up suddenly, Liz had noticed him sneaking glances at his watch. "Elizabeth, you must excuse me. I'm afraid I have to attend a meeting. My assistant would be happy to take you on a tour of the embassy, the paintings are really worth looking at and the library is most interesting particularly so for you as an author."

It was, in fact, a pleasant afternoon. Deirdre, his assistant, seemed to enjoy showing off the embassy and it became clear fairly early on in their acquaintance that she had a "thing" for Philip. Liz wondered if Philip was aware of it, probably not, she thought, men were surprisingly dim sometimes!

Liz admired the artwork, the library, the main reception rooms. She exclaimed over the flower arrangements and finally, thankfully, Deirdre suggested she might like to take tea in her suite and relax before the six p.m. reception. With a sense of relief, she agreed, perhaps with a shade too much alacrity. Deirdre probably expected her to want to see more. As it was they parted at the foot of the stairs, Deirdre to check and see if she was needed and organise tea to be sent up for Liz, and

Liz to find her way to her room. Fortunately, she remembered a specific vase on a small table and with a sense of coming home found herself back in the suite again.

In what seemed only a few moments later, the maid, prompted by the efficient Deirdre, arrived with some dainty sandwiches and a pot of tea – all beautifully laid out with Crown Derby porcelain. She returned to her favourite spot on the sofa, kicking off her shoes again, and poured herself a welcome cup of tea. She ate two of the dainty sandwiches with their smoked salmon filling then decided, after a quick look at her watch, to organise herself for the evening.

As she stood in the shower her mind turned to the lunch she had shared with Philip. They had talked of her flight, of Goa, of the Prime Minister, but although there had been no personal conversation she had felt his steady gaze and in some strange way she felt connected to him. With the water still cascading over her, she tried to analyse what she meant and found she couldn't! There was "a something" – what it was she didn't know – and didn't even know if she wanted to find out.

Tonight's reception was fairly low-key. The Prime Minister had asked for an opportunity before the big reception the following evening for local dignitaries, government officials and so forth, to meet with all the key embassy personnel. There would be about thirty people in total, one of whom was Liz. There would then be an early dinner at seven-thirty.

Liz was looking forward to meeting the Prime Minister, she had followed her meteoric rise to fame with a great deal of interest. She had certainly jolted the failing Conservative Party out of their apathy. She had broken a few rules and a number of Conservative traditions. She appeared outspoken but fair, she got rid of malingerers in the Party, dismissed spin doctors and returned to a consensus Cabinet. She made it clear she did not want yes – men and – women and she stated publicly that any member of Parliament who had complaints should, above all, direct their views to the Cabinet and not the Press. She had invigorated Parliament and was even met with grudging approval from a surprisingly large number of Opposition MPs. It was as refreshing as it was productive – and in her first three years, she had managed to get politics on to a more balanced footing.

Liz dressed with care, her red dress looking as elegant as ever. Her hair gleamed and the light tan she had acquired since living in India brought out the green of her eyes. She knew she looked good – but what now?

As if on cue the telephone rang. It was Philip, telling her they should go down to the gold drawing room. He said Tim would meet her at the foot of the stairs in five minutes. Liz was thankful she was ready. She gave herself an extra spray of Shalimar, picked up her evening purse and was, she decided, as ready as she would ever be.

With her heart beating a shade faster than usual in anticipation of meeting the Prime Minister, she walked to the stairs. Tim stood with his back to her and didn't hear her approach, the thick carpet blanketing her footsteps.

"Good evening Tim," she spoke softly, not wanting to startle him. He turned instantly and a look crossed his face that she interpreted as approval. He held out his arm and together they walked towards the gold reception room. It was one of the smaller public rooms and a perfect size for the numbers invited tonight. The buzz of conversation stopped briefly as they entered the room, but picked up again when those present realised it was "only" Liz.

"The Prime Minister," announced the butler, throwing open the doors with a certain panache as he continued, "Miss Julia Naik." The first Asian prime minister of the United Kingdom walked in. Giving her a gentle push from behind, Tim managed to keep Liz abreast of him, while she instinctively felt she should hold back.

Philip had been in meetings all afternoon with the Prime Minister but nevertheless greeted her gravely, almost as if for the first time. He introduced Liz, and Julia Naik smiled warmly. "I know your name, your books give me a great deal of pleasure. You live in India now I believe." They chatted away and it was several minutes before Philip could continue introducing the Prime Minister to the staff she had not yet had an opportunity to meet. "We shall talk again," the Prime Minister said to Liz, sotto voce, before moving dutifully on.

"It was fascinating," Liz told Ronnie on her return home. "To watch Julia Naik work the room. She spoke to everyone, asked appropriate questions and listened intently." Liz was utterly impressed. Later at dinner, Julia had made an apparently impromptu speech, quite short and to the point, basically thanking them for the work they did representing the United Kingdom and adding that, as far as she was concerned, their important role should be mirrored in every embassy across the world and equally British people travelling or living abroad should feel that there was a piece of the United Kingdom wherever they went. The final sentence, Liz noticed, caused a slight groan, a few glances and a raised eyebrow or two between some of the staff around the table. Liz got the impression that there was not total agreement about the Prime Minister's final comment amongst some of the colleagues. With a tight smile, Julia finished by saying that being in the diplomatic service did not mean they were in any way superior to their fellow countrymen and women.

Liz felt this was a light but well-aimed rap across the knuckles, and it confirmed for her that this was a "thinking" PM as well as a "doing" one. Julia Naik had achieved more than anyone would have believed possible. She had been born in Bermondsey shortly after her parents had arrived from India. Her mother spoke little English, hated the weather, didn't understand the life she was leading and was only there because she was married to Julia's father.

It had been an arranged marriage of second cousins, so the good thing was Julia's mother had not married a stranger, the bad thing was she didn't love him either. Julia though seemed to thrive in this wet colourless country, as her mother described it, and she soon had a baby brother to play with. Uday was as different from her as the sun from the moon and once he started at school their lives really parted company. It was odd really, Julia often thought, same background and parents yet all Uday wanted to do was have Asian friends and return to India. Julia made friends easily, but her friends were not just Asian despite the fact that the school was seventy percent Asian. She loved school, not just for the friendships but for the learning opportunities. By some standards, she could have been thought a swot but learning seemed exciting and effortless to her and she strove to do excellently in all subjects. Her relationship with her parents grew worse over the years, they neither understood her or could comprehend how much knowledge she appeared to have. This was without knowing what a scholar she had become. She jumped a year in school without her parents even being aware of it. The school gave up on making contact with her parents and concentrated instead on their star pupil.

At fourteen she took her GCSEs, and a year later she took her last school examinations before heading to Oxford University to read Law. Her parents, totally uncomprehending, tried to arrange a marriage for her. Her initial outrage turned to laughter and she packed her few items of clothing and left home for good, leaving behind her confused parents who thought they had produced a changeling.

How she survived her time at Oxford is now history. She worked in a restaurant and a takeaway to provide her with enough to survive and still managed to obtain a First. She also taught yoga to her friends and acquaintances for a small fee, but she felt it was a great way to make contacts that might, at some stage, be useful. She managed to keep her penury hidden from most people's view and she slept little, having to study whenever she could.

It was only in her last year when she had a bad case of flu that her fellow students found out about the jobs she had been doing. Julia's photo and a potted history (mostly false) appeared in the local Press and other struggling students wondered how she had coped.

Julia stayed on to study for her PhD and her lecturing fees paid for her keep. For the first time ever she had a real sense of independence and she also had her first affair. Paul was a West African first-year student. He was, in her eyes anyway, amazingly handsome. Still a virgin, she had no compunction about losing it with Paul and they had a passionate eight-month affair. As suddenly as it had begun it was over. Julia wept in private, in public no one could have known how she was hurting. Paul had finally found her too intelligent, he had the sort of personality that made him always want to be right. With Julia, however hard as he tried, in any sort of discussion she came out on top. This finally drove Paul away and Julia recognised the failure was hers. It was then she made the decision that future relationships would be with men who enjoyed her mind as much as her body – intellectual equals as well as lovers.

With her free time no longer taken up with Paul, she widened her circle of friends and became once more the social animal she had been at school. Coping as ever with consummate skills, her obligation to her students, her doctorate and an enjoyable social whirl.

The doctorate completed, Julia realised that she was being increasingly drawn to politics. Her views had changed. The radical "left" thinking, caused perhaps by her Bermondsey upbringing, had considerably modified and she felt more and more drawn to the Conservative Party and their aims and ideals. They had returned to power after ten years in the wilderness, and although stronger, they had been returned to power almost by default. So many memorable mistakes had been made by the extreme left-wing Opposition.

She actively pursued every by-election seat that came up and, after a few years, she was selected as a candidate for Solihull in the West Midlands. At the next General Election her campaign was vigorous, her energy unflagging, and justifiably she increased the majority by a clear five percent.

She was one of the youngest female members of Parliament. Her outspokenness, never dropping her Party "in it", but nevertheless thoughtfully provoking and independently minded, brought her not just to the attention of the Press but of the Party hierarchy. She became a PPS (Personal Private Secretary) to a Minister, then number two to the Health Minister, and, finally, during a reshuffle became a Junior Health Minister. She did so well that when the existing Health Minister retired on health grounds (alcohol, mainly), she was promoted to his spot. The NHS Executive trembled, rightly so. There had, in her opinion, been "too much fiddling while Rome burned", she announced in the House. In future, there would be major changes: bringing in hotel charges for in-patients – which meant patients, unless on benefits, would pay for meals and transport costs. Every visit to a GP would have a basic charge of five pounds, again unless on benefits or pregnant. Cosmetic surgery, i.e. removal of tattoos or breast enlargements, would no longer be free. Drunk patients would be sent straight to a special unit in the grounds on arrival where there would be necessary but minimal attention, and there would be a charge levied on them, dependent on how much time they were in the unit. Security guards would deal firmly with bad behaviour. There were other less significant modifications.

Chief Executives were asked for their opinions, and small modifications were made here and there, but in general, things proceeded as planned.

Nurses had an immediate five percent increase in salary as did doctors in hospitals. GPs' salaries were reviewed, with a varied and excellent incentive scheme to help provide more in-house care and fewer referrals. Bed blocking was to become a thing of the past under a new title, Social Health. All patients ready to leave the hospital were to be given an opportunity for nursing care at home for a period judged by their consultant. This service to be free for those on benefits or with an income less than the national average. Likewise, for hospital outpatient appointments, a fee of five pounds would be payable at check-in, with the aforementioned opt-outs.

The country had waited with bated breath – there were those who had screamed in protest, but for the majority, there was a sense of relief that perhaps, finally, something was really happening.

The polls showed the increasing popularity of the Party and at the following election five years later they won an outstanding majority. Julia became the Chancellor of the Exchequer. She thrived on the challenges and she lived every moment to the full. She seemed to find time to visit factories and schools, but she kept away from hospitals, leaving the new Health Minister to continue consolidating the radical changes that had continued to improve the service. People talked about Social Health in glowing terms. More and more nurses were recruited and the pressures eased on the existing staff as more nurses completed their training.

It was felt, in many quarters, that it was only a matter of time before she became Prime Minister. There were, of course, the usual detractors. The National Front reared its head at intervals, but with their majority and the support of other parties, the National Front was held well in check.

Another election was on the horizon. It was as if the country wanted Julia to become PM. At thirty-eight she was making history. The third woman PM, but the first Asian ever. She was proud of her Indian roots but felt wholly British. She had never hidden the facts of her Bermondsey upbringing and she encouraged young people from all walks of life to aspire to greater things. "If I can do it, you can do it," was a favourite phrase when she talked to young people at schools and colleges.

The election over, Julia spent her first night alone in the flat at number ten, Downing Street. For the first time she felt alone, not lonely but definitely alone. She would have loved parents to chat with or a brother to "fence" with, but those relationships were a thing of the past. Her brother had made one attempt to see her some years ago, but his militancy worried her and there seemed no common ground or even family bond between them. He had hoped to influence her thinking and was disappointed. He never contacted her again.

So tonight Julia stood alone at the window, looking down on to the street below, wondering how all this had come about, and how adequately she would perform her duties. Her mind went back to her meeting with the Queen at Buckingham Palace. She had been so gracious and encouraging. Julia had left with a glow in her heart and a feeling that they could be friends, in a Queen/Prime Minister sort of way…

chapter 16

Liz dressed with extra care – she decided to pile her hair up, and although she had been offered the services of a hairdresser, she declined, knowing she wanted the freedom to change her mind. She slipped the dress on, pleased that the tailor had made the fastening easier for her to do on her own, not having the struggle she had with the red dress.

She put on the quite high, heeled evening shoes and crossed to the full-length mirror to look at the total effect. She had, of course, had the dress on for the final fitting, but hadn't really *looked* at herself in it, merely admired the dress. Now she looked at herself in astonishment. The gold seemed to emphasise the glow of her skin. She looked taller with her hair up and the dress seemed to accentuate her slender figure with its gentle curves. Sham, the tailor, had worked his magic. The dress was better than the one he had so carefully and laboriously copied.

Liz looked at her watch. Tonight Philip was escorting the Prime Minister, and Tim was due any moment to escort her. She was officially acting as Philip's hostess, but couldn't quite work out her role this evening, so when Tim arrived it was the first thing she asked him. He grinned. "Philip wanted to get you here, it was a pretext, though of course, you acted as hostess last evening." For a moment Liz was taken aback and not a little cross.

"It didn't require that to get me here, a normal invitation would have done."

"Hey Liz, lighten up. Enjoy." He grabbed her hand and made her twirl. "If I wasn't gay I'd fancy you myself. You look stunning, you really do." The reassurance was good to hear. She had been pleased with the way she looked but it was always good to hear it from someone else.

With Tim she stood near the double doors of the imposing reception room waiting for Philip to escort the Prime Minister. The guests were due in fifteen minutes and Philip liked to be in situ when they arrived.

The door opened again and Philip and the Prime Minister, who looked elegant in blue, came in together. Leaving Julia Naik for a moment he stepped closer to Liz and inclined his head towards her. She heard his whisper clearly. "What a very beautiful hostess I have tonight," and he squeezed her hand. "We will stand here," he gestured a place a few feet away. "You on my left Liz, and the Prime Minister on my right, please Prime Minister," he said formally.

The guests started to arrive. Tim acted as "introducer". There were so many titles of Indian dignitaries and ambassadors and diplomats from other embassies that Liz found it impossible to grasp and remember more than a few of the titles and names that Tim had so assiduously learned and now introduced so easily. She didn't discover until later that he had a most carefully arranged and concealed crib sheet in case of a momentary lapse, which fortunately didn't occur. It was one of the most impressive occasions Liz had ever attended, with so many eager politicians and diplomats so eager to "press the flesh". It made the literary award ceremonies she had attended in the past seem quite mundane by comparison.

Liz was still feeling a warm glow from Philip's whispered comment and the warmth of the hand-squeeze. She knew she glowed that evening and she also was aware that Philip was looking at her constantly. She carefully didn't look his way too often but felt his eyes on her.

Julia Naik, Liz noticed, was working the room, pausing for sufficient conversation with each little knot of people, leaving them smiling and feeling they had been singled out. Finally, Julia arrived where Liz was talking to the Minister of the Interior and his sari-clad wife. She gravely shook hands with Liz, while Philip, she thought, gave her a quick wink. Julia flashed her a warm smile and said sotto voce, "How good to see a familiar face." She turned to the Minister who said that he had read that the Prime Minister came from his home city of Chennai. He was obviously very proud to have this fact at his fingertips. "My parents certainly did," was her response which Liz thought very tactful, she could have so easily replied that her parents had come from there but that she was British-born which would have disappointed him.

The evening seemed to go on and on. Liz circulated as much as she could. People asked her so many questions, some presuming she was Philip's wife. Many were fascinated that she spent most of her time in Goa. Finally, the last guest left. A simple dinner in the room where Liz had had lunch with Philip was now laid for four. It was for the Prime Minister, Philip, Tim and herself. Liz felt very honoured.

Julia seemed to relax. She chatted like any other guest round a dinner table. She had a lovely sense of humour and, as Philip filled her in on one or two of the guests she asked about, she had a quip or comment that was astute and interesting.

After a while, they talked of other things: the world in general, the meaning of life and other philosophical subjects that come up when people are relaxed in each other's company.

It was two a.m. before they headed towards their rooms, walking together along the broad corridors of the embassy.

Liz, true to form, kicked off her shoes as she closed the door behind her. It had been a memorable two days and she felt physically and emotionally exhausted. As she undressed she thought about Julia who had told them a little of her early struggles, shrugging them off with, "It probably provided the catalyst I needed to motivate me." Somehow Liz doubted that. Julia would, she felt, have risen to the top in whatever profession she had chosen.

She hung the gold dress in the cupboard, her fingers moving gently over the silk as she did so. What a success and there would probably be a photograph to show Sham. The photographer had been active this evening making sure every guest would have a record of the event. The newspapers too would have a photograph of the Prime Minister and the Ambassador, and possibly The Dress might be in that one as well. Sham would love the publicity!

Finally, she slipped between the cool sheets as naked as the day she was born. Her hands rested on her flat stomach then moved upwards and she hugged her breasts to her. She was suddenly filled with such a longing. She had been able to convince herself that the celibate life suited her, but tonight she realised she had been kidding herself all this time. She moaned softly and Philip's face swam in front of her. She wanted him here, beside her in the bed, holding her close and whispering sweet words of love to her.

For a long time, she lay quite still, willing him to come to her room. Finally, she drifted into a deep sleep and dreamt of Goa and the beautiful beach she so loved to walk.

Philip had been widowed now for three years. Tonight, for the first time since Helen's death, he found himself thinking seriously about another woman. A woman dressed in gold –

with gleaming black hair, green eyes and a smile that lit up her face. He tried to banish her image, but couldn't, so with a sigh, he let himself remember her from the first moment they had met. He remembered every word she had said at their first lunch. He remembered the first time he had seen her in the red dress – he had thought he was looking at a film star. She stunned him, not just with her looks, but with her ready smile, her wit, her ability to listen in such a way that he knew she was not just listening on a superficial level, but was really hearing what was being said to her.

Helen, he remembered Helen. His sweet, dear, lovely Helen. He had so loved her. Petite and as fair as an angel. He used to call her, "my angel Helen". When she became ill, neither of them had wanted to acknowledge it. At first, even after she was diagnosed they talked about the future. Of next year. The next "posting" for Philip. They were in Vienna at the time wondering if his next posting would be as an Ambassador. "I rather want to be the Ambassador's wife," she had laughed. "I've done all the lowly wifey things – I'm ready for the numero uno spot now."

"So you shall be my angel," he had replied. Yet in his heart he knew this was not the case, she was dying. It was, he supposed, mercifully fast. Four months from beginning to end. He would never, ever forget the day she died. She seemed so bright, it was almost as if she was getting better. She asked for a mirror and tidied her hair. Even put on a touch of lipstick. That was in the morning. She ate no lunch, and he saw something in her eyes he had seen before. He had seen his mother die – he had seen that look. He kissed her and excused himself for a moment. He left her there and in the corridor outside her room he wept. He wept for Helen, he wept for himself, he wept for the future they would never share.

The Sister found him and led him to a chair. Sitting beside

him she put an arm around his shoulders and he wept again like a child. He stopped as suddenly as he started. He was losing precious moments with his dearest Helen. He wiped his eyes, straightened his shoulders and stood up. "Thank you, Sister," he said quite formally. "Thank you," he repeated. She smiled kindly and said nothing.

He returned to Helen. "Darling," she said, "hold me." He held her fragile body in his arms. "Philip," her voice was weaker than he had ever known it. "Philip, will you promise me one thing."

"Anything," he said. "Anything, my angel."

"I will always be your angel, won't I? Your only angel."

"Of course," he breathed. "How could you ever doubt it?"

"But promise me, Philip, you will find someone else to be the Ambassador's wife." He was horrified, how could she even think of saying something like that? She felt him stiffen. "No Philip, don't be angry with me – you will need someone by your side to love and be loved – as long as I am your only angel."

He felt her body slump – he raised his head from where she had rested in the cradle of his shoulder. She was dead. His dearest Helen, his darling angel was dead. Gently he extricated his arms from around her, closed her eyes and looked at her. His Helen had gone, her soul had winged off leaving him totally and completely alone.

※

The bed felt cool and deliciously comfortable. He wondered if Liz was asleep. He could picture her – eyes closed, face in repose, black hair fanned out on the white pillows. He wished he could creep into her bedroom and just see her. He cursed out loud – how was he behaving? Hardly the behaviour of a forty-eight-year-old British Ambassador. He had found celibacy easy after Helen died. From time to time he thought about what she had said about a future Ambassador's wife, but no one had ever come close to his even contemplating along those lines. He was vaguely aware that Deirdre tried terribly hard to be Miss Perfect – but he had never remotely considered her as a life companion. They had had dinner together on one or two occasions, but not alone, instead joining a dinner party with friends, where she was included to even up the numbers and because she was a likeable person in her own right.

Once or twice people had referred to them as a pair and Philip had made a point of saying nothing, feeling a denial might fuel a fire more than an acknowledgement even in the form of a denial. For the first time since Helen, his body was telling him celibacy was not for him. He threw back the sheet and naked, as always in bed, he strode into the bathroom and turned the shower on full.

The icy needles of water seemed to pierce his skin with their force. For several moments he stood accepting their icy deluge like a penance. He rubbed himself dry, took a sleeping tablet from an emergency supply he rarely touched and went back to bed. This time he focused his thoughts on the breakfast meeting he was to have with the Prime Minister before she flew off to Pakistan.

The crisis in Kashmir had been officially solved – but it was a fragile legislation and the Prime Minister felt she should and could make a continued contribution. Just before he fell asleep he thought he heard Helen's voice. "You've found her darling, found her…" The pill knocked him out, and the next morning it was forgotten.

Liz had asked for fresh fruit, coffee and orange juice in her room for eight a.m. Tim was to escort her to the airport at nine-thirty. Philip, she knew, was in a breakfast meeting with the Prime Minister, she wasn't sure, after her "in-bed experience" whether she wanted to see him or not. It was a decision she did not have to make, as Tim informed her that the Ambassador and the Prime Minister were sorry not to see her before she left but they were in an intense meeting with the Indian Prime Minister. Tim put the "intense" bit in, and he added that the Ambassador had asked Tim to thank her for coming and would be in touch.

Liz felt instantly deflated. Now she couldn't see him, she quite perversely wanted to and felt, quite unfairly, a little piqued. She was quieter than usual on the way to the airport and Tim was concerned that she might be unwell, but when he asked her she assured him she was a little tired that was all.

They chatted about places they had both visited and enjoyed and, as they said their goodbyes, Tim handed her a small package along with a letter for their now mutual friend Ronnie. "Excuse me using you as a postman but you will see Ronnie several days before this would arrive via the postal system."

They said their farewells with a sense of relief, both perhaps feeling, in different ways, the strain of the last few days. Once more, on the plane flying home, Liz found herself looking forward to being back in her own household again.

The faithful Ashok was at the airport to meet her. She hadn't expected Ronnie, there was little point in making an unnecessary journey on Goa's infamous roads. Nevertheless, she wished he had been there. Her spirits rose though, as they always did, the nearer they got to the villa. Ashok was full of chat about the new air-conditioning. It had, he informed her, changed their lives even more. The children slept better, and he and Nina slept well too. They would also be able to cook indoors during the monsoon, for the first time, in comfort.

How little it had cost her in time and money, thought Liz,

to make a little Goan family so happy. She felt cheered up as her life started to return to normality.

Ronnie heard the car on the drive and was at the top of the steps outside the front door before she was even completely out of the car. Ashok carried her case up the steps and handed it to Ronnie who handed it to the hovering Anjali. She was home. "Anjali I would like lemon tea in my room, please. Ronnie, you will join me?" He nodded, waiting for news of Tim and also longing to hear all about her time in Delhi in total. He had learned who the "important" guest was as the television and newspapers carried the story of "The Reception" and several photographs.

"One of you," Ronnie told her. "Beautiful as ever, you are SO photogenic, darling." Liz laughed as she opened the door to her bedroom. She briefly went to the bathroom, then rejoined Ronnie as he sprawled on the chaise longue.

Anjali knocked and entered with the tea – served as usual with some of Aarav's dainty biscuits. "Come on darling, do tell," Ronnie was on tenterhooks, he hadn't mentioned Tim and Liz knew that was taking a certain amount of self-control. "Just a moment," she said, standing up and reaching for her handbag. She reached inside and handed Ronnie a letter and a package. He tore off the wrapping with unseemly haste and she teased him, saying he was like a child in a candy store.

He opened the small box and inside lay a silver fountain pen. She saw him looking at it more closely and realised there must be an inscription. In answer to her unspoken question, he muttered, "Just a date." He looked up with a smile. "But rather a special one. I shall keep the letter for later."

"Of course," Liz completely understood, he needed privacy for that. She poured their tea and started to tell him about the last two days. She answered his questions about Julia, the people she met, the food, and of course the dress; but on the subject of the Ambassador, she was strangely subdued. "Come on, tell Uncle Ronnie," he said reaching out and squeezing her hand. Unbidden her eyes filled with tears which rolled uncontrollably and, she felt, ridiculously, down her cheeks.

"Hey, sweetie," Ronnie moved closer and as he hugged her she turned and rested her head on his chest. "I'm soaking your shirt," she said between gulping sobs. He just held her until she calmed, then he fetched a face cloth from her bathroom which he had dampened with cold water. "Mop up," he said putting it into her hand.

"Oh, Ronnie I am such a fool. I think I've fallen for Philip."

"It must be something to do with the Delhi air," he quipped and wished he hadn't. But she smiled and that was a relief to both of them. Liz didn't tell him everything, not the intimate things she had thought and felt whilst she lay in bed. But she talked about Philip in such terms that Ronnie knew at last her heart had healed and then she had promptly lost it again.

"Oh love how fickle," he quoted from a poem he had recently read.

"I don't feel fickle. I feel desperate!" Even she laughed at herself which made them both feel a lot better. They had their tea and then talked about other matters. Ashok and Nina's delight with the air-conditioning. The nursery situation and Bernadette. Liz was feeling concerned that her original plan to be really involved with the little ones was not happening and should Bernadette decide to leave it would be a disaster. She had become a mother-figure to them, and Liz, a sort of special aunt.

Finally, Ronnie excused himself, longing to be on his own and open the missive from Tim. He was not disappointed. Tim was full of plans to meet again soon. He had a few days leave owing and wondered if Ronnie would like to fly to Nepal and, among other things, see the sunrise over the Himalayas which he had seen and found breathtaking...

Ronnie filled his new pen with ink and wrote an affirmative reply. Two weeks would seem a long time to wait but he had a painting he was working on and hoped to complete it and take it as a gift.

chapter 17

Dinner that night was quite a quiet meal, with both Liz and
Ronnie wrapped in their own thoughts. Liz had attended the
meeting as arranged with the group of mothers and at ten forty-
five she said a tired goodnight to Ronnie and went to her room.
Usually, she enjoyed having him as a semi-permanent house
guest, but tonight she could have done with being on her own.

The telephone was ringing as she opened her bedroom door.
She made her desultory way across the room rather hoping
whoever was ringing at this time in the evening might hang up
thinking she was already in bed. No such luck. Liz picked up
the phone. "Villa O'Mal," she answered automatically.

"Elizabeth." Only one person called her Elizabeth.

"Philip," she responded her spirits lifting and her heart
giving irregular thumps.

"I know it's late, but I remember you saying you were
seldom in bed before eleven." There was a pause. "Are you
there Elizabeth?"

"Yes, I was just surprised to hear your voice."

"I was so sorry and disappointed that I didn't have an
opportunity to say goodbye before you left. I was somewhat
caught up!"

"I know."

"So I just rang to apologise." Liz felt a stab of disappointment, he only rang to apologise.

"Apology accepted." There was a slightly uncomfortable silence, then they both spoke together, causing the tension to lighten. "Elizabeth I really wanted to tell you how wonderful you looked. Like a shaft of gold last night. You were wonderful too, the way you socialised. The Prime Minister took to you as well." The last sentence Liz could have done without, but she very much enjoyed the first part of what he had said. "Elizabeth, we need to see each other again don't we, quite soon?"

Liz threw caution to the wind. "I want to see you too Philip."

"Right, that is settled then. This is my plan – I just hope it will fit in with your schedule. Over the telephone is not the greatest place to have this conversation, but I have no option."

"Oh," was all Liz could think of by way of response, wondering what was coming next.

"I have two sons aged ten and twelve, they are at boarding school and I am taking them sailing for three weeks of the Easter holidays to Greece. I wondered if you would like to join us for a week. I've chartered a forty footer so there is plenty of space for us all. Do you sail?" he asked. "Not that it matters," he added hastily.

"I've been sailing a few times, I know how to leap off at a quayside and tie up. I am sure I can manage a week, and yes I'd like to come, and I'd like to meet your sons." She said it all in a rush. What was she thinking, the rational voice in her head was asking. You hardly know the man, yet you are thinking of spending a week on a yacht with him and with two boys in tow who could be a nightmare.

"I will send you all the details," Philip continued. "As we

will already be there, will you make your travel arrangements and we will, of course, meet you at the airport." It was, she felt, good that they were travelling separately – a long flight would not have been the best place to talk and get to know his sons.

Following her conversation with Philip, Liz had to make a number of phone calls, particularly to Kathy to let her know the exact timing of her stay in London. She had decided it would be an opportunity to have a catch-up with her agent and do a bit of shopping for the holiday.

She went through her bikinis and decided she needed at least three new bikinis and a pareo or two. Philip had told her that suitcases were unacceptable on board, so whilst in London she wanted to purchase a smart holdall. She had a soft Italian vanity bag she used from time to time – it was a well-known brand and she recalled seeing a pull-along holdall in the same brand which she thought might be good to have and she liked the idea of a matching set!

Her memories of sailing were of very limited hanging space and shelves, rather than drawer space, and extremely narrow bunks. Admittedly, her memories were of a thirty-foot boat with four healthy teenagers on board so, hopefully, Philip's charter would be more upmarket. Her wardrobe, she decided, must be limited but interchangeable. Several pairs of capri pants with a number of tee shirts. One long floaty and totally uncrushable skirt, with slightly smarter tees for a possible dressing-up occasion should there be one. Little makeup and loads of sun protection, a large squashable hat, and a baseball cap for when sailing would complete her wardrobe apart from undies which took up no space at all.

In London she and Kathy both had hysterics when they looked at the size of her bag compared with the number of things spread out on her bed. She started to cut back, the towels were replaced with smaller ones, that helped. Underwear was minimised. Philip had told her she had her own "head" – the marine name for a bathroom. When she showered she could wash out her undies too, which meant taking half what she had planned. Finally, all was squeezed in and, in case of cooler weather, she carried a particularly cosy fleece.

Kathy drove her to the airport and, as they kissed goodbye in the drop-off zone, Kathy murmured, "Be good sister dear." Liz smiled. "On a yacht sister dear, there is no alternative!" But as the plane took off her heart raced, she was looking forward to seeing Philip again with a mixture of pleasurable anticipation and dread.

She had not liked to speculate about his sons. They might resent her terribly, she must prepare herself for anything. With no knowledge of prepubescent boys, she had no starting point, which she concluded was probably no bad thing.

Her week in London had gone well, her agent liked the new material she had forwarded, though he was pressing her for more. Liz had promised once she returned from Greece she would work harder! She and Kathy seemed to grow ever closer and Kathy's modelling career was really going from strength to strength. There also seemed to be a new and mysterious man in her life who Kathy, unusually for her, was being circumspectly reticent about.

Liz herself had been fairly reticent too. Having confided her feelings to Ronnie, she was now able to chat about a widowed friend with two sons. Her sister had grimaced. "Keep it as friends – who wants a ready-made family." It was perhaps an astute warning and Liz thought about the comment as the plane flew towards Greece.

The airport was near Lefkas where Philip had promised to meet her and they would then drive the short distance to the boat. Customs did not take long and, as Liz had found her holdall very quickly, it was not long before she was walking briskly through the doors to the waiting area, where Philip seemed to tower above everyone.

His smile was warm and welcoming as he kissed her on both cheeks. "I am glad you are here safely," he said. "I felt bad about you flying out here alone."

"Oh Philip," she laughed. "What nonsense, I fly everywhere alone, but it was kind of you to be concerned," she added hastily, feeling perhaps she might have hurt his feelings. She need not have worried.

"A spirited, independent lady," Philip said. "How nice."

They walked outside, Philip pulling her holdall behind them. The heat hit her. It was not the heat of India, but a gentler, less humid heat. "Where are your sons?" she wanted to know.

"I left them on board, under threat of serious penalties if they got up to any mischief. They had permission to go ashore near the yacht to buy ice-cream and lemonade but that particular bar was as far as they could go." Liz could imagine him laying down the law to his boys. She had a feeling they would not want to get on the wrong side of him. She was right.

chapter 18

John and James were eating their second ice-cream apiece. They had decided two ice-creams and a drink on board was better than one ice-cream and a lemonade on shore. John and James, better known as Jack and Jamie, were wondering what this lady that was coming on THEIR holiday was like.

"Elizabeth sounds a bit of a 'grand' name," Jack commented.

"She writes books," Jamie said, speaking with his mouth full of ice-cream and nearly choking in the process.

"I wonder what sort," Jack speculated.

"Not the Harry Potter sort I'll bet," replied his brother. Jamie suddenly had "that look" on his face. Jack groaned inwardly. Jamie was going to talk about Mummy again. He hated it when Jamie did that. He missed her too, but he didn't like to talk about her out loud – only in his head.

"Do you think Mummy would have liked this lady coming on holiday with us?"

"How can I know?" answered Jack a bit crossly. He saw his brother's eyes fill with tears. He was sorry, but he hated to see his younger brother upset and it was a long time ago now. Jamie sometimes said he couldn't even remember what Mummy looked like anymore except for the photos. "You were only seven," Jack would say, feeling inadequate and always wishing Dad was around at moments like this, but he never seemed to be. Perhaps because the boys never mentioned their mother to Philip, and Philip never mentioned her to them, no possible issues had been resolved.

"Do the boys talk about their mother at all?" Liz asked as the taxi drove them towards the harbour.

"Never," Philip replied a shade brusquely.

"Do you talk about her to them?" Liz said softly, as if walking on eggshells.

"How can I?" he replied. "They don't want to talk about her." A silence – a slightly uncomfortable silence – ensued and Liz wondered if she had said the wrong thing, but something had prompted her to ask – and now at least she knew. She sighed briefly. "A penny for them," Philip said good-humouredly. The tension she had felt momentarily vanished. "Just a bit tired I expect," she replied with a smile.

The yacht was, to her eyes, amazing. She had enjoyed a bit of sailing in her teens in Lasers, which were one- or two-man tiny water-skimming yachts, very susceptible to a sudden gust of wind that would blow them over and deposit whoever was sailing into the water, and of course the sailing with teenage friends on twenty- or thirty-footers. This was a real yacht.

The boys saw the taxi arrive and decided to wait where they were, out of sight for the moment. They watched through a porthole window as their father and a slim woman with black hair tied back and dressed in navy trousers and a white top paused at the gangplank. "From here she is alright – but close up she is probably a witch," Jack spoke in a fearsome voice.

"Oh no," Jamie said, looking upset again. Jack was cross with himself – he hadn't meant to frighten his little brother who after all was only a kid of ten.

"I'm pretending Jamie. I suppose she must be okay or Dad wouldn't have asked her along." Jamie looked mollified.

Once on board, Liz followed Philip down to the main cabin which was surprisingly spacious with a bank of seating fixed to either side and a central table. Philip showed her the forward cabin. "This is where I sleep, and this," he indicated, "is a small cabin the boys share, and they have obviously tucked themselves away. Our head, or bathroom, is here, and now let's show you your quarters at the other end of the ship."

He collected her holdall, which had been left at the foot of the stairs, and she followed him in to a narrow corridor. The door at the end was open and he walked ahead of her, putting the holdall down before announcing, "This is your cabin Elizabeth, I hope it will suit." Liz was dumbfounded. A double bed that one could walk around and a cupboard fixed to the wall with coat hangers neatly lined up, with adjacent drawer space. "Now for the pièce de résistance," said Philip, opening a door within the cabin. "Your own ensuite!"

Liz was amazed. A fully tiled shower and enough space for a washbasin and loo with enough space to actually turn around. It was unlike anything she could have imagined and she was both delighted and relieved.

There was a thumping noise and, in the confined space of the cabin, it sounded like a herd of elephants. "The boys," Philip laughed. "They don't actually know the meaning of quiet." Quite unceremoniously, announced only by their feet, two boys looking to Liz like two of William Compton's urchins, burst into the cabin.

"Hello Dad," they chorused in unison, as if they rehearsed the moment.

"Boys, you are not elephants are you?" Philip asked. They grinned. Both had managed to get ice-cream on their shirts and the smaller of the two, Liz noticed, smiling at them, still had the remains of chocolate ice-cream around his mouth.

"We just wanted to welcome," there was a pause and the younger of the two added, "the lady on board the *Griffin*."

"Hello," said Liz. "Which is John and which of you is James?"

"I'm actually Jack," said John.

"And I'm actually Jamie," said James, aping his brother's words.

"Well, I'm actually Liz." She rather liked Philip calling her Elizabeth but that was far too formal for the boys. "Actually," she said, unconsciously mimicking their turn of phrase, "I brought you something from England." She hastily unzipped the side pocket of the holdall and produced two books. The latest Harry Potter books, and signed for the boys by J.K. Rowling, who had become a good friend of Liz's.

"They are a bit hard for Jamie at times," Jack said a bit uncertainly, "but of course I'll help him out." Their father smiled indulgently at his sons. One dark-haired as he used to be, and Jamie fair-haired and fair-skinned like his mother.

Ushering his sons out of the cabin and turning to Liz, Philip said that she could take as long as she wanted to freshen up but that they planned to set sail in about half an hour. Although it was on the late side to set off, he wanted to make a quick sail to a quieter place and get away from the somewhat noisy bustle of Lefkas. "We're all provisioned up so we'll leave," he looked at his watch, "at sixteen hundred hours."

"Aye-aye, Captain," Liz responded happily. "I will report to the Captain in twenty minutes."

"I'm the first mate," said Jack.

"I'm second," added Jamie, as their father pushed them out of the cabin ahead of him.

"They are wonderful," Liz mouthed at Philip. He flashed her a grateful smile, followed by a grimace implying he only partially agreed!

Liz unpacked quickly – putting to one side a pair of shorts, a tee shirt and a baseball cap which she quickly changed into and slipped on a pair of deck shoes before making her way back on deck within the allotted time.

Philip looked at her approvingly. "How is it you always look so good?" She smiled in response, not always quite sure how to deal with his directness, and said a quiet, "Thank you."

"What is 'tage'?" Jamie asked looking at the emblem on her baseball hat.

"Taj," she corrected his pronunciation. "It's a hotel quite near where I live in Goa, India," she added. Jack was looking at her closely and she was very aware that she was under scrutiny from both of Philip's sons.

They motored down the Lefkas Canal and then, finally, in the second hour were able to sail. "Jack is our navigator. Right first mate?" Philip said.

"Yes Sir, Captain," he gave a mock salute.

"Jamie, would you like to tell Elizabeth about Nidri?"

"There is a hotel where we can swim in the pool if we want to, and there are lots of places to eat, and we can have pizza for supper, and can I call you Liz?" They all laughed and somehow it broke the ice.

"I love swimming in the sea or a pool, I love pizza too, especially on holiday, and I would love for you to call me Liz. I can see we shall get on famously," Liz replied.

It was as if she had passed some test. They all suddenly seemed more comfortable together and while she was told all about Nidri being a great place to provision up, Jamie said, "It is isn't it Daddy?" Jamie sounded so young as he forgot, for a moment, to be as "grown-up" as his brother.

Both boys, now far more relaxed, were calling Philip "Daddy", which Liz found endearing – they obviously tried so hard to be older than they were and she could tell how important they and Philip were to each other.

By the time they arrived in Nidri the wind was blowing quite hard. The sails had been taken down for the last mile or so and now Philip was looking to drop anchor reasonably near the shore. He found the spot and, with Jack holding the wheel, he went "forward" to drop the anchor. The sound of the chain being released seemed to go on for ages, but, as suddenly as it started, it stopped when Philip jammed the winch off. "We'll have to wait for a while to see if she's settled," Philip explained to Liz. "So how about a gin and tonic? Boys, you can break out the cola."

Liz found the family atmosphere quite overwhelming. It had been a long time since she had been in a family group. She suddenly felt terribly tired – emotionally, mentally and physically. It seemed ages ago since she'd said goodbye to Kathy at Gatwick and now here she was, only a few hours later, in the middle of nowhere with two boys she had never met before and a man she hardly knew.

As if reading her thoughts, Philip brought up a gin and tonic from below and sat beside her. The boys were below sorting out their drinks and she could hear them arguing about who had the most. Philip sighed and called down for them to stop arguing and read their new books or something, promising them that they would all be going ashore before long for pizza. There was immediate silence below.

Liz, glass in hand, looked about her. The boat was swinging gently in the breeze and other boats, far enough away for safety but near enough for company, swung as they did, all of the prows facing the way they had come. The boats swung again and now the shoreline was in view, every movement a slightly different vista. "It's so peaceful," she said almost to herself. Philip nodded.

"It's what I like about this sort of holiday. It's good for the boys too." They sat in companionable silence. The boat had settled and now Philip was happy to go ashore. As Liz watched, he fitted a small outboard motor to the dingy they had towed behind them.

The boys were told to clean up and put clean tee shirts and shorts on. "And," Philip added, "something sensible on your feet! I have to add that," he explained to Liz. "Or I find them wandering around Nidri barefooted."

Liz stood in the shower, very aware that she must be careful with the water. By turning the tap on and then off several times, she finished up feeling pretty refreshed, deciding that the gin and tonic had definitely helped!

She pulled on a new pair of blue capris and a recently purchased shirt. She brushed her hair thoroughly and, after a touch of moisturiser and lipstick, a quick look in the mirror assured her she looked okay.

Liz thought she had been very quick, but not quick enough for the boys who were already in the dinghy. Philip helped her over the rail and as she stepped off the boat and into the dinghy it wobbled seriously. The boys loved the wobbles. "It's like stepping on a waterbed," she shrieked, laughing as she made an ineffectual attempt to move. "What's a waterbed?" Jamie wanted to know.

"Not now," Philip was laughing too as he stepped into the dinghy, making it wobble even more perilously. "Elizabeth will tell you later." He started the engine and it spluttered into life making the whole dinghy feel much safer.

Now they were all settled and the dinghy glided over the water, it seemed safer than Liz had thought it would. After only two hundred yards or thereabouts, they drew alongside a simple wooden jetty. Climbing out was as wobbly as getting in, but this time Liz was prepared and managed to be a little more dignified.

"That's the hotel," Jack pointed out. "We swim there sometimes."

"Not in the sea," Liz wondered aloud.

"Not here, I never feel it is as clean as it should be," Philip said by way of explanation.

chapter 19

Liz lay in her firm, comfortable bed. It should have been a lovely first evening. They were all relaxed enjoying their pizzas, which Liz found were surprisingly excellent. Nidri was quite a big town and they had wandered around for a while before choosing the restaurant. "We always do this," Philip confided as the boys made a firm choice of venue. "We look at all the restaurants along here on the front and then finish up at the same one every time!"

"You've been coming here a long time?"

"Really since the boys could walk. Helen was a great sailor, though she always said she wasn't strong enough to pull the ropes. She was very petite, but I used to tease her and call her lazy bones." A shadow crossed his face. It was, thought Liz, the first time he had mentioned her name and it was as if for a moment her memory, like a ghost, came between them.

The second jolt of the evening was as they came to the end of their meal. As they were about to leave, a woman at the next table called to them. She was French and spoke beautiful English with the accent the English adore – very Maurice Chevalier. "Oh what a charming family Monsieur. Two handsome sons and a beautiful *maman*." Philip gave a tight smile and Liz realised he didn't want to go into explanations, perhaps distressing Jack and Jamie. Jamie had not heard but Jack had. He stood up and moved to the small space between the two tables. "That," he said, pointing at Liz, "is not my mother, just a friend." His tone was aggressive.

"Jack," his father said. "That is enough."

"She is not my mother," Jack repeated, this time loud enough for several heads to turn and for Jamie to look distressed. Jamie stood up and Liz instinctively put an arm around him to guide him out of the restaurant. "Leave my brother alone," Jack snapped. Liz dropped her arm like a stone and looked helplessly at Philip who had, by now, shepherded the boys and Liz out of the restaurant. They were all upset in different ways and for different reasons.

Philip was angry with Jack, yet equally cross with himself for not realising this might happen. Jack was angry that anyone could think Liz was his mother. No one could be his mother. Jamie was sad and feeling something he couldn't quite understand. He sort of wished she was his mother and then felt sadder because he didn't think he should think like that. And finally Liz. Unwittingly she knew she was the cause of the evening's disastrous end and was upset for them all.

Jack said nothing as they climbed back into the dinghy then, once back on board the *Griffin*, turned on Philip and said angrily, "Why did you bring her here? We don't want another mother – we have a mother, she's just dead that's all."

Liz tried to say she didn't want to be their mother but Philip, with a look that said, "Don't say anything", stopped her short. Quietly, and with as much dignity as she could manage, she said goodnight to each of them and went thankfully to her cabin.

Now, as she lay in bed, she wondered how she was to get through the next week. Never had seven days seemed so long.

Liz never knew what Philip said to his sons that night, but whatever it was, the next morning although Jack was quiet he was respectful when he spoke to her. After a few awkward moments, Jamie was his sunny self again and there seemed to be a slight bonding between him and Liz.

Philip found a moment when the boys were swabbing the deck to apologise for the previous evening's episode. It seemed to Liz that the comfortable atmosphere that had developed between them had returned to a more formal one again.

Jamie liked Liz – Jack was disgusted and felt betrayed but Jamie didn't care. Liz was kind and beautiful and during the sailing on the previous afternoon, she had told him lovely stories about Goa, and about the mother cat and kittens she had befriended, and the little girls who shared her home because they didn't have a mummy or daddy.

Later that day, as Liz and Jamie sat together on the front deck, they shared a magical few minutes as dolphins leapt and leapt again in front of the yacht as it sailed along. Liz looked around and Philip and Jack were deep in conversation in the cockpit as Philip steadily held the wheel in the light wind. Liz tried to attract their attention but the wind didn't carry her voice and so she just hugged Jamie as they continued to enjoy the spectacle, leaving Philip and Jack to what looked like quite a serious conversation.

"Wouldn't it be lovely to swim with them?" Liz commented.

"Let's do it." Jamie was already on his feet. She pulled him down beside her.

"It would be dangerous here Jamie, but there are places where one can swim with them."

"I'd love to go there," he said, snuggling up to her. "I wish you were my mummy," he said, snuggling even closer. Liz smiled, he was such a warm bundle of love that needed nurturing.

"I'll be your special friend if you will have me," she replied.

"That's nice, but can't you marry Dad?"

"Well, Jamie that is quite a question. One, he hasn't asked me and two, I really don't know your father very well, he is just a special friend. And the other thing Jamie is that no one can take the place of your very own mummy."

"I suppose not," the boy said slowly, "but you could try couldn't you Liz, you could really try." He sounded so forlorn and she wanted to say the words he wanted to hear but, of course, she couldn't.

"I know," she said finally. "We'll have a secret you and I – when we are alone like this, I'll pretend you are my little boy."

"Big," he corrected.

"Big," she repeated. "And you can pretend, just like a game, that I am your mummy. But, it must only be when we are quite alone. You understand that is the rule of the game."

"I understand...Mummy." He seemed to savour the word and it sent a shiver up her spine. What was she doing? She consoled herself by remembering it was only a game.

As Jamie got easier, Jack seemed to get more difficult. He couldn't help noticing how close his brother was to Liz. He found himself feeling threatened. Mummy had died and now Jamie was leaving him for Liz.

Philip too noticed how close Liz was getting to his youngest son. It pleased him and he thought Liz was wonderful with the boy. He worried about Jack and had several serious conversations with him, pulling him up on his attitude towards Liz.

"I hate her," said Jack more than once. Philip felt helpless, he was more and more drawn to her but realised that perhaps the yacht was not the happy relaxed space he had hoped for. They had had such happy times sailing, he and Helen. He looked surreptitiously at Liz. She was chatting again to Jamie.

They seemed to have developed a closeness he almost envied. She suddenly threw back her head and laughed and Jamie looked at her with adoring eyes. "Share the joke," Philip asked.

Jamie looked at his father with a mixture of sadness and respect. "Sorry Dad, it's private." Philip felt left out. Liz felt concerned that Jamie had inadvertently caused a chasm between the adults.

She moved along the cockpit and sat next to Philip. He looked fit and bronzed in his shorts. "Would you like to take the wheel, Liz?" She had felt nervous when she first held the wheel, but now she took it with confidence, enjoying feeling the wind in the sails and the lean of the craft as it skimmed across the deep, almost navy-blue sea. Jamie went forward to look out for more dolphins. Jack turned his back on Liz and then went below.

Philip sighed. "I don't know what's wrong with Jack," he said. "I have never known him so difficult."

Liz bit her lip. "I think I may unwittingly be the problem," she said, trying hard to keep any emotion out of her voice. She didn't want him to know how frustrated she felt about Jack, but also how Jack was spoiling their relationship or, more to the point, their what-had-been burgeoning relationship.

Philip nodded. "It isn't you Elizabeth, it was that wretched French woman. Her comment made Jack feel that I was forgetting Helen, which of course is untrue. Helen will always have a place in my heart."

"Of course," Liz said, feeling even more melancholy.

"Elizabeth," he put his hand over hers on the wheel. "I think I am falling in love with you." Liz's heart missed a beat. She had felt things were spoilt but they weren't. She turned and looked at him and gave him such a wondrous smile that his heart melted completely. For a moment it was as if they were alone in the world. The tension and longing between them something almost tangible.

"The wheel!" Philip yelled, as the yacht was about to do an "about". The moment had passed but it had moved their relationship up a notch.

chapter 20

That evening, as they tied up at the quayside in Fiskardo, Jack's spirits seemed to lift as he leapt ashore to greet a school friend on a nearby yacht. It was not a pre-planned meeting, but Jack had known his school friend and family were sailing in these waters and it was such luck to finish up in the same port.

The Smythes came over to see if Jack could have dinner with them that evening. As they had a daughter the same age as Jamie they suggested he join them as well. "It seems a terrible imposition," Philip expressed concern. The Smythes – a plump and jolly couple – answered in unison that it was really their pleasure. Philip suggested they all had breakfast together and agreed breakfast at The Captain's Cabin, at eight a.m. the following morning.

"Breakfast ashore?" Liz queried.

"Family tradition, we always have breakfast at The Captain's Cabin – a full English-style breakfast too."

It was their first evening alone. In fact it was the first time they had been alone since the memorable lunch they had shared at the embassy in Delhi. They were both a little constrained at first but a gin and tonic on a "boyless" yacht seemed to break the ice.

"Do you mind, Elizabeth," Philip asked, "if I tell you about Helen?" If Liz was taken aback she wasn't going to let him see it. She nodded and smiled. "Jamie is the spitting image of his mother, his colouring and his amiable nature. I'm afraid Jack takes after me," he grinned.

"You must have been quite a handful then." Liz smiled as she spoke.

"In hindsight I probably was, but I had both parents to put me straight. Jack misses his mother more than he can admit. He never mentions her and when she died he wouldn't talk about it – never has in fact." Liz made sympathetic noises, wondering whether Philip had talked properly to the boys himself whilst he was in the early stages of grieving.

"It would be better if he could talk." Philip nodded in agreement, continuing by saying that Jamie talked about Helen at intervals, missing the mothering she gave him. "Helen was excellent with the boys, but she babied them. I am not sure she would have coped so well with Jack now. Probably would've made as much of a mess of it as me!"

Liz was silent. There was much she wanted to ask. She also would have liked to tell him about her pact with Jamie, but it was a secret she shared with Jamie and she was not at all sure how Philip would react.

"You and Jamie seem to have a good rapport," Philip said.

"I think we do," she replied.

"Elizabeth, let's go and have dinner. There is a small taverna just out of town, about a ten-minute walk. Are you game?" Liz nodded delightedly.

"I'll just get different footwear," she said, looking ruefully at her dainty strappy sandals. "Sneakers might be better," she said almost to herself as she went below to freshen up and find more suitable footwear for a ten-minute walk.

A few moments later she rejoined Philip who was waiting for her on the shore. He leaned forward and took her hand to steady her on the plank. She didn't need a helping hand, they both knew it, and they continued holding hands as they walked in companionable silence, passing the boys and their friends enjoying a good feast on board the catamaran. Jamie waved, Jack scowled and, wordlessly, Philip and Liz loosened hands. Wrapped in their individual thoughts, they barely spoke. The road was steep and stony which took Liz's concentration. Once, she paused to look back at the view. The twinkling lights of the village below, the yachts too with their lights on the masts – it looked almost unreal as if a sudden blast of wind might blow it all away.

The sound of laughter drifted on the light breeze and, turning back to the road, Liz saw lights a few hundred yards ahead. "The taverna," Philip said, as if reading her thoughts. The tension caused by Jack's scowling face, which had temporarily spoilt their pleasure, was melting away. Liz was determined to enjoy the evening, it might be a first and last such occasion.

Philip was thinking such different thoughts. He was determined that Elizabeth was going to stay as part of his life. He felt sure Helen would approve. Jack was a problem to be sure, but he would grow up, and, like it or not, would have to accept Elizabeth as part of their lives. Of course, there was always the matter of Elizabeth accepting him…

There was no menu, but after ecstatic greetings from the owners and introductions all round they were taken to the kitchen to see the food cooking and being prepared.

Liz was enthralled. It was such a perfect setting – high on the hill looking down on Fiskardo. The atmosphere was lively and the friendliness of the owners and their teenage children was exceptional.

They sat drinking ouzo for what seemed like hours but also, in some contrary way, seemed like minutes. The ouzo loosened their tongues and Liz told Philip of her warm relationship with Jamie. Philip reached for her hand and gave it a gentle squeeze. *Poor chap, he so misses Helen,* Liz thought, *though I fear his memories of her are rose-tinted.*

"That doesn't matter does it," Liz murmured. They didn't talk anymore about the boys. They talked of India, of her writing, which seemed to fascinate him. He wanted to know how she got started on a novel and she explained her research and card index system for each book with easy cross references.

"It sounds complicated."

"It isn't," Liz laughed. "It has to be simple enough for me to understand it."

The food, when it came, was piping hot and delicious. Stuffed peppers and aubergines with a feta salad. Followed by lamb stifado with such huge plates of crispy chips that Liz felt defeated before she had even started. She hadn't eaten chips for years, but once started they were so delicious that she was amazed at her capacity.

Finally, strong black coffee, with small sips of chilled water between sips of the delicious coffee. They both sat back feeling more relaxed than they had ever been. Philip produced a pipe. "Do you mind?"

"I didn't know you smoked," Liz remarked.

"Only a pipe."

"I always think a man with a pipe looks relaxed." For a moment he looked startled, then lowered his eyes to concentrate on the igniting. After several puffs, he looked her straight in the eyes.

"You women," he said between puffs, "are very intuitive." Liz was puzzled. "Helen used to say a pipe relaxed me."

"Ah," said Liz, wondering what else she was supposed to say. She didn't really want to be reminded of Helen just now, at the end of what had been a romantic evening.

Philip sensed the shadow. "I'm stupid and tactless aren't I? Talking of Helen to you."

"You are neither. Helen was your wife, the mother of your sons." He nodded, but they both knew that the atmosphere had changed. They walked slowly back down the hill, both wrapped in thought. When they reached the yacht he kissed her lightly on both cheeks before going to check on the boys who had put themselves to bed and were both sound asleep.

"A night-cap Elizabeth?" he called softly so as not to wake the boys. She hesitated, then shook her head. "It's been a lovely evening, I'm ready for bed though I think." She wasn't, she was wide awake, but she had a great need to be alone. Four more days and the week would be over. She would fly back to London, and Philip and his sons to Athens for "some culture", as Philip put it.

He looked a little crestfallen – but said a quiet goodnight. He kissed her again lightly and she turned away and walked to her cabin. She felt hot and sticky, so showered – keeping her hair dry as she hated going to bed with wet hair.

Putting on a light cotton nightdress she suddenly felt the need for air. Even with the portholes open there seemed to be very little breeze. She realised now why Philip liked "mooring out" – the air was so much cooler at sea, rather than cheek by jowl, yacht by the side of yacht, in the harbour.

On a sudden impulse, and noiselessly with her bare feet, she made her way through the cabin and up the stairs leading to the cockpit. For a moment as her eyes adjusted to the lack of light, she thought she was alone, until a sudden light sound made her realise she was not. Philip sat in the prow, his pipe in his mouth, still dressed as he had been. "I'm sorry," she blurted out. "Am I disturbing you?"

"To the contrary, did you want to be alone?" Philip responded. She shook her head, then realised he couldn't see.

"I just wanted some cooler air."

"Come here and sit by me." She sat down by his side and, putting down his pipe, he put an arm around her shoulders.

She felt herself shiver – it wasn't with cold but with a nervous sort of excitement. She felt eighteen again, nervous, tremulous even and as unsure as any teenager. "Elizabeth, I've been wanting to do this ever since I first saw you." His head moved closer and the aroma of the pipe smoke on his clothes filled her nostrils.

His lips were on hers, gently at first, then, feeling her response, they became more demanding. She turned a little, settling in his arms, they paused, then their lips touched in a succession of gentle kisses.

There were no need for words, it seemed so natural when he stood up and, holding her by the hand, led her below to her cabin. They made love and, for Liz, it was as it had never been before. His body was urgent, yet at the same time, giving and caring. He touched her in apparent wonderment, whispering tender words that made her long to feel him inside her again and again.

Finally, and inevitably, he left her as the dawn was breaking, and she lay in a drowsy state between sleep and wakefulness, feeling her body was on fire with a longing for him to return and quench reawakened desires.

She showered and dressed for breakfast. She could hear noise from the quay and the boys running back and forth along the gangplank, sounding somewhat like a herd of elephants. It was, she smiled to herself, impossible for them to do anything quietly, unlike their father!

Dressing with care, after all they were having breakfast at The Captain's Cabin with Jack's friends and family, she put on pale pink Bermuda shorts with a sleeveless cotton top. She tied her hair back with a toning pink tie and put on her smart navy deck shoes. They were due to meet at eight and it was seven-fifty. She had a ravenous thirst and Philip's first glimpse of her that morning was looking, he told her, about sixteen and drinking from a bottle of water as if she hadn't had a drink for days!

She took another great swig and polished it off. "There," she said satisfactorily, almost smacking her lips. He grinned and dropped a quick kiss on her lips. "You look pretty boyish yourself Philip." He looked pleased and blew her a kiss as he called Jack to come back on deck as they were off to breakfast.

It was good to see Jack laughing and fooling with his friends. Jamie looked at her across the table and she gave him a conspiratorial wink. He smiled back happily.

Breakfast was a full English, which seemed totally mad, but perfectly proper! They all ate to their maximum capacity, washing it down with copious cups of coffee for the adults, and milk or orange juice for the children. It was a good start to a happy day. Jack seemed to have got over his grumps and Philip and Liz made a point of not sitting together and avoiding a lot of eye contact. She stole occasional glances at him and, once or twice, their eyes met and it was as if their eyes were smiling at each other without their mouths moving.

That evening, after a good day's sail, Liz cooked her first meal on board. After the bustle of Fiskardo, the bay that Philip had chosen as their anchorage was a welcome piece of quietude. They also swam in the crystal-clear water. It was so hot that they could hardly bear to wait to see if the yacht had settled in its anchor, then all four of them jumped in together.

The spaghetti with freshly cooked tomato sauce, which Liz had spiced up with some herbs she swam ashore to gather before it was too dark, was eaten in record time and Philip promised that the next morning they would swim ashore to do a recce of the shoreline.

They played a card game called Slippery-Ann. "Its proper name is Chase the Ace," Jack stated, "and Mummy always won." It was a simple comment but meaningful, and Liz wisely made no response, except to ask Jack from time to time what would be the best thing to do as she showed him her cards.

By now Jamie was yawning and took himself off to bed while Liz, Philip and Jack had a game of Scrabble. Liz won by a mile and the other two decided that being a writer gave her a distinct advantage and next time she would receive advance penalty points. What had changed Jack's attitude Liz had no idea, but she was grateful for it anyway. It made for a happier boat and a happier crew. It was not to last for long…

Once both boys had gone to bed the adults, like conspirators, stole to Liz's cabin. They almost tore off each other's clothes – the restraint of the previous evening forgotten. They had just finished a marathon in lovemaking when Liz became aware of a voice calling. It was Jack. "Oh my God!" Philip swore as he leapt out of bed, and was standing completely naked when a knock, followed by the door opening, revealed Jack.

It was difficult to tell who was the most shocked. Jack's face showed total disbelief. Liz felt mortified as she reached for the covers to hide her nakedness. Philip looked and sounded angry. "What the hell—" he started to say.

"How could you?" Jack looked in disbelief as his father reached for his pants. "Jamie's ill," he said abruptly and left. Philip didn't even glance round as he gathered up his few items of clothing and left Liz alone and utterly shattered.

During the next hour she heard comings and goings, and finally, unable to stand it any longer, she got off the bed, pulled on a sweatshirt and some trousers. Jack was sitting alone at the table, his head bent. She could tell he had been crying but he neither looked up nor acknowledged her presence.

"How's Jamie? What's happening?" The boy didn't reply. She walked through the salon to look in the boys' cabin and then in Philip's. They were both empty. "Where are they?" she demanded, standing in the space on the opposite side of the table to Jack. He didn't answer and she repeated her question. "Jack I need to know, where is your father and where is Jamie?"

He looked up and she saw his face was filled with hatred. "They've gone to the hospital, and it's all your fault. He doesn't care about us anymore." And with that final damning statement, he got up abruptly, walked to his cabin and very deliberately slammed the door.

Liz sat in the cockpit alone and worried. The dinghy had gone, and of Philip and Jamie, there was no sign. The hours passed and she watched the beauty of the day as the sun rose in the heavens without even seeing it. Finally, she felt the yacht tremble as Philip climbed back on board. He had not bothered to use the engine as they were so close to the shore, which was why she had not heard him coming.

"It's alright," he said, anticipating her question. "Acute appendicitis – thank God I got him to the little hospital in time. Where's Jack?"

"Gone to bed," she didn't add any more, what was the point? She must get out of his life and that of his sons. The hours had given her time to formulate a plan. She had already packed her bag, she would take a ferry back from Fiskardo to Argostolion airport – if there was no ferry she would take a taxi for the twenty-three miles from Fiskardo. She would take the first available plane that would take her in the direction of London, even if it meant a transfer or two.

This man needed to be with his sons and they both, in different ways, needed him so badly. He demurred at first, but not for long and he rowed her the short distance to the shore where a taxi awaited her. They said a brief goodbye as Philip handed her the holdall she had bought when things were exciting and happy. Of Jack, there was no sign, and for that Liz felt a sense of relief. Philip seemed withdrawn. They didn't touch, they certainly didn't kiss, not even the customary kiss on the cheek.

In the end, the taxi took her all the way to the airport, where she found a flight within a few hours. First Class, Economy, she would take anything she informed the ticket office. Her mind was in turmoil, her emotions raw. Her only focus was home.

chapter 21

They weren't expecting her at Villa O'Mal. Liz had taken a taxi. She was beyond exhaustion, she had been travelling non-stop since leaving the yacht. She was worried about Jamie, although Philip had seemed happy with the hospital on Cephalonia and had been impressed by the efficiency of the Greek surgeon and his staff, and by the time he had left the hospital Jamie was asleep in bed, though still drugged up. She hoped by now he was starting on the road to recovery.

The taxi arrived in the early hours. Ashok came running out at the sound of wheels on the drive. Nina followed him looking, Liz thought, very beautiful with her long waist-length black hair flowing over her shoulders to her waist.

They both looked very sleepy and she sent them back to bed after Ashok insisted on carrying her holdall into the villa for her. Anjali came down the stairs as Ashok put her bag on the marble floor and said it was good to have her home again. If Anjali was shocked at the tired-looking, rumpled figure before her she did not let it show. Putting her arm around her mistress she propelled her up the stairs.

The bedroom had never seemed so beautiful, but she could only stand, too tired to even take off her clothes. After a moment's hesitation, Anjali guided her mistress to the bathroom and quickly undressed her, then washed her face and hands gently with a soft sponge before reaching for the freshly laundered robe hanging from a wrought-iron hook on the back of the bathroom door. She led her to the bed and took the robe off and, as Liz stood mesmerised, replaced it with a nightdress before turning down the bed covers and encouraging her to climb in.

Wordlessly, Liz did as she was told, asleep before her head touched the pillow – she tried to say thank you, but her mouth wouldn't behave properly. She thought she heard the click of the door but then blissful oblivion took over.

Anjali woke Ronnie with his early morning tea rather earlier than usual. Before he could protest and once he was properly awake, she told him what had transpired. "No, no," she said hastily, sensing he was about to rush to see Liz. "She must sleep, that is what she needs most. She will need you later."

Several times during the next twenty-four hours Liz thought she heard the click of the door, but when she opened her eyes there was no one there. Anjali and Ronnie checked on her every hour afraid that if she woke alone, whatever had happened might mean she needed instant support.

Ashok and Nina came to the house at intervals to check on her. They had been shocked at her haggard appearance and crumpled clothes. This was not the Madame O'Malley they knew.

The door clicked again, Liz dragged her eyes open, quite surprised to find she had actually arrived home. Ronnie had just come in. He looked so anxious that despite herself she smiled. "It's alright Ronnie, I'll survive, but I'm so thirsty." As if on cue Anjali arrived. She had a tray with two tall glasses of lemon with some added feni – the local drink. She felt perhaps Madame needed a kickstart!

"Ronnie," Liz patted the bed beside her. "Come and sit here. How are you and what have you been doing whilst I've been away?" Ronnie made a few brief comments. "But it's you Liz – what happened to you for you to arrive home in such a state?" he asked. She felt immeasurably tired.

"Not now Ronnie, dear." He sensed that she wanted to be alone and he was correct. She wanted to think. Just once she was going to go over the whole time she had spent in Greece.

Left to herself, she started thinking about the happy times. Jamie and the dolphins and their secret pact. Hugging him and, probably foolishly, letting him call her Mummy when they were alone. The lovely walk along the front at Nidri and the most delicious pizzas, then the whole evening spoilt by the Frenchwoman's comment about what a lovely family they were. What had she said, like a film-star family? It had caused Jack to resent her, had actually said he hated her.

The night they had made love, she and Philip. He had been so gentle, so caring, yet asserting himself, so that she felt taken as well as given to. The taverna, the lights twinkling below them in Fiskardo. Jack at the door of her cabin, seeing his father naked by the bedside of an obviously naked woman, albeit under the covers. She shuddered at the memory.

Her attempt to talk to Jack when they were alone, Philip having taken Jamie to find a hospital. Philip arriving back with, at least, the news that Jamie would be alright. Leaving the yacht without even a kiss or a squeeze of the hand. It was over before it had even properly begun.

For the first time, she allowed herself to cry. Not simple tears, but howls from deep within her – some depth she had never known before. With her face buried in her pillow, her cries went unheard, but Ronnie knew she was suffering and felt powerless to help. He telephoned Tim at the embassy in Delhi. Tim was mystified, as far as he knew the Ambassador was spending another week in Greece. He hadn't been informed about the appendix problem and the schedule had been to take his sons to Athens, then back to the apartment in Cadogan Square, before returning Jack to Eton and Jamie to his prep school in Kent. He promised to keep Ronnie abreast of any news.

chapter 22

Cadogan Square was their London home. Philip opened the door, and he and a still strangely uncommunicative Jack went in. Wordlessly, Jack went into the large drawing room where, hanging over the fireplace, was the beautiful painting of Helen with a two-year-old Jamie on her lap and Jack leaning against her, looking adoringly up at his mother.

Philip watched the boy. He couldn't ever remember Jack looking at the picture before and certainly not as he was now. Philip started to say something but Jack either didn't hear or didn't want to hear. He turned and picked up his travel bag which he had dumped by the door and went to his bedroom, firmly closing the door behind him.

Philip ran his fingers through his hair. The gesture reminded him of Helen, who always asked when he did that what he was worried about... It had been a hellish few days. Jamie had started to recover, but Philip wanted him home. He pulled every string he could pull and a helicopter was sent from the British base on Cyprus to fly the three of them to Athens, where he had paid a heavy but worthwhile price for a Red Cross team to collect and escort them back to England. The charter company had fortunately been understanding about him not returning the yacht to the base and had arranged for two of their flotilla crew to collect and sail it back to Lefkas.

He walked to the drinks cabinet and poured himself a stiff, and for him a rare, whisky. At least Jamie was in Guy's Hospital now, he had stayed with him long enough to make sure the exhaustion of the flight hadn't done him any harm. He had hated leaving him but explained that he must get Jack home. "I want Liz," Jamie had said, which gave Philip a real jolt. He'd almost forgotten all about her in the turmoil of Jamie and the convoluted arrangements of getting him home. "She's back home in India old chap," he had answered with more confidence than he felt. Jamie's face had crumpled. "I want her here," he had sobbed.

Now Philip was conscience-stricken. He had let Elizabeth leave, barely even saying goodbye to her. He had almost wanted her out of his life. At that moment his only concern was his two sons, especially at that moment, Jamie.

God, what must she have thought! He'd behaved appallingly. He wondered whether to telephone her and looked at his watch. No, she would be asleep at this hour with the time difference.

Jack came out of his room and went to the kitchen. Philip clapped his hand to his head. He had arranged for his cleaner to stock the fridge for his return, but of course, they were way ahead of schedule. "Jack," he called. When Jack didn't answer he followed him into the kitchen. Of the boy there was no sign – he had gone out via the staff exit. Where he had gone Philip had no idea and he felt a sense of utter despair.

Walking back in to the drawing room he looked at the portrait of Helen. "What a pig's ear I am making of everything Helen," his voice low and defeated.

Jack was hungry. He left the apartment without telling his father and headed straight for the food hall at Harrods. He was only thinking about himself and bought what he wanted. His father didn't care about him anymore so why should he care about his father. He bought pain au chocolat, orange juice, eggs and bacon. He was going to cook himself breakfast. He hadn't done it before but he was sure it wasn't too difficult.

By the time he returned his father was frantic and, of course, shouted at him for going off God knows where without telling him. "There isn't anyone to tell except you," Jack replied, "and you don't care."

Philip felt angrier than he could ever remember feeling in his life. He got hold of his recalcitrant son, marched him into the drawing room and pushed him down in a chair facing the portrait. "We've never talked, you and I, have we about your mother since she died?" Jack didn't answer, just looked down at the carpet as if the design was particularly fascinating. "Jack, look at me when I am speaking to you." With reluctance, Jack looked at him squarely in the face. "Jack," Philip spoke more quietly now. "Jack I loved your mother, you probably don't remember but I used to call her my angel." He saw Jack bite his lip to stop a wobble that was becoming difficult to control. "When she died it was like," he searched for the words. "It was like a light going out inside me. I had no feeling – nothing. It was only because of you and Jamie that I pulled through. Your mother loved you so much and I knew I had to try, not to be just a good father, but try to be a mother to you as well."

"You failed," Jack said bluntly.

"Yes I did, I have. But life is like that. I tried my best in my way and it wasn't good enough and for that, I am truly sorry."

"I don't like that woman."

"Jack, that woman's name is Elizabeth. She is a dear friend and she has left us, all of us, and has gone back to Goa, her home."

"I saw you…" He couldn't finish.

"Jack you saw two adults, behaving in a way adults do. No one can ever replace your mother." The boy gave a sob and, for the first time, he started to cry. All the pent-up tears he hadn't shed when Helen died were shed now. Philip knelt on the floor in front of him and held his son tightly in his arms, wishing above all he had done this a long time ago.

They cooked breakfast companionably together. Philip drank his coffee black without saying what he might have said previously: "You didn't get any milk." He had learned a lesson and they had crossed a bridge together, but he knew he would have to build their relationship again on a new and closer understanding.

chapter 23

It took time for Liz to recover – it was as if she had been ill and was convalescing – but slowly, after a few weeks, she appeared to be her old self. Ronnie had tried to draw her out, but Liz would not be drawn and Ronnie resorted to finding out what he could from Tim.

The Ambassador had delayed his return, staying in London long enough for Jamie to make a full recovery after his emergency appendix surgery performed in Greece. When he eventually returned to Delhi, the boys having commenced their new school terms, he looked a bit gaunt (according to Tim) and seemed to have lost a certain spring in his step.

More, Tim didn't know. Ronnie had planned to tell Liz on her return that he was moving with Tim to his new posting in London. They were planning to share Ronnie's flat for Tim's two-year Foreign Office stint. Now Ronnie had to tell Tim he would have to live there alone for a while, he just didn't want to leave Liz quite yet. The two men commiserated with each other about the fickle finger of fate, realising though it was only a matter of time.

Bernadette had fallen in love. There had been an inevitability about it, but now it had happened. Liz was so happy for Bernadette, but wondered what she would do without her. Fortunately, Bernadette had that all worked out. Shantaram was a doctor and he had long felt the need to provide family-style homes for abandoned babies. Not in any way like an orphanage but with a couple acting like father and mother. He decided the acceptable number would be eight to ten children only. "Marie and Therese are like my children already," Bernadette had said.

They agreed that once they had found a suitable house they could get married and start on their plan. They decided to call it the D'Souza Home for Children and Shantaram had plans to, one day, have them all over India!

When Liz heard their excited voices and exciting ideas she almost clapped her hands in delight. Dear Bernadette had given her so much and looked after the little girls so wonderfully that she felt determined to give them something special as a wedding present. Bernadette smiled happily, she would be delighted, she knew, with whatever Madame chose for them.

"I would like to buy the first of the D'Souza homes," she told the delighted girl.

"Oh Madame O'Mal you can't, you shouldn't. I can't believe it." Liz smiled at Bernadette's obvious excitement while Shantaram looked stunned.

"You must start looking straight away, and somewhere nearby so that I can visit you and the girls, and eventually all your children."

It was only a few days later that Bernadette came to see Liz again. She was bubbling with excitement. "There is a house Madame, half-built, so we can add more as we need it."

They handed the little girls to Anjali's care and Ashok drove them the ten minutes or thereabouts to the house. It was down a narrow track that led to the beach and it was on two floors. The roof was on but the interior was unfinished apart from the wiring and plumbing.

Shantaram was waiting for them, looking, Liz thought, a really earnest young man with his bushy moustache. He greeted her solemnly. His ready smile in evidence as he showed Liz around, explaining how and where additional rooms could be built, but that to start with, three bedrooms would be sufficient. He seemed embarrassed to talk about the price but finally was cajoled into telling Liz the total sum the contractors wanted for the land and the build. Liz's first reaction was a pleasant surprise and she confirmed that would be her wedding present to the young couple, with the proviso that Marie and Therese would be cared for as their own. She knew she could trust Bernadette, who adored them, and her gut feeling about Shantaram was good.

Within three months or less the house would be ready so the young couple could begin to plan their wedding day. It was, Liz told Ronnie a lovely new project. Ronnie felt relieved, for the first time for weeks there was a bit of the old sparkle. Soon, quite soon now, he would be able to return to England and be with Tim.

Liz started writing again. A new idea had been taking shape in her head and she started making notes. Whilst sitting at her desk, she came across the letter she had received from Philip shortly after his return to India. When it had arrived she had still been recovering and the letter had helped not one bit. Now calmer and with more time passed she re-read the letter:

My dear Elizabeth,

I feel so bad about the way I let you leave so precipitously, but my mind was totally on Jamie and thoughts of how to help him, maybe even flying straight back to London. Once the operation was over and he was beginning to recover a little I was able to make rather special arrangements to get him home and straight into Guy's Hospital. We obviously made it back safely and I won't bore you with the details.

Jamie, thankfully fully recovered, has returned to school. Jack was a problem for a while but he and I have done some serious talking, not, you may think, soon enough. I hope the experience won't put you off the Greek islands forever.

Kindest regards,

Philip.

She sighed, what a hopeless letter. Not even warmest regards. It was over before it had begun. Her first reading of the letter hurt her feelings but now she was angry and tore it into tiny bits, letting the pieces fall into her waste-paper bin. She mentally closed the book on their ill-fated relationship. Liz had wrongly presumed he would be in touch before long but the letter was of a finality that brooked no argument. Once again she picked herself up and resolved she would never, ever allow herself to be hurt like this again.

chapter 24

Ronnie had left. He had noticed Liz's new determination. She was writing three to four hours a day, she was visiting Bernadette's new house once or twice a week, and she had bought herself a horse, having had an air-conditioned stable built, and she was riding in the early mornings and evenings along the beach, often through the breaking waves.

Ronnie realised Liz needed things in her life to make her feel she was making a real contribution. It had started with the house and Ashok and Nina. Ashok's driving lessons and making their home even better with the air-conditioning. The two little girls she had "rescued", and the employment of Bernadette to care for them. Even rescuing the cat and kittens!

He was delighted she had started entertaining again which pleased Aarav who loved and excelled at special lunches and dinners. He liked nothing better than providing "party food", as he called it.

Finally, Ronnie told her he was leaving. She hardly demurred which made him wish he had left sooner, though in his heart of hearts he knew she had needed him until now. She didn't show her emotions like she used to, and he hoped she wouldn't develop into a withdrawn and lonely woman.

Ronnie was perhaps more aware than Liz was, that she needed life and vitality around her and to his mind there was not enough of either in her life at the moment. Liz had not wanted him to know how much she would miss him and almost managed to convince herself that it would be good to have the Villa to herself again, though she knew she would miss his cheerful and good company desperately.

Reading the letter from Philip had depressed her as well as making her angry. She hadn't bothered to reply – it somehow didn't seem appropriate but she had written to Jamie. In their many conversations, he had told her the name of his prep school and she had dropped him quite a brief note, saying she hoped he had made a full recovery and that she would always remember their time with the dolphins.

To her surprise and immense pleasure, she had received a letter back, almost written by return. It was such a sweet letter, and it brought the memories of the warmth between them flooding back. Soon they were corresponding regularly and it was from him that she first learned that Philip was moving to Paris. A few days later she received a formal invitation to a farewell party for the out-going Ambassador. Across the bottom, Philip had written. "Had you heard I am off to Paris? Hope to see you at this event." No signature, nothing. She sent a formal refusal stating a prior engagement – then regretted it – but it was too late, she couldn't undo her refusal.

*

It was, thought Philip, quite wonderful to be in Paris. He had always loved the city, indeed he and Helen had spent their honeymoon there. He even visited the small boutique hotel where they had spent a few halcyon days. He tried not to think about Liz. She had not come to his farewell party, which he had quite deliberately not pressured her to attend. If she wanted to come it would be because she wanted to see him. When she sent her apologies claiming a prior engagement he took it that she did not want to see him again – so that was that.

He tried not to dwell on their lovemaking and the few happy hours they had shared. He remembered putting his hand over hers on the wheel of the yacht and he smiled mentally, as it had caused a momentary loss of concentration on her part and the boat almost went "about", the sails flapping frantically.

He remembered the perfume of her. The smell of her newly washed hair. The soft silkiness of her skin and her responsiveness to his touch. He banished thoughts like this regularly, but as time went by, when he saw a figure in a crowd that for a split second he thought was her, his heart would miss a beat. Then when he drew closer, or the woman turned around and it was not Elizabeth, he would feel bereft, a feeling almost like losing Helen again, and that made him feel guilty.

The only good thing was Jack. He seemed happier these days. He was glad his father was in Paris, which meant exeats could be taken at home, rather than having to stay behind in school or stay with friends and their families who probably he felt, incorrectly, were having him, and sometimes Jamie too, out of a sense of duty.

It was on one of these exeats that Philip found the letter. He was helping Jamie repack his small bag to take back to school, when he noticed a letter under some shirts he had picked up to hand to his son. Jamie saw him spot it and reached for it, just as Philip picked it up. "That's mine," Jamie said, a little panic in his voice. He just didn't know how his father would react.

"What is Elizabeth doing writing to you?" Philip asked, his voice registering genuine curiosity.

"She just does," Jamie answered resolutely, tying his

shoelace as he was trying to think what to say. "Because she likes me, that's why." He added a shade defiantly.

"Well," said Philip with a smile on his lips which he didn't feel. "She doesn't write to me does that mean she doesn't like me?" The now eleven-year-old Jamie looked puzzled.

"I think she does like you," he said carefully. "But she doesn't ever say it." Philip thought the subject best left alone, he longed to know what was in the letter but didn't feel he could ask to read it, and Jamie didn't offer to show it to his father.

Philip found he felt hurt and then had to rationalise things to his satisfaction. *She doesn't write to me because*…it was like a game. He kept starting the sentence off and when he got to the "because" he put different endings on the sentences. She didn't like him. She was cross with him. She was offended. She had other things to do with her life. She had a new lover. It was all most unsatisfactory, particularly when he realised the last thought was probably the most accurate!

He tried again to erase her from his thoughts, but at night she would feature in his dreams. Occasionally, wonderfully, they were making love as they had that amazing night on the yacht. He felt the warmth of her kisses, he felt her touches and her responses as he touched her. Other times she was running away from him, glancing back then running again, always elusive.

chapter 25

Jamie's letters arrived, full of the exciting exeat in Paris. He loved the Metro. He loved Montmartre. He loved the Eiffel Tower and the Bateau Mouche that went up and down the River Seine. He thought the embassy even grander than the one in Delhi and he had made some friends in Paris already. He still loved her and he enclosed a photograph of one of the school cats he had painted. Liz felt he had really caught the animal's personality. It looked a real feline, which Jamie said was its name. *The cat*, Jamie explained in his letter, *is called Feline and people say he is. What do they mean Liz, please? Oh, and by the way M* – which was what he called her nowadays – *M, could you please send me a photo of you? I have a frame and I'd like to be able to say goodnight to you – please, like the other boys do with their mummys.*

Reading it, Liz felt a lump in her throat. She had thought about sending a photo when he had mentioned it before and she realised he was not going to give up. She looked through her selection and found one of her cuddling the mother cat, who she could tell him was called Mother Cat – about as ridiculous a name as Feline she thought.

Jamie looked forward to her letters. She always signed them "Lovingly L". He understood that the "L" really stood for Mummy, which is why she didn't sign Liz, which would have spoilt it. One of his friends saw a letter once: "Why does your mother sign herself like that?" he wanted to know.

"It's a big L meaning 'big love'," Jamie had responded quickly. His friend accepted it in the way friends do. When he received a letter from India they would say, "a letter with a big L Jamie." He didn't care – he knew deep down Liz loved him like a mother should, and he thought of her and wrote to her in those terms. He was asked sometimes if his parents were divorced and he was able to answer quite truthfully, "No". He explained that his father used to live in India and now lives in France and L goes between the two countries. He knew it was a lie and it was certainly wishful thinking, but he convinced himself that it was acceptable. His friends were suitably impressed and soon the subject was forgotten.

One of his friend's mothers was slightly mystified when she heard of the supposed living arrangements of Jamie's parents, as she remembered when the very sad news of Helen's death was made public, but wisely decided to keep her own counsel and say nothing.

Jack had grown up during the last twelve months. At thirteen, sex was often a topic of conversation amongst his friends. There were times when it seemed, apart from sport, the most major discussable "thing". With the space of time, he began to understand a little better that his father wanted to fuck Liz. He acknowledged she was pretty in an old sort of way. One night he told his closest mates how he had found his father stark naked by the side of the bed, with the obviously naked body of a woman, partially covered by a sheet. He hadn't noticed more than Liz's horrified face peering out of the covers, but a good story was always better for embellishments. He had to tell the story several times, adding a little more with each telling because they were all laughing so much.

Jack's description was not graphic enough, so they wanted details. "Had he got a hard-on?" one friend asked, whilst another wanted to know about the smell. "Did it smell of you know – sex?" Jack made up what he couldn't remember and, somehow, though the whole incident had been blown out of all proportion, it all began to seem less important than it had at the time when he was so shocked to see his father in that light. Now talking about it with his friends put the whole episode into better perspective.

He found, to his surprise, he was beginning to forgive Liz – just a little. He had already forgiven his father, for they had grown closer after the showdown in London some months ago. He blushed, remembering how he had sobbed in his father's arms and even felt the wetness of his father's tears too.

Now he had his friends rolling on their beds with laughter. Liz was now totally naked too, and as his father got off her as Jack had entered the cabin, he saw his father's cock was wet and glistening. No one bothered to remind him the story had changed, they enjoyed it far too much for that.

Jack knew Liz wrote to Jamie – he had found a little stack of letters under his brother's clothes in a drawer. Jamie had been out, so without any compunction, he took them to his room to read. He noticed Jamie had numbered them in the top left-hand corner. This was very helpful as he wouldn't muddle them up.

He started with number one. It was written to Jamie at school, asking if he was fully recovered, hoping she had the correct address, saying how much she had enjoyed being with him on the yacht. She would never forget their secret pact and how she so loved sharing the dolphin experience with him. Jack felt real pangs of jealousy. The second and subsequent letters were even warmer, more loving. Like a mother's letter. Jack went through a gamut of emotions. He wanted to burn the letters or tear them into tiny pieces. He wanted to kill Liz and punch his brother for his disloyalty. But, the more he read the more envy he felt, and he decided that every holiday from now on he would make sure he continued to read the letters that were written since the last number he had noted.

There were sometimes references to him. One letter, obviously in reply to something Jamie had written, read: *Of course, Jamie darling, I love Jack. I only wish I had been able to get to know him like I've been able to get to know you. I hope one day Jack will forgive me and know, as you do, that I never wanted to either "steal" your father away from you or to take your mother's place. That is inviolate and always will be. If you don't know what that means sweetheart – look it up!*

The letter continued cajoling him to work hard, so that in due course he could join Jack at Eton and then went on to tell him about the second horse she had bought. *It's silly really*, she wrote. *I can't ride two horses at the same time, so I ride one in the morning as the sun comes up, and the other in the evening as the sun is setting. Coco is great at following when I am riding Guinness. But when I ride Coco I have to put Guinness on a long rein as he goes swimming out to sea and won't come when I call. I hope he will soon learn to behave better because it is a nuisance having him on a leading rein.*

Perhaps, when you are older you can come and canter on my beautiful Benaulim beach with me and feel the magic.

Jack could visualise her, black hair streaming, she didn't seem old anymore and he began to realise why his father had been attracted to her vibrancy. If Jamie noticed the letters were not exactly as he left them, he never said and it was only years later when they were both married and with families of their own that Jack told Jamie that he had read the letters, and Jamie confessed he knew.

Liz's letters brought them closer because, although it was Jamie she wrote to, she never failed to mention Jack, almost as if she knew he was reading her letters too. Liz opened Jamie's letters with a smile. He always had so much to say. This time he was full of news of Eton. He was going and she would, he informed her, have to write to his new address from September.

He also wrote that he had thought for some time that Jack was reading the letters she wrote to him, which, he informed her, he kept in chronological order, carefully numbered. Because of his suspicions, he had placed a hair through the elastic bands that held them together, and when he returned from some event or other, the letters were as they had been, but the hair was missing.

It was from then on, particularly, that Liz started thinking of Jack for a portion of the letter. Jamie noticed and commented that it was nice for Jack, but of course Liz could never comment back. Over the next year or two, on one pretext or another, Jamie would make sure the last few letters from Liz were available for Jack to read. He loved the conspiracy, unspoken of, of course, but apparent to Jamie in every letter. He loved her more than ever, but with his new friends at Eton, he didn't lie. He could face the truth better now, Liz was Liz – a very special friend was how he described her, but in his head, he knew that Liz was a second mother to him and he felt very happy with that thought.

Jamie often wrote that he would like to see her, and one day she decided to succumb. She would be in London in June on book business, as she called it. Why, she suggested, didn't he meet her for tea at a tea shop she named in Windsor? Jamie could hardly contain himself and Jack, when he read the letter, started to work on a plan to see her himself.

chapter 26

Liz arrived in Windsor just after lunch. Having finally found a parking space she went straight to the tea shop. She reserved a table for three-thirty, hoping that the atmosphere and tea would be rather better than the dour-faced woman who took her booking. She explained it was a booking for two but it was possible that they might need a third place. "I'll have it set for three then."

Liz explained as carefully as she could that if the third person arrived she needed to seem surprised and therefore she would really appreciate some cooperation. With a hurump and a shrug of the shoulders, the woman agreed, writing something down on the reservation book on the desk. "It all sounds a bit odd to me," she said somewhat sourly. Liz did something she had never done before. Pulling out one of her cards and giving her brightest smile she said sweetly, "I so appreciate it. I am a well-known author and this is an important occasion for me." With a warm thank you, Liz left the tea room with a sigh of relief, smiling inwardly at the change of expression that her words and the card had made, even extending to the offer of a special cake the woman had suggested, consulting her watch. Liz had shaken her head. "They will choose from your excellent menu, thank you."

Wandering around Windsor gave Liz a rare opportunity to browse, checking the time regularly as she wanted to be first to arrive. The bookshop, she noted with pleasure, had several of her books on display and a small boutique prompted her to buy a rather beautiful scarf.

At exactly three-forty she was sitting at the table in the tea shop, and at precisely three-forty-five Jamie arrived. She hadn't seen him arrive, being momentarily distracted by the menu just delivered by a pretty young waitress. When she felt a tap on the shoulder she stood up immediately and they hugged each other before they sat down.

"I can see the road perfectly from here," Jamie said. He was almost as excited about the possibility of Jack turning up as he was to see her, but that didn't matter to Liz. He was here, grown so tall in a relatively short time. "It's so good to see you Mother," he said, savouring the word.

"Oh dearest Jamie, you are the son I never had – the baby I craved just about the time you were born." They grinned at the stupidity of the conversation, though in their hearts they knew a special bond existed between them.

"He's coming," Jamie whispered urgently. He leaned slightly forward nearer the window, he wanted to be sure Jack would see him without any difficulty. Liz's heart gave a leap. *Please, God, we are doing the right thing.* Jamie waved – he wanted to be sure Jack saw him. The tinkle of the bell announced his arrival. "Hi there, bro what—" He stopped in his tracks. "Liz, what a surprise!"

As Liz would say to Jamie afterwards, Jack deserved an Oscar, his look of feigned astonishment was a wonder to behold. "Hello Jack," Liz said quietly. "Won't you join us for tea?"

"There isn't a place," he began. On cue, at a raised hand from Liz, the previously dour woman came forward with a smile.

"Are you ready to order now Madam?"

"We would like another chair and place setting first," she replied. The woman nodded and bustled away. "That old battleaxe is never as polite to us Etonians," Jack commented in mild surprise. "The advantage of age," Liz answered smoothly.

For a short while the conversation was a little strained, but with the arrival of tea, cucumber sandwiches, scones with thick clotted cream and strawberry jam, followed quickly by fruit cake and another round of scones they relaxed a little. They were like hungry boys the world over and Liz, sipping her Earl Grey tea, watched with contentment. She couldn't help but laugh at the speed with which everything was consumed – she had eaten only one small cucumber sandwich and enjoyed two cups of tea in comparison with their mountain of consumption.

Finally, every plate was cleared, every crumb tucked away. It was, of course, Jack who raised the subject – overly casually he asked, "So how's Dad these days? We haven't seen him since exeat."

"Then you have seen him a lot more recently than I have," she replied. "The last time I saw him was on the yacht in the bay we sailed to from Fiskardo. Remember that Jack?" He had the grace to look abashed and to Liz's astonishment, he suddenly blushed bright scarlet. She surmised he was remembering seeing his father standing naked in his cabin. She would have been horrified if she had known he was blushing from remembering the embellishments he had given to the story.

Possibly as a result of his guilt he turned on the Broderick charm. He looked so like his father, his gestures, his mannerisms – even the way he laughed. It gave her quite a jolt and the empty space in her heart longed to see Philip.

She walked back to school with them, hugging both before saying goodbye. She didn't know about them, but she certainly had tears in her eyes as she walked back to where she had parked her car.

Writing to Jamie had never been difficult, or even a chore, but now Liz decided that, as Jack had obviously enjoyed the letters she had written to Jamie, she would write to Jack too. At first, it was not always easy, but Jack wrote back, stilted at first, but gradually becoming more fluid and relaxed. He wrote mainly about school, his sporting activities and languages which, like his father, he was developing a flair for.

He managed to drop in, casually, of course, mention of his upcoming birthday. She sent him a book of Hindi which she thought he might find fun, bearing in mind he had spoken a little when they lived in India. Over the next year or two, it became a regular occurrence to meet up once or twice a year. If her sister wondered why she made these short visits from India she didn't question it, for Liz seemed happier again now.

Liz had grown increasingly fond of Jack, who decided she should have an official title. Adopted Mother, he finally came up with which was soon shortened to AdMo. Liz wasn't sure this was either right or proper, pointing out that when their father married again they would have a new mother anyway. "He won't get married," Jack announced confidently one cold wet afternoon over tea.

"Only to you," Jamie piped up.

"I'm afraid that was over a long while ago, and if he does find someone to make him happy you two had better behave. None of that old Jack treatment." They both looked at her carefully.

"I think Dad still loves you," Jamie said solemnly. Liz burst out laughing.

"And why, young man, do you think that?"

"Well, every time he takes a lady out he always says she can't hold a candle to you."

"It's true," Jack added. "I don't know if he just says it to put us off the scent or whether he means it." Liz nearly choked on her scone.

"You two are priceless, I shall refuse to let this conversation continue or it's no more cake for either of you."

chapter 27

Ronnie rang just after she arrived home. Tim was going to Italy but beforehand he had some leave due and they wanted to travel around India for a while. Could they, Ronnie wondered, come and visit Liz for a few days? "Tim has never seen your lovely villa or the beautiful beaches there."

Liz was delighted. It would be great to see Ronnie again and she had always liked Tim. They talked dates and time of arrival and Liz said she would lay on a party of some kind. They were, she knew, party people.

A few days later she had another unexpected telephone call – this time from her new agent. She had hoped to meet him on her last visit to England as her previous agent had retired and his nephew, whom she had not yet met, had taken on his uncle's clients. It seemed he was taking a holiday in India and rather wanted to mix business with pleasure. Could he visit her and could she recommend a hotel nearby?

"I can, of course, recommend a hotel," she replied. "But why don't you stay at the villa?" After a moment's hesitation, he agreed and she realised his visit would coincide with that of Ronnie and Tim. She just hoped he wasn't gay as well – she didn't feel she could cope with a gay triangle.

Aarav was in heaven. At last Madame O'Mal was going to do some real entertaining again. They would have three house guests plus one dinner party for twelve, and, even better, a large luncheon buffet for around seventy, with music, lights in the garden and tables overlooking the beach and sea. He immediately requested that Nina be allowed to help him, she was, he told Liz, a really good sous chef these days, apparently delighting in learning about foreign foods and particularly good with a whole range of desserts from crème brûlée to terrine of lychees.

Even Liz was getting excited. It had been a long time since she had held a big party, she hadn't been in a party mood for a while. She looked in her wardrobe and knew she could wear neither the red or the gold dress, so she moved them to the back of the cupboard. Even looking at them brought back too many memories.

Bernadette came to visit, bringing Marie, Therese and two more little girls she and her husband had already taken under their wing. She seemed troubled about something and Liz knew that she must be patient, waiting for the girl to speak when she chose.

They sat in the shade of the palms watching the little girls play whilst the babies slept in the big pram they shared head to toe. "It seems I can't have children," Bernadette said quite suddenly. The response "but you already have four" almost slipped out. Liz bit her tongue it would have been a thoughtless and flippant comment. "Oh Bernadette, I am sorry, so very sorry. Are you sure?" Bernadette nodded wordlessly. They were silent. Liz knew that in her own good time Bernadette would talk, it was why she had arrived unannounced today.

The girl pulled herself up straight, and with her eyes cast downwards said in a low tone, "I was raped you see, by my uncle. I was very little three or maybe four, but I still remember. It happened later too, then my parents found him one night because they heard me crying and he was sent away. I was badly hurt by him physically I mean and had to go to the hospital."

It was Shantaram who had thought there might be a problem because of what had happened, she continued. "We have tried so hard to have a child of our own. The hospital did many, many tests and now, finally, they told us yesterday there was no hope."

"Oh, Bernadette, I am so very, very sad for you both."

"I know Madame, Shantaram said you would understand."

"Shantaram is a kind man Bernadette, you are fortunate to have found him – and he you."

"He is sad, but do you know Madame that yesterday he told me that the next child we take in, he is sure will be a boy and he will be our son, as the girls are our daughters." Liz hugged Bernadette to her and they both cried. Marie and Therese stopped playing and came to look, fascinated to see "grown-ups" crying. They looked so grave and concerned that Liz and Bernadette wiped their tears and each picked up a little girl to hug. "Perhaps that is why God sends me children," Bernadette said quietly.

"I am sure you are right," Liz reasoned.

*

Alex Wylde arrived a few days later. Liz hadn't known quite what to expect. He was tall, fair-haired and blue-eyed behind round glasses. He was, she thought, quite serious looking and probably about her age. She later found out their birthdays were a few days apart, although he was one year younger.

Ashok had met him and Alex confessed to being slightly shell-shocked at the state of the roads and the occasional mind-blowing moment of Ashok's driving, which, in truth, had not improved a great deal since his early driving lessons with Ronnie.

Liz showed him to his room, giving him the opportunity to shower and change after his overnight flight – it was now mid-morning in Goa. Before leaving him she asked if he would like a late breakfast or an early lunch. He decided on lunch but insisted it be at the Goan time as he wanted to adjust quickly. He would however like a cup of Earl Grey tea if it was possible. "A man with good taste," she responded smiling.

Alex looked refreshed after his shower, and after a few pleasantries over Earl Grey, they started discussing the first chapters of her latest book. It was, unusually, based on a boys' boarding school and his first comment was that, as per her reputation, she had obviously researched her subject with her usual thoroughness.

Liz felt a pang of guilt – seeing the boys regularly, hearing their comments on the masters, senior boys, sport and general "boy" language had sparked the idea of a missing boy and a diplomatic incident. "Your synopsis is different though, Liz."

"Really?" she replied, a shade dryly, knowing full well what he was going to say. That the ending was unclear and, of course, she could not explain to herself, let alone to him, that she had no idea what the final scenario would be. She decided to come clean. To her relief, he seemed unperturbed. "In a way Liz, that's good – it leaves you with more flexibility. I must say I want to know who the villain of the piece is."

"So do I," Liz joined in his laughter. She poured them more tea and they both felt more relaxed now that their first business conversation was over, though she knew before he left he would be pressuring her for a completion date for the first draft.

"Did I see stables from my window?" Alex asked.

"You did. I have two horses, do you ride?" When she learned that he did they went outside to admire Coco and Guinness enjoying the cool air in their air-conditioned stables. Having admired the horses, Alex wanted to know where and when she rode. Having explained her routine she invited him to join her pre-sunset ride. He had no idea how privileged he was, the companionship of her horses was sacrosanct. Liz always rode alone, she loved the peace and solitude – the company of her horses all she desired.

When she returned from her ride she would wash them down; this had caused consternation in the household when she had her first horse, but now they accepted that Madame O'Mal did things her own way. Although Ashok designated two garden boys to keep the stables clean. There was, he told Nina, no way Madame was going to do that chore. Liz had explained that washing down and grooming a horse was part of the relationship between rider and horse, and that in England most people did what she did and that it was their choice. Liz told Ashok that riding in the winter months could be challenging and that the horses sometimes rolled in the mud for sheer pleasure. He was surprised to learn they had special blankets for the horses to wear if it was too cold, and at the end of the winter the blankets all had to be washed ready for the next winter. Ashok couldn't even begin to picture it, but if Madame O'Mal said it was so, it was so!

Grooming her horses, she checked their unshod feet carefully. They had not been shod as they only ever ran or walked on the sand, so was for her an everyday pleasure. She worried about them when she was away, but she had trained Ashok and one of the garden boys and they would walk them on the beach morning and evening and would let them run free in the sea later. Neither horse was big – both around fifteen hands. Liz explained to Alex that, as she had only one saddle and bridle, she was more than happy to ride bareback, which she quite often did anyway, and she would just hold on to the halter of whichever horse she rode, deciding to give Alex his choice. "I am looking forward to sunset as never before," he admitted, thinking with pleasurable anticipation of the ride ahead.

They ate lunch in a relaxed atmosphere. He was, he said, starving. "Aarav will be delighted, he is always disappointed with my appetite." For lunch, they had a cold soup of carrots and coriander with cream and herb croutons, followed by a vegetable and chicken biryani and, for dessert, passion fruit and pomegranate shrikhand.

"This has to be the most delicious dessert I have ever had," Alex commented, and insisted on going to the kitchen to both thank Aarav and ask how he made such a succulent, almost souffle-type, dessert.

It was eleven-thirty p.m. when Ronnie and Tim arrived. Alex had disappeared to bed several hours earlier – jet lag having finally caught up with him. They were on good form, arriving in high spirits, and it was very evident that their relationship had moved on apace since Liz had last been with them.

They were a real duo, a couple in every sense of the word. They both hugged her and gave her presents that surprised and delighted. "Opal earrings to match your ring," Ronnie said. They were perfect, the colour of opals varies so much and these matched exactly – neither too pale or dark and, like her ring, each opal was surrounded by tiny diamonds. "I don't deserve anything like this," she protested. "You do, you do," they chorused. "Without you, we would never have met," Tim stated quite soberly.

They also brought a picture of the villa painted by Ronnie. "Tim chose the frame," Ronnie added, handing it to her and watching with pleasurable excitement as she started opening the package with particular care and attention. "Oh Liz, you are impossible!" Ronnie grabbed it back and unceremoniously tore off the packaging. "That's how you should open things. With gusto!"

"I like a bit of finesse in my life," Liz teased. He had handed her the picture upside down, turning it around, she exclaimed with delight. "Why it's beautiful, Ronnie." It was a painting of the house bathed in the soft late-afternoon sunshine with the tubs of flowers and the tall spirals of bougainvillea adding colour to the quietude of the rest of the painting. "Oh Ronnie," she said, getting up to hug him. "What a perfect gift. It is beautiful, really beautiful, and the frame exactly right." Tim smiled, feeling immeasurably pleased with himself, as he had chosen the frame with a great deal of time and thought put into it. He so wanted Ronnie's painting shown off in the best possible way.

The three of them talked about where it should hang and, after pacing around and much umming and aahing, decided the dining room was the perfect setting. Ronnie went off to track down Ashok to ask him to make a fixing for it for Madame, meanwhile the other two made a small mark on the wall, indicating exactly where it should hang.

They sat down for a very late supper in the kitchen. Aarav had left several covered and labelled bowls in the fridge, and whilst Liz drank a glass of dry white wine, the two men tucked in to chicken tikka sandwiches and salad washed down with chilled sandpiper beer for Tim whilst Ronnie shared the bottle of wine with Liz. They finally wended their way upstairs at one a.m. trying to make sure they did not disturb the sleeping Alex.

chapter 28

Of course, Alex heard them. He had heard them earlier in the evening and, for a moment, had been tempted to join them, but had decided it would not be appropriate to interrupt the friends' reunion. He found himself thinking about Liz. He had seen her photograph on the back covers of her books but they didn't do her justice. She was beautiful, calm – the adjectives to describe her continued in his head as he lay in bed. The last adjective being sexy. He sat up in bed with a jolt. God dammit, she was a very sexy woman.

He lay down again, savouring the memory of her riding bareback along the beach, cantering her horse Coco. He visualised her hair, tie undone, streaming out behind her. The splashes from the sea, soaked her loose cotton shirt and he could clearly see her body outlined with the wet shirt sticking to it, moulding every curve.

She had turned to see if he was alright and he realised she wasn't wearing a bra. He was close enough to see her nipples standing proud – the cool water stimulating them. She had waved and he had waved back, enjoying every moment of this rare experience. Guinness, responsive to his touch, leapt forward until they were cantering and galloping side by side, both laughing and happy – the world forgotten for a short space in time.

Alex had enjoyed the ride but now was enjoying the culminating fantasy perhaps even more. After they had cantered for what seemed like an eternity, Liz slid off Coco's back and walked him to the shade of some palm trees. She didn't tie him up, letting him roll on his back in the sand, enjoying his own bit of heaven. In his fantasy, Alex followed her, watching as she undid the girth and removed the saddle from Guinness, who, like his stablemate, neighed happily and joined Coco in a roll around in the sand, drying off the sweat from the ride.

Then the fantasy seriously took over. Alex noticed that a cool-looking sheet lay on the ground, several yards away from where the horses stood nuzzling each other. There was an ice bucket and a bottle of wine cooling. They sat. Alex opened the bottle easily and, instead of glasses, they passed the bottle between them. It spilt and wine ran down her damp shirt highlighting her high, firm breasts. He heard himself groan, but this fantasy was too good to stop. She stood and, leading him by the hand, walked towards the sea. There, as the waves crashed over them, they made love – the movement of the water adding to their pleasure. He didn't remember where the fantasy ended and sleep began, he wondered if he would ever dare look at her again.

The fantasy had been the most vivid he had ever had – so vivid it seemed real. As the dawn broke he dressed hurriedly, not wanting to keep her waiting. When he arrived at the foot of the stairs he found Anjali was hovering in the hall. "I'm afraid sir," she greeted him. "Madame O'Malley will not be riding this morning she was very late to bed last night because of our other guests." She smiled seeing his crestfallen expression. "It's alright sir, Madame says please ride whichever horse you like and let the other horse follow you. They will both do that now," she explained.

Alex was disappointed, but didn't want the housekeeper to realise how much. "Fine," he responded, as nonchalantly as he could, wondering at the same time whether he would be able to "tack up" properly. Normally when he rode some stablehand had put on the saddle and bridle for him and he kicked himself for never bothering to do it for himself. On impulse, he decided to do as Liz had done the evening before – she had appeared to almost leap on Coco's back and ride with just one hand on his mane. Being taller than Liz he couldn't envisage any problems mounting a horse.

Thankfully, both horses were wearing head collars. For a moment he wondered if he should postpone this ride, then a vision of Liz on Coco came into his mind and he knew he wanted to feel a horse's body beneath him as Liz had riding bareback the previous evening.

As he led both horses out of their air-conditioned stable, he sensed them looking around for Liz. "No chaps it's me and the two of you today!" He put his hand on Coco's mane, as he had seen Liz do, and quickly realised he could no more leap on his back and not fall off the other side than fly to the moon. He spotted quite a nice sized rock so led the mystified horse to it. Using the rock as a step, he managed to climb on quite easily.

Liz, who had woken early despite the late night, happened to glance out of the window at that precise moment and put her hand over her mouth to stop herself laughing out loud at the spectacle – not that he would have been able to hear from that distance, but he might somehow have sensed her.

As if on cue he looked up, and she moved hastily back out of view. He couldn't have seen her, of that she was sure, but she was amazed he was riding bareback. She watched discreetly as the trio – man and horses – walked down the path that led to the beach.

Alex had never been so uncomfortable in his life. Coco's spine seemed to dig right into him. He daren't get off in case he'd never be able to re-mount. The horses were prancing now, waiting for their full-stretch canter. Finally, with only the headcollar to try and steady the horse and himself, he had no choice. He let him run. It was an unforgettable experience and he thanked God he had strong legs. He had never gripped like it before. He turned Coco's head towards the sea and Guinness immediately changed direction too. For a few blissful minutes the horses swam, and the buoyancy of the sea lifted his body slightly off Coco's spine.

He insisted the horses walk back and he had never been, in his entire life, so thankful something had come to an end. He slid off and found his legs were trembling with the exertion. He knew he would suffer in a few hours. He rubbed both horses down as he and Liz had done the evening before. Ashok arrived to give them their breakfast oats. "A good ride on this lovely morning sir?" Ashok enquired politely. "Yes, excellent, thank you. It's Ashok isn't it?"

"Yes, sir. I am Ashok, my wife is Nina and my children—" he began. Alex cut across him. "Sorry, Ashok, I need a shower before breakfast." If Ashok was offended he didn't show it, but as he said later to Nina, "That is a man I do not like so very much. First, he is troubled by my driving of the car, now he has no patience to learn the names of our children. I hope Madame O'Mal does not like him very much either." Nina soothed him in the quiet way she had and soon he had forgotten Alex as he played with his children and ate the breakfast Nina had prepared for them all. "You are such a wonderful cook Nina. If Aarav leaves this establishment you should become the cook."

"Yes, Ashok, that is my thought too. That is why I work so hard for Aarav – to learn all he knows, for he will not stay forever, he has ambitions, he tells me so."

chapter 29

Alex bent down in the shower, letting the full force of the water hit his back and rear with its powerful jets. He was already beginning to ache and wondered how he would cope with even walking, let alone sitting, if he was as sore as he suspected he might be.

Ronnie and Tim, looking remarkably refreshed, arrived in time for breakfast. They were in high spirits and with all sorts of plans for the day, but wanted to check with Liz first if it was alright with her. It was Wednesday and Ronnie wanted to take Tim to the market in Anjuna, and then to Panaji to see the cathedral.

The market spread over several acres and was held once a week. Snake charmers, pickpockets and, probably, drugs were all part of the scene, but look beyond that and there were bargains to be had and fascinating people to see. They had already decided to take a taxi. Neither felt they could "steal" Ashok for the day, and Tim was not sure, even if Liz could spare him, he could take his driving for a whole day, despite Ronnie being more sanguine about it.

Alex arrived in the dining room walking, Liz felt, with a certain care. "I understand you rode bareback this morning," she said, not wanting him to know she had witnessed his several attempts at mounting. "Yes," he lied. "I thought riding bareback would be rather fun."

"And was it?" Tim asked, grinning from ear to ear in what Alex felt was rather a leering kind of way. These gays had only one thing on their minds, he thought. He had actually met a pair who had paid a fortune for a beautiful stone statue of a girl – then, when they placed it in their garden, had displayed it back to front so that the bottom was the focus, even illuminating it at night with the spotlight on the bottom and the rest of the statue more or less lost in the foliage. So Alex was not amused.

Tim sensed this, of course, and teased him mercilessly, with Liz finally intervening with "Enough, children, enough!" Tim had the grace to look somewhat abashed and Ronnie changed the subject by talking about their proposed day out. Ronnie, kindly Liz thought, suggested Alex might like to join them for the day. Alex almost shuddered. A day with these faggots, he could think of nothing less appealing. Anyway, he wanted time with Liz.

Alex declined quite gracefully, but Ronnie and Tim could read the signs. They knew how he felt and it indicated quite clearly to them someone whose nature was not all that pleasant. They mutually thought he was not quite the nice, charming guy he appeared to be, and they hoped Liz would not be swept away by his apparent charm and good looks.

"Mind you," Ronnie commented later, as they drove off for their "day's adventure" (Tim's phraseology). "We could be mistaken, you know." Tim was noncommittal.

"We could be," he said darkly. "Then again we could be right."

"Let's not waste time talking about him anyway," Ronnie added hastily, determined their day should be fun.

The taxi driver insisted on taking them via a fabric and jewellery warehouse run by his cousin. Why not, they decided, after a few half-hearted demurs. They bought Tim's mother a pashmina and they bought each other some silly little presents. Then Ronnie spied the ring. It was gold but set (quite discreetly for India) with small rubies all around it. Ronnie saw Tim looking at it and when he wandered off he quickly bought and paid for it. Trying it on one of his little fingers first, he knew it would fit Tim and he slipped it, carefully wrapped in tissue, into an inside pocket of his linen jacket.

Tacky it might be, but Tim adored Anjuna – from the snake charmers to the spice sellers, from the musicians to the children pleading "come to our stall, come to our stall" and other calls "no, no, come to mine."

They bought beautifully made trinket boxes. They bought carved elephants and camels and finally, when the heat of the sun had worn them out, they found their air-conditioned taxi with an immense degree of satisfaction.

They laughed over some of the ridiculous things they had bought. "The spices for Nina," Ronnie decided. "One of the papier-mâché boxes for Anjali," Tim suggested. They mutually agreed on a carving for Bernadette and the rest they might keep for other gifts, or even take them home.

Sorted to their satisfaction they headed for the cathedrals which stood either side of the road. They proved welcomingly cool and culturally exceptionally different and equally fascinating. They arrived back at the villa at four-thirty p.m. to find Liz and Alex deep in conversation over tea in the shade of the palms.

"Perfect timing," Ronnie said cheerfully. "A cup of Earl Grey tea, the right of every Englishman!"

"Every Scot too," said Tim, reminding him of his extremely remote Scottish ancestry. They had paid off the taxi, giving the driver a more than generous tip. Ronnie kissed Liz warmly, said they would be "down in five" and disappeared into their room carrying their spoils.

Both wanted the bathroom so, it being a question of age first, Tim stood impatiently waiting for his turn. Washed, refreshed and about to go downstairs Ronnie remembered the ring he had slipped in his pocket. "Here Tim, catch," he said, throwing the ring wrapped in its tissue paper. Tim caught it easily, opened it and flashed Ronnie a loving smile. "Oh, you clever fellow, how did you manage that without me seeing?"

"Try it on," Ronnie begged. Tim slid the ring on the small finger of his left hand. "With this ring, I thee wed," murmured Ronnie. Tim kissed him lightly on the lips.

"My thanks will be expressed tonight," he said teasingly. "Think about that from now till then!" and with the flash of a wicked smile, he left the room, leaping happily down the stairs like an exuberant schoolboy.

Despite the pain, a hangover from the early-morning ride hardly reduced by paracetamol, Alex had had a perfect day. Also, despite being driven by that maniac Ashok, Liz had taken him for pre-lunch drinks at the Taj Exotica where her friend, the general manager, had joined them near the stunningly beautiful pool. They had previously visited Bernadette, and Liz explained the plan for a series of similar houses to provide homes for abandoned children, rather than the more impersonal and larger orphanages. She was obviously so proud and happy to waste her money like this that Alex listened with flattering attention, making astute and sometimes useful observations.

They also visited the primary school attached to the church and met Father Julian – an Indian Christian, which surprised Alex. Father Julian explained that the primary school had come about because of the generosity of Madame

O'Mal. They looked on her presence in Goa as a gift from God himself, the priest explained solemnly.

If Alex found it all rather nauseating he hid it well. Liz found his encouraging remarks and comments helpful. She had to explain why she was called Madame O'Mal, but he felt she should insist on her full name, after all, Anjali used it correctly. "Anjali is a very educated woman. You must underdstand, the first people who helped me when I bought the villa. Ashok and Nina, for example. It was just easier for them to say Madame O'Mal, and it just spread. Hence the name of the villa." Alex was silent, although he nodded, pretending to understand her rationale.

Liz had enjoyed the day. Alex was so attentive and perceptive, he had made one or two suggestions and observations that she felt were thoughtful, if not necessarily correct. During the day he explained why he had not saddled up and she decided he had been courageous, if somewhat foolhardy.

"You should have called Ashok, he would have saddled up for you." Alex bit back a comment he might regret about Ashok, who, for some reason, he was beginning to dislike more and more. He had met Ashok's eyes in the rear-view mirror and realised the feeling was mutual. If this was his place, he thought, Ashok and Nina would go and he would import a decent driver from England.

He let his mind dwell on the thought. He had fantasised about Liz, but how about a permanent relationship? He was aware he should be thinking about marriage – he could spend the time between the two countries, as Liz did now, and he could sort out her household. Once he had thought of the idea he couldn't let it go and he started working on his strategy.

chapter 30

Dinner that night was a jolly affair. With the party planned for the following day, they made the most of being a small group. Ronnie and Tim would leave the day after the party and Alex, who had originally planned to leave on the morning of the party, postponed his travel plans for a few more days. This was the official line anyway, to himself he planned to stay indefinitely.

Ronnie and Tim had them all laughing talking about their day and all the nonsensical things they had bought in Anjuna. Tim's description of the snake charmer beggared belief as he made himself a turban out of his napkin, sat cross-legged on the floor with the bread basket in front of him, and played an imaginary flute with such consummate skill he almost convinced them a snake was rising up, swaying to match Tim's music. Even Alex enjoyed the show. They laughed and applauded whilst Tim modestly took his bows and passed the bread basket around for tips!

They sat on the terrace in the cool of the evening enjoying their brandies. Ronnie talking to Alex and Tim to Liz. Actually, it was Alex talking to Ronnie rather than the other way round. By the end of an hour, Ronnie knew all he ever wanted to know about publishing – the rip-off publishers, the unsupportive agents (of which he was not, of course, one). Plus, difficult authors who would either not deliver on schedule or were overly demanding – imagining he was available as and when they wanted. Once, and only once, Ronnie tried to intervene, in part to defend the authors who were perhaps struggling with unforeseen difficulties, perhaps domestic or financial, but he gave up. Nothing, he felt, would stop the flow!

By the end of the evening, Ronnie was seething with a mixture of anger and boredom. He found Alex pompous and manipulative and was somewhat concerned about leaving Liz alone with him, for he had already announced he was staying at the villa longer than originally planned. "I think Liz wants me here," he winked at Ronnie as he spoke. Ronnie who was, by nature, a generally mild man felt like punching him, and by the time he got to bed he was so uptight that it took all Tim's efforts and cajoling to relax him so that proper thanks could be made for the ring that had been proudly worn all evening.

When the other two had gone to bed, Alex moved to the chair vacated by Tim. "Are we riding in the morning?" Alex asked. For a moment Liz was put out. She so loved the solitude of her rides, but never one to be churlish, she smiled and said, "Of course Alex, same time, same place." She made as if to rise, but he put his arm out to stop her. "No Liz, stay a bit longer it's so peaceful now the others have gone." Liz bit back a retort but allowed herself to be prevailed on to stay.

She was annoyed when Alex leaned across and put more brandy in her glass. "Oh, Alex I really didn't want any more."

"It will do you good, relax you!" The minute he said that she was immediately tense, so she downed the unwanted brandy in one gulp and stood up before he could protest. "I have things to see to, I shall see you in the morning," she snapped. He cursed under his breath, he must take things steadily or he would frighten her off.

*

Life in Paris was a round of social event after social event. After some of the tensions in India with Pakistan as its neighbour, problems that arose seemed just minor irritations. Europe, in capital letters, still had its problems though, with the Euro now accepted as the currency, with the exception of the United Kingdom, no one complained about currency restrictions affecting trade anymore. There were those concerned about the sovereignty of the UK, indeed he was one of them, though in diplomatic circles he kept his own counsel.

It seemed as if every female in Paris was trying to either pursue Philip themselves or, perhaps even worse, trying to get him married off. He met beautiful woman after beautiful woman and although he enjoyed their company – even flirted a little here and there – it was Liz's face that haunted him at night. It was Liz he wanted between these pristine sheets. He blamed himself entirely for their non-relationship, he had let her slip silently out of his life whilst he sorted out his own relationship with Jack and worried about Jamie's health.

Both these issues were now resolved. Jamie seemed taller every time he saw him and looked more and more like Helen, whilst Jack with his flair for languages and his love of sport was more like Philip every day. He came across the Hindi phrasebook on Jack's bookshelves when idly looking for something to read one evening. It was the usual eclectic mix that any sixteen-year-old would have. From Harry Potter to science fiction and several sports biographies, which both surprised and pleased him, and then suddenly to come across the Hindi phrasebook. His first thought was that it must have come from his time in India – though he couldn't remember it. He flicked through the small book and there on the inside of the front cover a cryptic message: *Jack, lovingly L.* He was totally mystified now. Who sent Hindi phrasebooks – lovingly – to his son, and who the hell was "L". Not for one moment did he think of Liz – he always thought of her as Elizabeth anyway. Curiouser and curiouser. He took the book to his bedroom. There were quite a few pencil marks in Jack's untidy hand. Philip looked with interest at the phrases he had underlined.

"May I introduce my Father. May I introduce my Mother". By this, there were several exclamation marks. "May I visit you?" More exclamation marks. Philip was slightly concerned along with being a little amused, and he determined to ask Jack about the book and its "add-ons" during the next holiday. The following morning he returned the book to where he had found it and promptly forgot all about it.

chapter 31

Alex made a painfully slow recovery which he made the most of. It sadly meant he was unable to ride and Liz, well aware of his aches and pains, went off alone for her usual morning ride. He didn't hear the horses go on the soft sandy path but from his window, he glimpsed a flash of a white shirt through the trees. He determined to do the evening ride and took extra arnica tablets from the bottle Liz had given him, but decided to leave the painkillers to help him through the next ride.

On her return, he was waiting for her by the stables and rubbed down Guinness whilst she did the same with Coco. "I thought you were still sleeping," Liz said conversationally, feeling slightly selfish as she was aware she had crept out of the house, endeavouring not to wake him so as to enjoy her solitary ride. She was correct in her assumption that Alex would want to ride with her at sunset. It was, she had to admit, pleasant to have an attractive man around. Ronnie and Tim were such good company but Alex made her feel like a desirable woman again. She couldn't help wondering what sort of lover he would be!

Thoughts of Philip flooded her mind. Why had he never, in all this time, even contacted her again? She consoled herself with thoughts of his sons, who almost seemed like her sons too. Jamie and she had been close from the first, but during the last two years Jack had become very special to her. His letters always included a Hindi phrase or two and he had written that there was an Indian boy at Eton who had become a good friend. Asif was teaching him Hindi and Jack confided that he could now carry out quite a reasonable conversation.

I shall visit you when I have saved enough money, Jack had written, *and you will hear for yourself.* Liz was thrilled that he was being so positive these days. The old truculent Jack was a faint memory now.

Alex rode Guinness, the painkillers had worked their magic. Liz rode ahead, bareback of course. Once again, hair flowing and the sea-dampened shirt clinging to her body. Alex was reminded of his fantasy. Had he but known Liz was fantasising too, she could hear the sounds of Guinness pounding behind her. She could imagine Alex, his earnest face hiding the pain his body undoubtedly was in. In her fantasy he would come alongside her and the horses would turn towards the shade of the palms.

They would dismount. He would unbutton her shirt and kiss her full breasts and they would make love. She slowed Coco and turned him out towards the sea, the balmy cool of the water calming her senses as, beneath her, the horse started to swim. Tacked up with saddle and bridle, Alex watched, sighing inwardly, wishing he could join her but of course could not risk spoiling the tack. The woman and horse blended into the landscape against the setting sun and Alex sighed, thinking he had never seen anything so beautiful.

*

174

It was the holidays, Jack and Jamie were back in Paris and there seemed to be a new woman in their father's life. Remembering what Liz had said, they tried to be civil and friendly but her attitude to them was hardly cordial. The first thing she ever said to them was: "When do you return to England?"

"Hardly welcoming," Jamie commented to Jack. They really tried to be pleasant and friendly despite their growing dislike of Jutta. She was tall and very skinny, her hair was blonde and cut straight in a rather boyish cut, but worst of all, she bossed their father around and he didn't even seem to notice.

Jamie was worried. "I think I will stay at school for the holidays if he marries her." He sounded so serious that Jack, who felt much the same, felt he must come up with some sort of plan before it was too late! He told his younger brother not to worry. "I'll think of something," he said with more confidence than he felt. "In fact," he added. "I may have a plan already." When Jamie questioned him he refused to be drawn – "Wait and see," was his somewhat cryptic response.

Jutta had arrived in Paris after her divorce. She was now a very wealthy divorcee and, speaking fluent French, decided France would be a pleasant place to live. She liked French fashion and the food was good too. Not that she ever ate much – she was a size four and intended to keep that way. Her enemies would describe her as bones covered with skin, but she carried clothes well and could have, if circumstances had been different, been a model rather than a client at the major fashion houses.

All the fashion houses liked her. She had, it seemed, a limitless budget and a real eye for what suited her. She bought regularly at Armani and Dior and, from time to time, patronised Versace and Chloe. She liked Burberry raincoats and Ferragamo shoes and she was seen regularly in the front row of the fashion shows. Jutta was of course on the German embassy A-list, her father having been a well-known politician, and it was at one of the embassy functions that she first saw Philip.

She recognised him from Press photographs and had done some research on him so that when they met which she knew they would, in the relatively tight-knit diplomatic community, she would be prepared. She worked her way through the assembled guests, talking for a moment here and there so as not to appear obvious. As he moved, also socialising, she adroitly manoeuvred her position until, apparently by chance, they were in the same small group of people. Jutta continued her conversation with a diplomat from the Russian embassy, appearing fascinated by his conversation. Philip wondered who she was, he was sure he hadn't seen her at any of the embassy functions before.

"I don't think we have met," Philip took the opportunity to introduce himself during a brief pause in the conversation. "Philip Broderick," he added, holding his hand out to meet hers.

"Ah, the glamorous British Ambassador," she said shaking his hand and smiling warmly.

"I have never thought of myself in those terms," he laughed good-humouredly, rather enjoying the compliment. "And you are?"

"Jutta Weidenfeller." Philip looked puzzled.

"That name strikes a chord."

"My father was quite a well-known politician."

"Of course, how stupid of me."

"Not at all. He has been dead for five years, why should you remember him?" She noticed him glance at her hands. "No, I am not married," she said, waving her left hand which had until quite recently borne a wedding ring. "I am divorced and have reverted to my family name. And you, where is your wife?" Jutta knew full well he was widowed – she had done her research well and discovered he had been widowed for some years and had two sons who were (thankfully) away at boarding school in England. She had no intention of revealing the research she had undertaken when she first received the invitation to this event. She also had no intention of making the same mistake twice – a boring businessman husband, although wealthy, had not provided her with the upmarket life she sought, and certainly no children. She shuddered at the thought of putting her body through that sort of "thing". But now she was charm personified. Philip thought that the company of such an intelligent and elegant creature might cheer him up, and anyway, he was attracted to her.

After the reception, he invited her out to dinner. With real regret in her voice, she told him that she had a prior engagement – but would adore to have dinner with him on a future occasion. She handed him her card and he promised to be in touch with her soon.

The taxi took her straight back to her apartment where she sat curled up on one of her elegant sofas for several hours, planning how she would ensnare the Ambassador. Of her supposed previous engagement there was, of course, no sign. She needed to play this "catch" with care – she would let him "land her" eventually, when she was ready, not before.

Philip ate a lonely meal. His aide de comp was out somewhere and although there were plenty of people around they were all embassy staff and he did not feel like socialising with them, lovely though most of them were.

He brightened at the thought that the boys would be home in a few weeks for the summer holidays. Jack had already written to tell him that he wanted to go climbing with friends. He was sixteen now and Philip realised the boy must be allowed to do things on his own. Still, it was good that they were to spend two weeks on the French canals first.

Philip smiled to himself, thinking how Jack had changed, he had grown up so much and seemed so responsible these days. Even Jamie at fourteen seemed such a confident young man too. He felt immensely proud of them both. Helen would be proud too. He seldom thought about her these days, then felt guilty as he did tonight.

Suddenly depressed, he put his head in his hands. He was so lonely perhaps Jutta Weidenfeller had arrived at just the right moment. He had, he decided, been impressed with her cool attitude and Teutonic good looks, at her pride in her father and at her interest in what they chatted about – and her obvious disappointment that she could not join him for dinner.

chapter 32

Jack and Jamie were on the flight to Paris. They didn't seem to have seen much of each other this term. Jack had been on a week's climbing in the Cairngorms and, at the same time, Jamie had been canoeing.

Jack had been studying hard. He had decided he wanted to teach languages – not just the standard French and German, but Russian and Chinese too. He had started Russian already and was picking it up easily. He found his photographic memory helped him, for once a word was written down and he knew the pronunciation, he seldom forgot it. He was no swot though – he loved tennis and rugby and, best of all perhaps, climbing.

Five of his school friends plus a games master had planned a climb in Wales during the summer holiday and he was pleased when his father had said it was alright. So, after two weeks on the canals, he would return to England for the climbing holiday and then fly back to Paris for the remainder of the holiday with two of his closest friends – who he had rashly agreed he would show the seedier side of Paris.

Jamie was looking forward to seeing his father, but best of all, would be being on the canal boat – although he wished for about the umpteenth time that Liz would be with them too.

They were met at the airport by the embassy car with a message from their father saying he was with the Greek Ambassador but would be home in time for dinner. True to his word Philip was back by six p.m. and his sons threw themselves at him with great delight with hugs and friendly punches, making for a noisy and happy reunion.

The trio sat down and talked for half an hour, when Philip, glancing at his watch, realised Jutta would be here at eight o'clock. "I must shower and change boys, we have a dinner guest tonight."

"Not on our first evening home Dad," they chorused. Philip felt a pang of misgiving. Jutta had thought it would be "such a lovely family thing", as she put it, to share the boy's first meal at home.

Philip, after some initial misgivings, had then also asked her to join them on the canal cruise. At first, she had been delighted, but when she saw the size of the boat and realised two horrible boys were going to be there too she suddenly had an urgent need to return to Germany on important family business.

Their relationship was now one of mutual satisfaction. She didn't particularly like sex, but put on a good act, constantly telling Philip he was the best lover she had ever had. He thought she meant it but felt the relationship was not as wonderful as he had expected. Helen had been a follower in sexual adventures, now from time to time the picture of Liz came back to haunt him. It had been a match of equals. He tried not to dwell on thoughts of her but strangely Jutta coming into his life had brought back so many memories of her.

Jutta arrived when Philip was still in the shower. He had been delayed by a telephone call from the French Minister of Human Rights about a point of legislation. He had tried to keep it brief but was now twenty minutes behind his planned schedule. He comforted himself with the thought that his sons would equip themselves well in his absence.

Jack and Jamie were in the drawing room when Jutta arrived. They had heard via their father's valet that he would be down in fifteen minutes. The butler had informed Jutta of the same information when she arrived.

"Master Jack and Master Jamie are waiting for you in the salon," the butler said. Jutta was annoyed but knew she mustn't show it.

"Ah, you must be James," she said, addressing Jack. "And you John, the younger one." She smiled a fixed smile at them both, shaking them by the hand as she did.

"Actually, I'm Jack—" Jack began, but Jutta wasn't listening.

"And when do you return to school?" she asked. It was probably the most unfortunate question she could have asked, they had only been home a few hours. The young Jack would have slammed out of the room, but with a warning glance at his younger brother, he answered as calmly as he could. "Several weeks yet, but we shall be coming and going quite a bit you know." It was politely said – yet Jutta sensed she had put the older boy's back up. At least now she had the names right.

"Well James—" she said brightly.

"Jamie," he corrected. Jutta didn't appear to notice the interruption. "You are the apple of your father's eye – yes?"

"Only," said Jamie afterwards. "She said 'apfel' and I'm not – we both are, Jack."

"It's alright," Jack said. "She's just a stupid woman, but she's clever too and she has set her cap at Dad for sure."

"You said you had a plan Jack – you better do it before it's too late." Jamie said and Jack nodded. After the evening that lay ahead, he knew he just knew he had to get Liz back into his father's life.

If dinner was strained Philip did not appear to notice it. He thought it quite quaint that Jutta used the boys' formal names of John and James. "Why not?" he said afterwards when the boys questioned it. They didn't complain, though they would like to have done. They were doing what Liz had suggested – she had told them they should behave properly when and if another woman came into their father's life.

After the boys had said their goodnights and left to go to bed, Jutta put on rather a sad and reproachful face. "I'm afraid your sons do not like me."

"But Jutta – dinner was fine, the boys were really well-behaved. Frankly, I felt proud of them."

"My poor Philip you saw what you wanted to see. Before you came down..." She took a small lace-edged handkerchief and dabbed a non-existent tear. "They were so, how do you say it – churlish."

Philip was furious. "I will speak with them in the morning, I won't have them distressing you." His heart warmed towards her – he had not thought she was this vulnerable, it made him feel protective. He held her close and could feel her body trembling and there were occasional restrained sobs.

She didn't stay that night, she needed solitude she said. "I have to think Philip – I do not want to divide your family."

"There is no question of that," Philip replied, becoming even more furious with his sons. They had really let him down. He really didn't need this, he was very busy and life had been going smoothly until the boys came home from school.

The next morning, as Jack and Jamie sat down with Philip for breakfast, the atmosphere seemed chill. Jamie cast anxious glances at his brother and Jack signalled with a slight movement of his body to keep quiet.

After a few moments, Philip spoke. His voice was colder than either of them could ever remember. "I am exceedingly disappointed," he began. Jack signalled to Jamie again to keep quiet. "I am not just disappointed, I'm angry, very angry."

Jamie could contain himself no longer. "Why Dad? Why are you angry?" Philip looked from one to another. "I suppose being without a mother all this time could explain a little, but to insult a guest under my roof – in our home. I find almost beyond belief."

"What are we supposed to have done?" Jack asked as politely as he could, though he was seething too. What on earth had the bitch said to alienate their father? She had been the one to be rude. "If you don't even know then I feel helpless – I have failed as a father," Philip continued. "She wept, Fraulein Weidenfeller wept after you had gone to bed. I felt ashamed of my sons. I am tempted to cancel the holiday. I'm not surprised Jutta didn't want to come for two weeks with you heathens." Philip could contain himself no longer. "I have work to do. Keep yourselves out of trouble and I will see you at four p.m. for tea. I shall be out tonight."

Jamie couldn't help it – he began to cry. He knew he was too big to cry but he couldn't understand his own father believing someone else over them. "He didn't even ask us," he sobbed.

"Come on," said Jack, put off by the tears but angry too. "Come on Jamie, I'll think of something."

chapter 33

It was over breakfast that Alex began to express his concern at Liz's lack of writing time. At first, she was cross, feeling justifiably that she had given up writing time to show him around and spend time with him generally. She had even, following several hints from him, suggested he stay a week or two at the villa rather than sticking to his original touring plan. He had said on a number of occasions he loved it so and wished he had not made plans for the rest of the month.

So now, when he started to suggest, albeit gently, that she should try and have three to four hours uninterrupted writing time every morning after their early morning ride and breakfast, she said, a shade angrily, "How can it be uninterrupted? I have a household to run. Anjali consults me on one thing. Aarav talks menus. Ashok wants to know if I need taking anywhere or needs to talk further planting or cutting back."

"Then why don't I, for the short time I am here, act as your shield? I can take on Aarav, Anjali and Ashok too for that matter." Liz hesitated, but the more she thought about it the more sense it made.

After breakfast, she spoke to Anjali, explaining that in the short term Mr Alex would be taking over the reins from her so that she could concentrate on her writing. If Anjali was dismayed she didn't let Liz know by a word or look, but later in the kitchen with Aarav, she confessed her uneasiness. Aarav was more philosophical. "He is only here for two more weeks what can go wrong in that short time?"

It was lovely to be able to write totally uninterrupted. Liz wrote with extra vigour – her plot deepening as the story developed. There was to be a heinous crime and murder was afoot. The story unfolded in her head as she wrote. She had identified the hapless victim and was now building a series of alibis for the main characters.

The morning flew by and when Alex came to tell her it would be lunch in five minutes she was amazed. He was delighted with the morning's word count and she confessed she was too. "You are a dear Alex, this is a pattern I will have to adhere to when you leave."

"Don't talk about my leaving yet," he laughed a shade ruefully. "I shall think you want to push me out!" Anjali, hovering at the foot of the stairs, saw Liz rest an arm lightly on that of Mr Alex. She realised this was not the opportunity she was seeking to talk to Madame O'Malley alone.

The atmosphere in the house changed in only a few days, only Liz, now totally immersed in her writing, didn't seem to notice. Aarav banged his pots and pans in the kitchen. Anjali walked round unsmiling, quietly attending to her duties and trying to keep well out of Alex's way. Even Ashok looked glum. According to Mr Alex, the stables were not cleaned well enough, the car was filthy inside and out and the gardeners lazy. The final insult – Mr Alex had taken a taxi to Madkal this morning because Ashok's driving was so terrible. "The worst driving I have seen in my life," Ashok was informed.

Ashok was frightened. This man could influence Madame O'Mal. They might lose their home, their jobs, everything. He didn't dare tell Nina, who was full of the problems Aarav was having in the kitchen.

Liz began to wonder how she had coped without Alex and when one evening, an hour or so after they had said goodnight, he knocked on her bedroom door, there seemed to be an inevitability about him sharing her bed.

At that point, Anjali hit rock bottom. "He will," she confided to the others, "never leave, she will want him to stay as her lover." Anjali had never lowered herself to gossip, but now she couldn't help it, and now every member of staff knew "he" had moved into Madame's bed and was ruling the household.

The morning and evening rides had changed. Now Alex had her in the bedroom he no longer fantasised as they rode. Instead, he made her talk about her novel and questioned some of her ideas. For the first time ever Liz began to doubt her ability to write and the rides ceased being a pleasure, but more a time of inquisition.

Even the horses sensed the difference. Instead of the wild canters and sea-bathing, they now walked sedately to and from their stables and they seemed restless. Alex had bought another saddle, bridle and bit which he had Ashok put on Guinness. Liz gave up riding bareback as Coco was pulling these days. She was grateful Alex had bought extra "tack" for Guinness. The horse hated his new bit, which pulled at his mouth and he didn't like the new rider much either. They were now two separate entities, not man and rider "as one" – which is what both horses had always enjoyed with Liz.

It was very hot and humid – the monsoon season was almost upon them. Liz was surprised with the menus. Tomato soup with herby croutons was fine, though she might have chosen crisp iceberg lettuce with a few roasted peppers. The main course, however – roast beef, Yorkshire pudding and roast potatoes – defeated her. She said nothing, presuming that Aarav had made a gesture to the English guest. Judging by Alex's reaction to the food she was right. He tucked into his dinner with gusto, seeming not to notice Liz only playing with her food. Dessert was apple pie and custard. Aarav had scoured his library of cookery books to find the requested recipe.

Liz felt she must compliment Aarav on the individual Yorkshire puddings and the custard which was superbly made, if not to her taste anymore – well not in Goa anyway.

"Well done Aarav," she complimented him when she visited the kitchen after dinner.

"As long as Madame O'Malley is pleased," Aarav answered formally, leaving Liz feeling that something was being left unsaid and surprised at his calling her O'Malley in full.

Anjali and Aarav ate together when everything was cleared up from Madame's dinner. "So," Aarav said in a very disappointed voice. "After all this time I find that what Madame really wants is an English menu."

"I wonder," Anjali replied enigmatically and would be drawn no further.

Liz didn't understand herself anymore. Alex was technically an excellent lover, yet Liz felt lonely when he rolled away from her after lovemaking. Lonely and somehow empty, she needed to be held tenderly, and found herself with silent tears rolling down her cheeks, unable to cope with her own emotions of sadness.

The more Alex thought about it, the more sense it made. He could stay with Liz in Goa. With modern communications he could keep in touch with his other authors by email and three or four visits a year to England would suffice. Using his laptop he emailed his thoughts to his colleague in England and the reply was encouraging. Gradually he was taking over things at Villa O'Mal – that name would have to change for sure, he decided. Villa Wylde (his surname) had a much better ring to it. He extended his stay to a month, then another month, and by then Liz had completed her first draft of the book, which was now due to be sent to England for editing. It was, Alex thought, her best book to date although he didn't tell her this – just that it was good but needed a fair amount of editing. It wasn't that he wanted to put her down, but consciously or subconsciously he certainly wanted to have a hold on her.

Liz emerged like a butterfly from a chrysalis. She greeted Anjali on her first morning's freedom with a hug. Alex was still sleeping. He had been almost aggressively passionate last night and Liz wondered if she was heading for an early menopause, because she neither enjoyed it nor actually – and not for the first time with Alex – did she climax. Alex had started hinting that she was frigid and had it not been for remembering her time with Philip and her marriage to Steve she might have believed him.

There was a seed of doubt growing within her. She felt she was being manipulated these days; she hardly saw the staff whom she had regarded as friends as well as staff, and when she did it was almost as if they avoided her. Ashok wouldn't look her in the eye. Aarav she never saw and his menus had undergone a most, to her, unfortunate change. As for Anjali, she seemed to have lost her sparkle. She had always been respectful, but they had laughed together in the past and even on occasion wept together.

With a look up the broad staircase that Liz had just walked down and with a sense of urgency in her voice, Anjali spoke very quietly. "Madame O'Malley, a word please, in private." To Liz's astonishment, she led the way to her own bedroom with its sitting room off. She almost pushed Liz into a chair and sat down opposite. Liz was thoroughly mystified – Anjali never sat down with her mistress despite Liz begging her too on occasion.

Anjali cleared her throat. "Madame O'Malley, I need to talk to you privately – it is very important." As if on cue they both heard Alex calling her from the hall. Liz looked at Anjali and saw a certain fear there. Liz put her finger to her lips and tiptoed to the door silently turning the key. She turned back with a smile and was about to say something jokingly – for she still felt the situation was odd enough to be comical – when she realised Anjali was crying. "I'm sorry, Madame. I'm sorry."

For a few moments, Liz thought Anjali must have done something very wrong. "It doesn't matter, it really doesn't – whatever it is you know I will stand by you." Anjali cried even more, stuffing a handkerchief into her mouth to subdue the sound. Liz heard Alex again, he sounded angry this time.

The sound of his voice seemed to finally spur Anjali into conversation. She began at the beginning, telling Liz how Alex had changed everything. Menus, the running of the house, Ashok and driving, the stables, the garden. Liz was stunned and horrified in equal proportions. How could all this have happened under her nose? How gullible, how foolish she had been – even within herself she had known something was wrong. Her rides had changed, at first subtly, now they were like "hacks" through Hyde Park. The menus, how she had hated the food of late. Stodgy puddings she hardly touched but Alex enjoyed. Anjali so quiet. Ashok so withdrawn. What a fool she had been, an unmitigated fool. She was kneeling on the floor with her arms around Anjali. "It is over," she said softly. "He will leave today."

Anjali looked up – the tear-stained face wreathed in a sudden smile. "Oh, Madame O'Malley I thought perhaps you wouldn't believe me." Liz believed her, she herself had been undermined on a personal level. He had questioned her response in bed. It was him who was the arrogant bully, she pulled herself up short. She left Anjali's room through the garden door and when Alex spotted her she was apparently strolling through the garden. "Here you are, Liz. Where have you been? Didn't you hear me calling you?"

"No," she answered sweetly. "I was just enjoying the serenity of *my* garden." He didn't appear to note the emphasis. "Let's have breakfast," she continued smiling at him brightly.

"I have a surprise for you, Liz."

"What a coincidence. I have one for you too!" Something in her tone made him look at her sharply but she was smiling.

They walked into the dining room where Liz ate chopped fruit as usual. Pineapple, watermelon and papaya with a few pomegranate seeds. That and coffee was what she enjoyed most at breakfast. To keep Alex company she occasionally had an egg, but this morning she declined.

Alex finished his second soft-boiled egg and said, "I can't wait any longer. Liz, I have a very important question to ask you – then you can have the present." He thought Liz looked at him a bit strangely but he assumed it was curiosity, fascination or excitement. There was an expectant hush. "Liz I want you to marry me." He held up his hand when he saw she was about to speak. "I've arranged everything. I can live here and just go back to England two or three times a year. I can take all your worries and stress away – and here, look."

He jumped up and went to a package in the corner. "Here is an engagement present." Still stopping her speaking she sat appalled. What monster had she created? The wrapping was off, he held the "engagement" present triumphantly above his head. She looked in total disbelief. "Villa Wylde, your new name, or it will be soon."

Liz stood up. She had never felt so angry, her voice sounded cold even to her. "You have gone too far Alex." He tried to interrupt, this time she stopped him. "I have one request, please go upstairs and pack – I want you out of my home and my life forever both personally and professionally."

He looked dumbfounded. "But Liz you need me!"

"I neither need or want you, you have done enough damage. I will hear no further discussion. There will be a taxi here for you at ten o'clock, you have exactly half an hour," she said, looking at her watch as she spoke.

Liz swept out of the room and went to her study for the first time, locking the door behind her. There was a light tap on the door. Liz took no notice. "Madame O'Malley, it is me, Anjali." Liz opened the door and locked it once the woman was inside.

"He will be gone in half an hour. If he is not ready I want Ashok and two of the garden boys to make sure he gets into the taxi. If he isn't packed then throw his things into a bag and throw it into the taxi after him," Liz said.

Anjali beamed, but could hardly bring herself to speak. She let herself out of the study and Liz relocked the door. It wasn't as if she was frightened – she just couldn't bear to ever see him again. She saw the taxi from the window. She saw Alex, suitcase in one hand, laptop case in the other. The sound of the wheels on the gravel indicated he was gone and she emerged from her study determined to rebuild the relationships and happiness at Villa O'Mal.

chapter 34

Philip had never been so glad to see the end of the long summer holiday. Admittedly the canal cruise had been good and they, father and sons, seemed to grow closer again. They fished – usually unsuccessfully – from their canal boat. They worked as a team at the locks, one of the trio handling the lock gates, one guiding the boat into the lock and the third using a boating hook to fend the boat away from the lock walls to prevent damage.

At lunch time, they ate huge quantities of baguette with cheeses and salads, washed down with local wine for Philip and generally lemonade for the boys. In the evenings they would tie up near a village or small town and, following delicious aromas, would track down a restaurant. Jack was allowed occasional glasses of wine, whilst Jamie, in true French fashio, was allowed a watered-down version.

They returned to Paris all determined that things would continue as happily, but it was not to be – Jutta saw to that. She and Philip were invited everywhere as a couple these days. Jutta, very carefully and apparently not saying anything at all, let it be known by innuendo that she, in the not too distant future, would be living at the embassy.

She was aware that people pointed to her at social events. "The British Ambassador's fiancée," she had heard on one occasion. She was delighted, though cross that Philip was moving so slowly. They had, of course, slept together. He was, in her opinion, an okay lover but too conservative for her rather more exotic tastes. However, that was not a problem. She could always go elsewhere for the "extras" as she liked to think of them.

Philip tried to tell her about the holiday she had missed but she didn't seem particularly interested so he stopped talking about it. What she did want to talk about was the continual and constant rudeness of his sons. "I don't see it," Philip said.

She smiled cynically. "Of course not Philip, they are perfect in front of you, but when you are not there – the things, the hurtful, terrible things they say…"

He spoke to them and they completely denied everything their father mentioned. She had been very specific, he mentioned those things. Both boys denied saying or doing any of the things they were being accused of, but they realised they were not being believed.

It was actually Jamie's idea. "He needs to hear her say the things she does, how can we work that Jack?" he said, appealing with total confidence to his older brother.

"Jamie I always knew you were brilliant." Jamie looked bemused. "Listen," said Jack, and told Jamie "The Plan".

"Do you think it will work?" Jamie wondered dubiously.

"It's got to – it is our only chance."

The following morning there were two rather unusual conversations. "Dad," Jamie said over breakfast. "I need to talk to you about a rather personal matter." Philip raised his eyebrows.

"Really Jamie, well I'm listening?"

"Oh no," Jamie said quickly. "Privately please." Philip

looked mystified and a concerned look crossed his face. The boys were not exactly in his good books at the moment, but his younger son had a worried look on his face that Philip could not ignore. "I have a busy day, how about six p.m. in my study? I shall be leaving at seven with Jutta."

"That's perfect," Jamie grinned, then, remembering he was meant to be worried, added, "I mean that's perfectly okay with me. Thank you, Dad."

*

The second conversation was conducted in German. Jack had never been so pleased that his language skills would be put to such special use. She certainly would not recognise his voice over the telephone because she would not anticipate him speaking German to her.

"Fraulein Weidenfeller?"

"Yes," she answered abruptly.

"Ah Fraulein Weidenfeller the British Embassy here. The Ambassador has requested that you arrive one hour earlier than arranged. He has a surprise, I understand he wishes to share with you."

"Who are you? Why is a German working at the British Embassy?"

"Actually, Fraulein Weidenfeller, my mother is English and my father German, but as I was educated in England, I joined the British Diplomatic Service. I am the Ambassador's new personal assistant. I look forward to meeting you," Jack continued smoothly. "You are, I believe, to become the Ambassador's wife." There was a gasp at the other end of the telephone. Jack cursed himself – perhaps he had gone too far.

He need not have worried. Jutta was so sure of herself that she presumed the new personal assistant had been taken into

Philip's confidence. She almost purred down the telephone, "Tell the Ambassador I shall be at the embassy promptly at six."

"Auf wiedersehen Frau Weidenfeller," Jack said quietly, putting down the telephone.

His brother, who had been listening to the entire conversation, whooped with delight. "We've done it! We've done it!"

"That is only part one," Jack said seriously. "Let's hope part two goes as smoothly."

It was a long day for the two boys. Philip was ready to see Jamie at a quarter to six so Jamie had to hide until six p.m. for fear of spoiling "the plan". Promptly at six p.m., the embassy bell rang and as per instructions from Master Jack, the butler showed Fraulein Weidenfeller into the salon. Jack was standing under the portrait of his mother, which he had been looking at before she arrived as if to draw strength from it.

At precisely one minute past six, Jamie knocked on the study door. Earlier, Jack had opened the interconnecting door between the two rooms about an inch. "Where is the Ambassador?" Jutta asked Jack. "Your father!" Philip, in the study, thinking he had heard Jutta, started up from his desk. Jamie came round and laid a restraining arm on his father's. "Dad, this is my time with you, remember?" Philip sat back in his chair with half an ear to a rather strange conversation that seemed to be taking place in the next room.

"Why are you so horrid to us, except when Dad's there of course?" Jack's question was heard clearly in the study. "Because I can't stand you or that little brother of yours," Jutta replied. Philip made as if to stand and once again Jamie laid a restraining arm.

"But this is our home," Jack said.

"Not for long, little boy. I will soon be Philip's wife, and as far as I am concerned you can stay at school, you certainly won't be welcome here." Her tone was cutting and as frigid as it always was with them. "Now, where is your father? I don't like to be kept waiting."

"You think my father will marry you?" Jack asked quietly.

"I have him in the palm of my hand, he will marry me very soon and you will be out!"

Philip had heard enough. He walked into the room, leaving a grinning Jamie behind him. "Jack," said his father. "Leave us." Jack joined his brother in the study, making sure the door was still slightly ajar. "Jutta, you will leave this embassy immediately. Our relationship is over, I am horrified that I believed you over my sons – you have done so much damage it is unforgivable. What is more, I shall see that in future you are not included in this or any other embassy's functions, so, knowing your ambitious nature, I suggest you find another capital city, but I hope for his sake you don't find another fool."

He rang the bell over her protestations and denials and she was shown out of the embassy for the last time.

chapter 35

It had taken time to get Villa O'Mal back on an even keel again. Ashok felt he should no longer drive Liz, so she had to make up reasons that meant he had no option but to. In a strange way, Alex had done her a favour where Ashok was concerned, for once he got over the worry about driving her she noticed he actually was a steadier and more thoughtful driver than before.

Aarav had to be cajoled back into his former style of cooking, which he happily returned to once he understood what had taken place. Liz started enjoying his cooking again and to make him feel better she threw a series of luncheons and dinners encouraging him to be as adventurous as he liked. He had developed an interest and delight in Chinese cooking, and lotus stems in honey became not only a favourite of Liz's but of guests too, who hoped it was to be on the menu when they came to dine. Chicken wonton soup, followed by chicken in chilli and honey was another favourite. Nina, too, was back in the kitchen having, unbeknownst to Liz, been banished from the house.

Anjali was the first to recover. Realising that Liz needed support herself, she rallied, and the house seemed to give a sigh of relief and settle down again.

As for Coco and Guinness, once more they cantered along the beach. Liz seldom bothered with saddle and bridle, meaning all three of them could swim in the sea. She felt renewed and cleansed and life became good again.

The letter from Kathy when it arrived gave her quite a jolt. It enclosed an article supposedly written by the literary agency but in fact, Liz quickly recognised Alex's style. Alex had supposedly been interviewed about new and existing authors. In it he said, "Of course Liz O'Malley is a 'has been'" and they were no longer her agents and extremely unhappy with her latest submission.

Liz had seldom been so angry. She telephoned England and spoke to the senior partner of the literary agency. In no uncertain terms, she explained how she had thrown Alex out of her house and refused to let him handle her book. The senior partner promised that the matter would be put right but she had little or no faith in his protestations and informed him she would be taking her business elsewhere.

It was the article that was actually a turning point for her. An American publisher who had long admired her work contacted her by email. He was representing a large and highly reputed publishing house and, at his request, Liz promptly sent him a copy of her latest novel. Three days later she was offered a contract of such immense proportions that she had to sit down rather rapidly.

The small print stated that on publication she would be expected to do a publicity tour of the States. She emailed back saying that if her lawyer approved the contract she would be delighted to comply with their wishes. She was no fool. The contract seemed straightforward, but nevertheless she had her English lawyer look it over before signing.

Three months later she set off on her big adventure. Before she arrived, there had been plenty of pre-publicity but as she was not all that well known in the States her personal appearances would boost the sales.

She flew into Boston for the start of the tour. It would be a long time before she returned home to Goa.

*

Life in Paris had settled back into its steady rhythm of diplomatic encounters and pleasant social events – at which there was no sign of Jutta Weidenfeller. It was as if she had never been. If Philip had any regrets about the woman, it was that he had been taken in by her. He had been gullible and it had almost caused a rift between him and his sons. Thankfully, that had been healed and he saw them whenever possible.

Jack was now seriously into languages, not yet sure how he would use them, but determined he would. Jamie was still uncertain about what he wanted to do but was showing a flair for the sciences. Philip rather hoped he would not go into research – eminently worthwhile, though he felt it might be rather a lonely life for such a gregarious young chap.

He never made observations of this nature to Jamie, leaving it to the boy's good sense. They had grown up so much. He felt Helen would be proud of them. He certainly was.

From time to time he would think of Liz, and wonder what she was doing. He wished they hadn't lost contact, for a short and precious time there had been such a bond between them.

*

Boston, the first city Liz visited, had been such fun. Vivien Brown, a personal assistant at the publishing house met her from the plane and never seemed to leave her side. She was a highly efficient young woman of around twenty-five who had Liz's itinerary at her fingertips.

Fortunately, the two women hit it off instantly. Although at first Liz found her general breezy and apparently boundless energy exhausting, she soon found it was a delightful stimulus. Together they attended literary luncheons where Liz was the guest speaker. She had been interviewed by local television and radio companies and signed more copies of her book than she could believe, and this was only the start!

Vivien had planned the tour down to the last meticulous detail, allowing a day or two at the beginning or end of each stop to give Liz a chance to become a real sightseer. Visiting the Boston Tea Party Museum on the quayside and listening to the somewhat negative recorded "declarings" regarding "the British" made her smile and reminded her of learning about the Boston Tea Party at school. As she listened to the saga of the bales of tea being dumped overboard, she thought it seemed so much more interesting actually being in situ.

They ate lobster at the restaurant Pier Four and the bell clanged at intervals announcing another ship coming in. Many of the clangs were unrelated to what was happening outside, but it certainly made for an entertaining atmosphere.

By car, they traced the route of the Paul Revere ride and Liz was charmed by the clapboard houses built around village greens – the early settlers trying so hard to re-create the country they had left behind. Names like Plymouth, Newcastle and Dover speaking volumes. Liz knew she must return here one day, ideas for future books darting in and out of her brain.

From Boston, they flew to Chicago. There, the huge expanse of river and the moored riverboats, evocative of another age, excited and stimulated her. The book was already selling well and she had three solid mornings of book signings in different parts of the windy city. Her right hand felt quite numb with the effort, but it was, she felt, worth it to see the pleasure on people's faces. Once again she spoke at a literary lunch. About two hundred women attended. The questions were, for the most part, fairly straightforward: the "where do you start?" and "do you plan the whole book in advance?" and "do you find the experiences in your own life influence what you write?"

Liz met some charming and interesting people and dinner invitations followed. On Vivien's advice, she refused them all. "To accept one means you offend others, and," continued Vivien, "you need the evening space to have a quiet meal, go to the theatre, watch television or have an occasional early night."

Liz, a social animal, felt a momentary pang but she also realised Vivien was right. Certainly, she was tired by evening and the two women often shared a room service meal. Vivien always left her by ten p.m. saying they both needed space.

Once again Liz found her professionalism comforting, knowing she was being "managed" but preferring it to floundering on her own, which she would have done without VB, as she began to call Vivien.

Liz had adored New Orleans. The music, the way people spoke, permanently sounding relaxed and laid back. An illusion, she knew, but one she enjoyed. The Creole food was delicious, spicy and different and she searched for a Creole cookbook to take back as a present for Aarav. The spices were different too and with Vivien's help, she chose a small selection of the rarer ones.

She was tiring now, her voice was even tired, and Vivien, anticipating this, had suggested before travelling to Phoenix that they could spend a few days in Sedona. Liz had heard of Sedona of course. The red rocks, the place where countless films had been made and, of course, the Grand Canyon.

Liz thought it a fabulous idea and when they finally arrived at the log-built hotel with its spa, masseuse and straightforward American food, Liz realised how much she needed to relax. She slept for twelve hours the first night, putting it down to the wonderful air and the fact that she had five whole days to wind down.

She swam for an hour every morning, going gently up and down the pool. It was set into rocks and it was so cleverly designed it looked almost as if it was a natural pool. She enjoyed the spa too and had a daily massage when she let her mind wander and thought of Philip. For a short while, she had felt loved and felt she loved him too. The boys had written their different accounts of Jutta and her unseemly departure. What she loved was that each boy credited the other for having been instrumental in "getting rid of her". What pleased her most though was it had, in a way, brought their father closer to them, and she noticed they both seemed to write of him more frequently with a sense of fondness as well as filial respect.

Liz had written to Kathy and the boys giving them her itinerary for the two months she was travelling and also the contact details of her publisher – she wanted to be sure they could always get in touch with her. The boys were her sons, maybe in spirit only, but they were her sons…

Before leaving Boston, the ever-efficient Vivien had asked for her next of kin. When Liz raised her eyebrows, Vivien had explained it was quite usual with writers on tour. "We've never had any sort of incident – but once one of our writers developed chicken-pox and we had to fly him home in the company plane."

Liz had come to enjoy the company plane. It had six passenger seats and enough space to walk around. Checking in at airports was so easy and Liz decided it was definitely the way to travel. After a moment's hesitation, she provided not only Kathy's details, but contact details for Jack and Jamie. She could not imagine any reason for them to be contacted but felt in the event of "something" they should at least "know".

Now, the tour was drawing to its conclusion. Lying in a jacuzzi, Liz reflected on some of her experiences. New York, The Plaza Hotel, the Broadway shows, the splendid dinner with the Chairman of the publishing company, along with his wife and senior colleagues at the famous Mama Leone restaurant. Would she ever forget the finest Italian food she had ever eaten? Her mouth watered at the memory.

Her New York audiences had been her toughest though. The usual literary lunches but the questions were perhaps more penetrating at times. Questions, too, about her change of publisher, someone produced a copy of the newspaper article written by Alex and asked what had caused her to change her agent/publisher. "After all," the disembodied voice from the audience continued. "Alex Wylde is respected and well known. He has stated that your writing is now passé. Have you changed this novel in any way as a result?"

Liz grimaced as she thought back. She had, she admitted afterwards to Vivien, been knocked off course. For a moment she had stumbled over her words. "I shall be frank," she had said, finally pulling herself together. "Alex Wild Wylde was a guest in my home in India. I threw him out because he overstepped the mark." – *Let them think what they want*, she thought – "I chose to remove my book from his agency and his 'revenge' was to write that article. That," she had continued, "is the truth and I am not prepared to discuss it further. Next question?" she smiled, remembering the moment of total silence, and when she finally left the podium she was still shaking.

Vivien had been brilliant. "Well done, Liz," she had said. "Sometimes it pays to speak out – it will stop speculation and gossip. Now tell me," she had continued. "What on earth did he do?!"

It had been good to tell someone the truth, for after he had left she had so much to do repairing all the damage and hurt he had caused to her friends that her own feelings had been pushed to one side. Vivien had listened in horrified fascination. "What a sod," she had said finally, causing them both to fall about. It had been good to talk, Liz thought, as the jacuzzi jets continued pulsating around her, it had been quite a cathartic experience – washed it out of her so to speak.

She smiled happily. Yes, she was feeling great. Better and happier than she had felt for quite some time. She mentally paused. Better than before Philip or rather after Philip. She was, at last, realising irrevocably that she would never see him again.

chapter 36

Over breakfast the next morning, Liz and Vivien were enjoying a desultory conversation when Vivien suddenly asked about Liz's life in Goa. Liz had mentioned it of course but now at Vivien's insistence, she described the villa, the gardens, the beach and Ashok and his family and the little home they had in the grounds. She talked too about Anjali and Aarav and even Bernadette, her husband and the children they were caring for.

"Oh Liz, you must write about it all. It sounds so heavenly."

"It is my bit of heaven," admitted Liz. "I miss everyone and everything – even my horses."

"You have horses too! Where do you ride?" Vivien wanted to know. Liz told her about the sunrise and sunset rides, about riding bareback and swimming in the sea with Coco and Guinness. The more she talked about it the more homesick she became and the thought of another month in the States was suddenly unbearable.

She looked reflective and Vivien intuitively knew that Liz was feeling really homesick. "I ride," she said, quite suddenly.

"Really?" said Liz her mind still on thoughts of Goa.

"I have a brilliant idea, why don't we leave here two days earlier than scheduled and we can go via Wickenburg en route to Phoenix. There is a super ranch there and I'll ring and see if they can fit us in for a couple of days."

Liz looked slightly dubious, "I really don't want to ride in a line—" she began.

"Leave it to me," Vivien said cheerfully and, taking her mobile out of her bag, she pressed a number of digits. "Hi Nancy, Vivien Brown. Yes, I'm fine – now something special." To Liz's embarrassment, Vivien explained that she was looking after a famous author who had her own horses but was missing them and would love to have a couple of days riding at the ranch. "Free riding," she continued. "With a wrangler of course. Just a moment, Nancy," she paused, realising Liz was frantically signalling to her.

"Please ask her not to tell anyone – I really would like a private two days," Liz said. Vivien passed on the message and it was quite clear that Nancy understood and would guard Liz's privacy.

Liz didn't usually mind people knowing who she was, in fact usually it was an important part of the necessary publicity, but if she was to have two days riding she perhaps acknowledged, rather selfishly, that she did not want to hear from other guests the oft-quoted, "Oh, I was thinking about writing a book if I had the time." When this comment cropped up when she was lecturing her response was always the same: "If you really want to write, you will. If you feel a need to write – you will always find the time." But now with the prospect of a riding break she wanted to savour every moment of "freedom".

They left for Wickenburg soon after breakfast going via "slide rock" where they enjoyed watching both adults and children sliding down the large smooth rock into the river that flowed steadily past.

"I would love to have done that as a child," Liz laughed.

"I did," Vivien confessed. "The first time I came here with my parents and twin sisters. The three of us spent the entire day sliding and swimming and ruining our shorts and tee shirts, in fact, we finished up with no seat in our shorts."

"Your poor mother." Vivien laughed.

"She wasn't best pleased for sure but I think she has forgiven us by now!"

They drove into Wickenburg, eating lunch at a Mexican restaurant that Vivien knew. She then insisted they visit the museum which was in memory of Henry Wickenburg who had set up and mined Vulture Mine many years before. It also provided a picture of times gone by with posters displaying requests for orphans to ride for the pony express. The death rate was appalling, Vivien explained, hence the need for orphans – who would not be missed… "Poor boys," she continued. "If the Indians didn't get them exhaustion frequently did."

A little later they were driving along a bumpy unmade road. Liz had no idea what to expect and the first glimpse of a beautifully tended lawn with a pool set in the middle of it was in great contrast to the barren and dry landscape they had passed on the drive.

The sound of their car brought Nancy and her husband John out to meet them. Vivien was the recipient of warm hugs whilst Liz was made to feel her visit was a real treat for them! "We've put you in the homestead VB," Nancy said. "Perfect," Vivien answered, as John took a bag in each hand and the four of them walked across a small dusty quadrangle to the door of an adobe house.

The smell of horses filled the air and Liz breathed in heavily, the smell transporting her to her own stables and horses. Here, she could see the horses lived in spacious corrals and stood in small groups, with shade provided by the scattering of bush-like trees and shrubs.

"We always do an orientation here," Nancy explained to Liz. Liz nodded, Vivien had explained the practice with new guests. "If you folks aren't too weary we could always do it now so that you can ride first thing in the morning."

Liz nodded happily. A quick freshen up and she would be all set to go she informed Nancy, delighted that they would be able to ride first thing in the morning. "Great," enthused Vivien. "I'll do the orientation as well John. It's always good to have a brush-up and have a few reminders." John looked immensely pleased – he always liked guests who entered into the spirit of things.

In the adobe house, which was comprised of a sitting area with fireplace and television and two bedrooms with a shared bathroom, the girls quickly changed into jeans and tee shirts. Neither of them had riding boots with them but they were each able to find a pair in the "loaner" box specially provided for guests who hadn't their own. Liz thought the adobe house, built of local mud years before, quite perfect and the atmosphere of the ranch and the welcome they had received made her relieved that VB had come up with such a happy idea.

Within half an hour of their arrival, they were on horseback. Liz on a quarter horse called Eclipse and Vivien on Hosea. They spent an hour in the corral which gave Liz a chance to try a western saddle for the first time and learn to hold the reins with just the left hand. It seemed strange at first but soon she had totally adjusted and they cantered around with John making the occasional encouraging comment.

John and Nancy were surprised by how quickly Liz adapted to the western saddle but when they learnt she frequently rode bareback and therefore with a "long leg" they understood. She told them how she rode morning and evening on the big expanse of beach, frequently finishing off by going into the sea with both horses.

"It sounds fabulous," Nancy confessed. "I can't even imagine being that free, yet we feel free here, don't we John?"

"Sure do," he answered in what Liz was beginning to realise was his normal monosyllabic way.

They had a glorious two days. Liz had already become fond of Vivien but the two days on the ranch cemented their friendship and they enjoyed their rides together. Climbing high, looking down at the town of Wickenburg or looking out at the mountains all around them. Best though, they both agreed, was cantering along the dry sandy river bed of the Hassayampa River.

All too quickly the two-day vacation was over. Of the week's break they had had, Liz acknowledged that, as much as she enjoyed the beauty of Sedona, the ranch in Wickenburg had been the highlight – a real oasis of peace and pleasure – and she promised her hosts she would definitely return, either at the end of the tour or she would make another visit to the States just to ride on the plains and mountains of Arizona.

As a thank you for their warmth and kindness, Liz left them a copy of her book, inside she wrote: *For my dear new friends Nancy and John Loftis, with thanks for two of the happiest days of my life. Liz O'Malley.* It may have been a bit over the top but she couldn't remember being so happy for a long time.

From Wickenburg, Vivien drove them the hour or so to Phoenix, where Liz was due to appear on television that evening on the Larry King Show. His reputation as a searching questioner was well known and Vivien advised that if he needled her in any way she should stick to the subject of the book and the tour. It was sound advice. He had picked up the Alex story, but she refused to be drawn. He presented her with a copy of her own book for her to sign and she made him laugh when she said he was taking advantage of her, that he should stand in line like everybody else.

He wanted to know how her book sales were going and, primed by Vivien, she was able to give exact figures. "Very well," was his conclusion at the fairly phenomenal sales. Finally, just when she thought the interview was about to end he asked her why she had never married. "You are," he said tantalisingly, "what would have once have been described as 'on the shelf!'"

Fortunately, Liz's sense of humour came to the forefront. She thought for a moment, not wanting to talk about her failed marriage to Steve which he obviously didn't know about, so replied firmly. "Mr King, whenever I let men into my life they either spoil things themselves," – thinking Philip – "become possessive," – thinking Alex – "or are seeking fame by associating with someone relatively well known" – thinking Steve – she concluded modestly.

"Thank you, Elizabeth O'Malley, enjoy the rest of your American tour and I hope you will come back again soon." The lights changed and the applause was warm. Liz rose thankfully from her seat glad the "ordeal" was over.

Liz had not enjoyed the experience and although Vivien assured her she had equipped herself well she made a mental note not to be interviewed on the Larry King Show again. She and Vivien had a light meal and turned in early, as there was a literary breakfast the next morning. "It could only happen in America," she thought.

As it happened it went particularly well. Whether it was because everyone was very wide awake at eight in the morning or whether she was on particularly good form she had no idea, but it seemed somehow easier and more relaxed.

Towards the end of the two hours, a red-haired woman rose to ask a question and the microphone was handed to her. "May I ask Miss O'Malley if you were encouraged to write when you were at school?" Liz laughed. "I don't know what prompted your question – but to be honest the answer must be no. I think I was forever 'scribbling' and my English literature teacher felt I should be putting my writing to better use. May I ask what prompted the question?" She was wondering if perhaps this was the mother of an aspiring young writer. Young writers she was hoping to meet when she lectured at Flagstaff.

The woman stood again. "Do you remember a dormitory in a boarding school in England where a young Irish girl came on an exchange visit for one term?" Liz inclined her head in acknowledgement. "Do you remember seven girls night after night asking the eighth girl, the Irish girl, to continue the story from the previous night?" Liz was startled. She couldn't see the features of the woman as clearly as she would like – but there was something about her. "Were we at school together?" Liz asked. By now the audience was turning to look at the redhead. "Do you remember Judy Greenhalgh?" "Judy!" Liz momentarily forgot herself. "Judy!" Everyone laughed and Liz gathered her scattered thoughts.

"You will have to forgive me, ladies and gentlemen. Judy and I share some happy memories. Judy, please stay behind afterwards." The event was at an end. There was laughter and applause as Judy wended her way through the tables to Liz, and there was more laughter and light hand-clapping as the two women hugged. Liz quickly explained she had a book signing now and Judy insisted on being first in the queue and then waited patiently as another hour passed by, as on request she wrote personal messages as well as her signature.

Finally, the last book was signed. Vivien started the clear up leaving Liz and Judy to properly catch up. They hugged and laughed, both talking at once in their excitement. Judy hadn't changed much – still as slim as ever with her freckles now discreetly covered. She invited Liz back for lunch and Vivien nodded when she looked her way. "Give me your address," she asked Judy, "and I will come and collect you around four o'clock if that is alright," she continued, looking at Liz.

It was, and saying goodbye to Vivien who was still in the throes of packing up and sorting out various papers, the old friends drove off to Judy's home in the neighbourhood of Scottsdale. Judy was now married to Gregory Raventos and Liz learned they had two daughters and she adored living in America. They chatted non-stop for the forty minute drive. Greg apparently worked from home so Liz would have the opportunity to meet him too, Judy informed her friend happily.

Judy was full of questions about Liz's life in India and Liz was equally curious about Judy's life in the States. "Where did you meet Greg?" she asked curiously. It transpired that they both had worked for the same bank in Hong Kong, "And then," Judy continued. "When he was transferred back here he asked me to marry him and live in the States. All my family flew out for the wedding – gosh that seems a long time ago," she sighed.

"You are happy though?" Liz queried, slightly worried about the sigh.

"Oh yes, Greg is a dear, it's just where do all the years go! The children were like babies only yesterday and now Sarah is four and Jenny is six."

Greg charmed Liz. He was a big, outgoing American, adored by his wife and apparently delighted that she had brought Liz home with her. Judy chatted as she busied herself in the kitchen making a pot of coffee and producing some home-made soup accompanied by some lovely crusty bread. Apart from the study, the whole of the downstairs was open plan with the kitchen in the middle providing real focus. It was so very different from the villa which, at their request, she tried her best to describe to them.

At Greg's insistence, she even drew a floor plan of the downstairs and she described the gardens which led on to the beach. She mentioned her horses and Ashok's home in the grounds. "Are you married?" Judy asked suddenly.

"No, but I sort of have two adopted sons, so I feel very lucky." They both noticed a certain sadness as she spoke and felt the subject was not up for discussion. After she had left Greg and Judy talked about it for a while and concluded Liz had had to deal with some sort of tragedy in her life.

Vivien arrived promptly at four and as they drove off Liz turned to wave to her old friend. Greg was holding a copy of the book she had signed for them and he raised his arm in a sort of salute. Judy had shed tears when she had read what Liz had written in the book: *To a dear school friend, who has reminded me of happy and fun days. Do keep in touch and visit me in India. Much love, Liz O'Malley.*

She felt rather sad as the car turned the corner and they were hidden from view, she wondered if she would ever see them again, she thought perhaps not. She was wrong...

chapter 37

The company plane flew them up to Flagstaff. Liz was feeling a bit emotional and a little despondent. Lecturing literature students at Flagstaff University would be challenging – they were apparently doing a course that had them studying writers in different genres and covering a vast period in history and their relevance to present-day writers. Liz had been asked to talk about contemporary literature and where she fitted in. She imagined they might be a tough group – but she hoped they would gain something from what she was proposing to talk about.

She planned to start her talk by telling them of her "Three D Guide". "I know from your tutors that most of you here today hope to become writers, even great writers, but the word rejection will be a keyword for most, if not all, of you at some time in your writing careers. So my first piece of advice to you is. Don't be Despondent, Disappointed or Desolate. Instead, remember the 'C guide'. Be Courageous, Committed and Confident."

The plane flew smoothly onwards, an occasional drop in air-pressure causing the plane to rise or drop slightly. Liz's eyes were closed and Vivien noticed how tired she looked and determined that, after Flagstaff, there must be a short break before the final reception in New York and before she flew back to India or England.

Liz didn't open her eyes until she felt flaps go down and noticed the change in the engine noise. Vivien proposed another few days' break. Liz beamed. "But VB we only had a break in Sedona and the ranch recently." "I know, I know," Vivien responded, "but constantly being on the move is tiring me and I don't have to lecture, be interviewed or attend literary events." "True," Liz said happily. "What shall we do, where do you propose we stay?"

Vivien smiled, she had an idea she wanted to check out, something really special. She knew she would enjoy it too even though she had done it once before.

While Liz unpacked yet again and arranged to have a few things pressed, Vivien talked with the front desk and made all the enquiries she needed to. Armed with a telephone number she made a phone call and "the plan" was put in place. She couldn't wait to tell Liz.

That evening Liz ordered room service and for once did not invite Vivien to join her. She wanted to go back in her mind to the meeting with Judy and realised she felt a pang of envy for her friend's obvious happiness in her marriage and with her children and her life in general.

Liz felt a sense of aloneness that she never experienced at home and felt slightly sorry for herself. She'd had enough of America, from its cheery "have a nice day", to the large meals that seemed forever presented to her. She longed for Goa – she longed for home.

The students were such fun, it quite lifted her spirits. Many of them planned journalistic careers, a number were not quite sure which direction they wanted to go in but were enjoying the course, but there was a small group, easily identified by their questions, who were novice writers. She gave them her three Ds and three Cs, and talked about her early disappointments and frustrations. How sometimes when a manuscript was returned for the third or fourth time, she would put it in a drawer and try and forget about it for a while.

"But," she continued. "If you have written it, you have put your thoughts and energies into it. Don't leave it lying in a drawer, a dusty manuscript found after your demise seventy years on is not going to do you any good, though it might make millionaires out of your descendants!" This made them laugh and broke the ice. Questions spewed forth about researching ideas and developing a personal style.

Liz continued by saying that even if they did not become full-time writers but had a longing to write, then they should find a part of every day when they wrote, if only an hour. "If you really want to succeed, you will." She concluded by adding how she wished them all the success they deserved, whether they became professional writers, or hobbyists, or told stories to the children they might have one day. There was a groan and laughter to which she responded. "I know that must seem a lifetime away! But anyway, I would like to thank you for having me here and I look forward to meeting as many of you as possible."

After the inevitable book signing Liz returned with Vivien to the hotel, to have a rest before showering and changing to have dinner with the Principal and staff, at which thankfully, she remembered, she did not have to speak. It was, Vivien assured her, a purely social affair and she, Vivien, would not be accompanying her. A car would collect Liz and bring her back to the hotel at the end of the evening.

It turned out to be a relaxed and informal affair. Principal Betty Enfield and her husband Derek were gracious and charming and she met so many friendly people, most of whom assured her they had read several of her books. It was all quite good for Liz's flagging ego – flagging only because the end was in sight and she could hardly believe how well it had gone, and how much she wanted it to be over.

From time to time during the evening her mind went to Vivien, wondering what particular excitement was planned for the next afternoon. Vivien had suggested she have a lie in, breakfast in bed and then be ready, casually dressed at noon.

Finally, back at the hotel, Liz had another shower, then she picked up the TV remote control and climbed into bed to catch up on the news or even watch a movie. In the end, she did neither, watching only a few minutes of local news before the remote slipped from her fingers on to the floor and she was asleep.

At noon the following day, after a deliciously lazy morning, she went down to the lobby. Her hair was tied at the nape of her neck. She wore light cream trousers and a cream silk blouse with a Hermes scarf tied loosely at her neck. She carried a lightweight jacket and shoulder bag with the things she would never be without: a small pad and ballpoint for notetaking; her diary which she carried in case she needed to consult it regarding an engagement; her tiny travel address book, for wherever she was in the world she would send postcards to the boys, her sister, a favourite cousin and staff at the villa; lipstick, a clean handkerchief (she hated tissues) and a small tube of moisturiser as she found all the air-conditioning in the States very skin-drying. Finally, a small hairbrush in case she needed to tidy up if she got too blown about.

Vivien looked her up and down as she returned to the lobby from outside. "Right Liz, perfectly dressed as always – the car awaits!"

If Liz felt anything it was that she hoped the drive would not be too long. Twenty minutes later they arrived at an airfield.

It was not the one they had arrived at two days before, but a smaller one and the only thing Liz could see was a helicopter. She was mystified. "Right," said Vivien, thoroughly enjoying keeping Liz in suspense despite her earlier entreaties. "We are going to fly to and over the Grand Canyon. The copter will fly us around the rim then go down a bit so we can have a really good look around. I've done this trip before," she continued, "and it is FANTASTIC."

Liz was overwhelmed with excitement. She knew some people walked right down and even stayed overnight at the base, but this sounded much better and certainly, feeling the way she was at the moment, agreeably less tiring!

The pilot came over to meet the two women and give them a briefing. He went through various safety procedures with them and then they were climbing in. The blades were rotating, the roar blocked out by the headphones they were wearing. Liz sat next to the pilot with Vivien behind. Although when the helicopter took off, Liz's stomach gave a leap, she soon adjusted to the angle the helicopter was flying at and settled back to enjoy the flight. It was about twenty minutes before Liz got her first sight of the Canyon from the sky. First they flew around the huge perimeter, then their pilot made a series of swoops so that they were able to see the depth and colour of the rocks, even seeing the small figures of people walking up or down the path to the base.

Liz clapped her hands in delight. "It's wonderful," she said into her microphone. The pilot turned and gave her a thumbs up. A little while later she noticed him speaking into his mouthpiece. The helicopter banked quite steeply. Liz took off her headphones to hear the pilot saying, "Mayday, Mayday," then repeating and repeating. The helicopter seemed to be falling, falling like a stone, and that was Liz's last conscious thought.

*

The telephone rang at the school. She hated having to do this but Liz's sister knew that it was what Liz would want. She still hadn't grasped the awfulness. Her telephone ringing at three a.m. had shattered her sleep – it was a telephone call from New York, Liz's publishers. She had been dragged into awful reality by the sympathetic voice at the other end. "Yours was the 'next of kin' number she gave us. It is very grave news I'm afraid." She heard something about someone being "dead" and she heard someone screaming – it took a few seconds for her to realise it was her.

The scream woke her, and she asked "the voice" to repeat everything slowly. There had been a helicopter crash over the Grand Canyon. The pilot was dead as was Vivien Brown. "But my sister, Liz?"

"She is alive but critically hurt. The rescue was tricky because of the difficult terrain – it took quite a long time to reach her."

"Where is she?" Kathy demanded. The kind voice gave her the name of a hospital in Phoenix. "I shall come as soon as I can get a flight."

By early morning Kathy had her flight arranged, packed a small case and then, just as she was about to leave the flat, thought of Jack and Jamie. She telephoned the school and eventually was put through to someone who at last said he would locate Jack. "It was," he questioned, "concerning a family member?"

"Absolutely," Kathy lied. Jack, who was just finishing breakfast, was summoned out of the dining room. His language master, looking very serious, told him a close family member had been in an accident. "Your aunt is on the telephone." Jack was mystified, as far as he knew he had no aunt. Then he knew without a shadow of a doubt it must be Liz's sister. He had never met her but Liz often mentioned her. Jack followed the master to his study. "Jack Broderick," he said, picking up the phone.

"Oh, Jack you don't know me. It's Kathy here, Liz's sister." With a sinking feeling, he knew he had been right. It was Liz. "What's happened to Liz?" he asked without preamble.

"There has been a bad accident, I'm flying to Phoenix this morning. I'll call you from there. I promise I will keep you informed all the time – Liz would want that."

"Thank you," Jack replied putting the telephone down and wondering what to do. He must tell Jamie of course, but there was one other person he must tell. He must tell his father.

He found Jamie and together they sat on a bench outside. They had been told they could miss the first lesson of the morning. "We have to tell Dad you know," Jamie said.

"I know," Jack answered, knowing that he, as the eldest son, would have to make the call.

"Let's do it straight away, he'll know what to do. He'll have to give us the money – we have to go, Jack, we have to."

Jack nodded. Getting his mobile out of his pocket he pressed the code for Philip's private number at the embassy. Philip, sitting at his desk looking at the day's mail his secretary had left for him, sighed when his mobile rang but, seeing Jack's number on the screen, smiled as he answered. "Are you having time out for good behaviour?" he asked good-naturedly.

"Dad, listen." There was something in his tone – he sounded upset.

"Jack are you alright? Or Jamie?"

"Dad it's Liz!" For a moment Philip's mind was a blank. *Liz, Liz who?* "You are talking about Elizabeth?"

"Yes." Jack explained about the accident. He and Jamie wanted to go. "Please, Dad will you give us the cash?" Philip's mind was in a turmoil. He pictured her in the boat happy and carefree – then his imagination took over and he saw her poor body torn and hurt. "Jack," he said firmly. "I shall go. I shall go for you and Jamie. I shall tell her that and I will telephone you every evening. Jack are you there?" He heard a sob. "Jack, it's alright, old chap, I'll go and look after her I promise. I will look after her for you and Jamie," he added to himself, *I will look after her for me as well.*

Philip found the flight to Phoenix endless. His thoughts ranged from his conversation with Jack and his son's obvious distress, to his subsequent conversation with Elizabeth's sister – her coolness which he sensed despite her distress too. He wondered at the coolness and her surprise that he was flying to Phoenix. "What about Jack and Jamie?" she had asked and he heard the real concern in her voice. It was almost as if she knew them, yet how could she?

Of course, he thought of Liz – he saw her in his mind's eye leaping off the yacht, helping with the ropes. He remembered, even though he had been in conversation with Jack, how he had seen her "forward" with an arm around Jamie's shoulders. He couldn't hear the shrieks of delight as they watched the dolphins – but every now and again as their heads turned he had caught glimpses of such joy, and he had felt a momentary envy that it was she and Jamie, and not himself who Jamie's joy was shared with.

He thought about the night they made love. Her soft responsiveness. Her trust – the way she gave herself and the way she touched his body – giving him something that made him crave her more and more, and as their bodies became one he had no idea where he ended and she began with a total "oneness" of body and mind.

He had acknowledged later, much later, that it had never been quite like that with Helen. She had been more reticent and he was never convinced that she really enjoyed their lovemaking. She had adored him, he knew that. She hung on his every word. She wanted nothing more than for them to be happy and she clung to him when they made love, but he felt there was, on her part, a sense of relief when it was over. Her happiness came from being with him and being his "angel". Now, after all these years, he knew he had loved her, but he had let slip away the only woman he had ever been "in love" with.

Once again he remembered the night when Jack burst into the cabin. Him, naked as the day he was born; Jamie and the operation for a burst appendix in the tiny hospital with one doctor and nurse. He remembered coming back to the yacht; his anger at himself for being in such a compromising position when Jack found him and Jamie needed him – an anger that spilled over and caused tension between him and Liz. She, he remembered, had her bags packed when he arrived back at the yacht. He should have stopped her, but didn't. His guilt over the way he treated her, mixed up with his guilt over Jamie and Jack which left him feeling furious with himself, had caused him to act so stupidly and selfishly and prevented him from holding on to a most precious love. Now it was probably too late. He stiffened, a new resolution taking place inside his head and heart. He would not let her die, he would do anything, everything, to save her and he would never let her out of his sight again.

She was a fighter – she would come through. For the first time since the news, he suddenly felt exhausted. A new peace filled him now that he had resolved what to do. He slept, he continued to sleep and, only as the aircraft landed and the light bump made him aware that they had arrived, did he wake feeling refreshed and ready.

chapter 38

He may have been ready, but nothing could have prepared him for the shock of seeing her. He was allowed in, despite the fact that he couldn't claim to be family. He used his diplomatic title, feeling this was definitely not an occasion to hold back. He also explained that he was to marry Elizabeth O'Malley. The nurse looked sympathetic. "I am so sorry," she said. Philip was startled, something in her tone made him realise how bad it was and, knowing this, he walked into her room.

A young woman who bore some resemblance to Liz sat by her bed. Philip only glanced at her briefly, the still, slight figure in the bed, covered to her waist with a light cotton sheet, was his only focus. "Elizabeth," he could hardly believe her frailty, he had imagined of course, but this... her beautiful black hair had been shorn and he could see a large gash, neatly stitched, went right across her head.

She had another gash right down the left side of her face, she was bruised and, perhaps most awful of all, her eyes were covered with taped-down dressings. She seemed to have drips everywhere, tubes up her nose, cannulas in her arms. Her bare arms were lacerated and stitched, and the yellow of the antiseptics used covered most of the skin he could see.

She moaned and the sound pulled him out of his reverie. "Oh Elizabeth, my darling, darling girl," he moved to the bed and kissed her gently on her forehead. "Why is she moaning?" he wondered aloud. "The doctors say it is a good sign, it will hopefully mean she will come out of the coma before too long. You must be Philip – I'm Kathy, Liz's sister." She added a shade coldly: "So you finally, now she is near death, crept out of the woodwork did you?" She sounded bitter and Philip knew she was right. He bowed his head in acquiescence. "She was as stubborn as you. You have no idea how many times I told her to contact you."

"What did she say?"

"She said she would wait until you contacted her." He put his head in his hands in total despair.

"I've been such a fool."

"You've both been fools. Let's hope it's not too late."

*

Liz was having a wonderful time. When Ashok had first put the hammock in the garden, suspended from two of the tall palms, she had been just a shade disappointed. The hammock was made of corks joined by strong black threads. She didn't like to tell him that, although she loved the motion of the hammock rocked gently by the breeze, she had never found it truly comfortable. That was until today. It was as if it was made of silk. She nuzzled into its comfort. Looking up, she watched as the palm fronds moved lazily in the breeze – they reminded her of huge ostrich feathers. For a while, they lulled her and she rested feeling cool and comfortable.

It was the sound of the *caw-caw* of the rooks that woke her. The pair sat on fronds above her. "I wish I knew what you are saying," she said out loud. *Caw-caw* they repeated. "Oh, you want some fruit." She went to move, happy to chop up some apples for them, but she was so drowsy and comfortable that once again she drifted off to sleep.

Next time she opened her eyes she was amazed to see Coco and Guinness. She was surprised that they had left the coolness of their stables with the whirring roof fans she had decided were better for them than air-conditioning. They stood at the foot of the hammock in the shade of the palms. "What are you doing here boys?" she asked them. "Did you just want company?" As if understanding every word they moved their heads up and down in perfect unison. "Oh, you are so clever," she exclaimed, marvelling at their understanding.

A flutter of wings made her look across to the lawns on her left where the family of egrets were out searching for their favourite grubs hidden among the grasses – not hidden well enough though. Poppa and Momma egret now had three young to feed and, like a family of swans, they processed in a stately line. She loved them. With their eager walking and their serene flight they reminded her slightly of miniature storks.

She heard the sound of tinkling ice. Anjali was coming down the steps and across the lawn towards her. She carried a tray with two tall glasses of lemonade and, over her arm, she carried Liz's favourite blue pashmina.

For a moment Liz was disappointed – she was so enjoying the peace and tranquillity. She wondered who had arrived to disturb her serenity, for Anjali had made up a second glass for a guest. She looked beyond the housekeeper but could see no one.

Anjali put the tray on the small round table and sat down on a chair that Liz couldn't remember noticing before. "Why Anjali are you going to stay with me and have a glass of lemonade?"

"Yes, Madame. I wanted to be with you." She put out her hand. Liz held hers out and grasped the slim cool hand. "Oh dear Anjali, how fortunate I am to have you as my friend."

"I am the fortunate one," Anjali answered. "But you are cold, Madame. Here let me cover you." She gently laid the blue pashmina over her mistress. "I will stay with you, Madame." With a contented sigh, Liz closed her eyes, she was so tired she must sleep again.

*

Anjali received a telephone call from America. It was Philip Broderick. "You may remember I was the Ambassador in Delhi," he said, by way of introduction. Anjali never forgot anything so she knew immediately who it was. "Sir Philip," she began. "I'm afraid Madame O'Malley is touring in America at the moment, she will be so disappointed to miss your call."

"No, Anjali," Philip spoke gently. He remembered Liz talking of her housekeeper so warmly. A friend as well as an employee she had said.

"There is no easy way to say this Anjali. Elizabeth, Madame O'Malley, has been in an accident. She is very ill I'm afraid." Anjali felt fear clutch at her heart.

"Bring her home sir, please. We will look after her." As gently and as firmly as he could he explained that she was still in a coma but he promised that, when it was possible to bring her home, he would bring her himself. "I will telephone again, Anjali, every few days."

Anjali couldn't tell the others, not yet. Feeling a slight shiver, she went to her bedroom and collected her blue pashmina, the one Madame had so kindly given to her on her birthday. She wandered aimlessly down the steps, collecting a small chair from the veranda as she went. She carried it over to Madame's favourite place under the palms. She pictured Madame lying in bed. Closing her eyes, she willed herself to the bedside. She searched for the fragile white hand which seemed cold and clammy. Mentally she took the blue pashmina and laid it gently over the still form. In her head, she heard Madame O'Malley's voice. "I am so fortunate," she said, "to have a friend like you."

"Oh Madame," Anjali said. "It is I who am fortunate."

*

Philip sat by the bed, hearing every sound, seeing every movement. Sometimes she smiled and he wondered what thoughts were making her happy. Other times she moaned a little as if she was trying hard to form words. She had been in surgery again this morning, he had learned to dread surgery days, for he was always uncertain what condition she would return in.

With the cage over her legs to keep the sheet from touching her burned flesh, he had no idea how bad they were. He knew she was on strong medication to alleviate as much pain as possible and they were using the most current techniques in skin-grafting they could.

That morning they had removed the pads that covered her eyes. Amazingly, the operation to remove shards of glass from her eyes seemed to have been very successful and the retina appeared to have been undamaged. "When she opens her eyes," the surgeon told Philip, "she is likely to have blurred vision at first, but that should clear in a couple of days, hopefully." He added as a cautionary rider.

Philip watched helplessly as she seemed to search for something – she kept plucking at the sheet. What, he wondered, could she be seeking? He asked if he could look at the things of hers that had been taken off the burning helicopter, amazingly they had found her suitcase flung yards away as the helicopter crashed and before the subsequent fire.

He felt rather awkward, as if he was prying – but he determined there might be a clue to be found there. Everything was neatly folded. Shoes in cloth shoe-bags, blouses and tops, each in their own zipped pochette. The blue pashmina had been on the top and it was only when he could not find anything obvious that he returned to it. Lateral thinking he reminded himself. The pashmina was on the top, perhaps because it was important to her, or perhaps she put it around her when sitting up in bed. The air-conditioning could sometimes feel a little chill.

Clutching at straws, he took the pashmina over to her bed, leaving the bag open in case he could find something else. The pashmina was fortunately very light so, opening it out, he spread it as gently as he could over the sheet. He lifted one of her hands and placed it on the pashmina. He watched the clutching fingers despairingly. It was no good, it had been a crazy thought. Suddenly, her fingers stopped their restless movements. The other hand joined its fellow on the pashmina. He watched as her fingers curled the pashmina within them and, looking at her, he saw a smile of pure joy.

Despite her scars and her poor shorn hair – which was beginning to grow back a little now – despite all that he had never seen her look more beautiful. For the first time in a very long time, he knelt by the bed and thanked God for her life, vowing he would never leave her side.

After he had made his usual evening call to the boys, Philip rang number ten, Downing Street. His call with the boys had a more optimistic tone and he was able to say, quite genuinely this time, that there was an improvement. Jack and Jamie didn't ask this time, they demanded that at the end of the term in three weeks they would join their father in Phoenix. Philip didn't demure, he realised that there was something special between his sons and Elizabeth that he didn't fully understand, in fact, he didn't understand at all but felt that whatever it was it was good, and they certainly must be allowed to visit.

The call to Downing Street was difficult for Philip, who had always believed his career must come first. He originally decided that he must offer his resignation as he planned to stay with Elizabeth indefinitely. After some discussion when the Prime Minister expressed her concern about Liz, whom she had, of course, met in Delhi, she suggested Philip take an indefinite leave of absence. His deputy could take over in the short term and she insisted that he must put Liz first. Philip was both relieved and surprised at her generosity.

Julia herself was in the midst of some rather unpleasant matters dealing with a hitherto supposedly respectable politician, who had been found to be dealing in a people-smuggling ring. She had been horrified to learn about Liz and the Foreign Office had not thought to inform her that Philip had taken a month's compassionate leave. He smiled ruefully on hearing this, knowing that someone was going to get their knuckles rapped – at the very least. After a little more conversation about the temporary handover, Philip agreed to her various suggestions, and then, putting any contemplation of his professional life out of his mind, and with Julia's blessing, all thoughts of his Ambassadorial role went out of the window.

The following morning yet more flowers arrived, this time not from students at Flagstaff University, or people she had addressed during the tour, or even the chairman of the publishing house, who was still trying to deal with the trauma of losing his favourite PA, Vivien Brown, but still sent regular messages and flowers. No, this time the flowers were from Julia, the Prime Minister. The accompanying card read : *Get well, dear friend. The flowers are golden, for I shall never forget you in your gold dress. I wish I could visit you, we shall meet again I promise. Warmly, Julia.*

Of course, Liz could not see the flowers, nevertheless Philip knew that the perfume of the golden roses filled the air and he had them put on a side table as close to her bed as possible.

chapter 39

She was warm at last, it was good that Anjali had put the pashmina over her whilst she rested on the hammock. She thought perhaps it was Anjali's pashmina, a slightly different shade of blue than the one she had bought for herself. When Anjali had admired it she immediately decided to buy one for her, and on her birthday when Anjali had unwrapped it, she saw with pleasure the delight her gift was giving. She wondered where her pashmina was, it was so kind of Anjali to share hers.

She was so tired and she so wanted to sleep. People kept talking to her. She knew she must be dreaming again, she was having so many dreams. She tried to get back to the peace of her garden. The hammock was empty, she could see it moving slightly in the breeze. The voice again – calling her – she tried to concentrate but the darkness kept coming back. "Elizabeth." Yes, someone was calling her. She tried hard to think who it could be.

Yes, yes, she remembered. That's what my father called me. How can he be calling me now? The darkness came, blessedly, and she didn't have to think anymore.

He watched silently, only ever leaving her for a few hours. Kathy had returned to England for a photographic assignment, but they had parted on good terms after a few awkward exchanges when Philip had first arrived. He kept her up to date with what was happening on an almost daily basis and they had finally reached a rapprochement.

Philip would go back to his hotel for a few hours – shower, set his alarm and close his eyes. Three hours later he would order room service and try and eat something. It was usually wasted as he was anxious to return to the hospital.

Judy and Greg took it in turns to stay with her whilst he was away. When the red-headed woman had first appeared at the hospital he had thought she was yet another well-wisher. Judy explained the school connection and, after some hesitation on his behalf, Philip "allowed" Judy or her husband, Greg, to stay with Liz during some, if not all, of his absences.

"I wish he'd have a proper sleep," Judy confided to Greg. He put his arms around her.

"I know honey, but imagine if it was one of us – would the other leave?" Judy hugged her husband.

"Of course not." After that, the pair of them, to Philip's eternal gratitude, took over from him every evening for a few hours.

The boys would have been enjoying the flight had it not been for worrying about Liz. "He said she was getting better," Jamie said happily.

"What he said is not necessarily the full truth," countered the more realistic Jack. Jamie went very quiet and Jack could have kicked himself, he adored Liz and he knew that Jamie really looked on her as an "almost mother". Try though Jack might, he couldn't cheer his brother and finally they both closed their eyes as night fell and the plane took them ever nearer to Liz and their father, and they would face whatever it was that they would face.

*

It was that voice again. "Elizabeth, come on my darling – the boys are coming to see you today. Jack and Jamie will be here in an hour or so. Wake up, my sweet, please, we all need you so much."

It was so warm and cosy in the dark. She clutched the pashmina, her comforter she used to call it when she put it over her shoulders. The air-conditioning in these American hotels was too chill for her.

*

He saw her tremble. "Nurse," he called urgently. "Something different!"

"It looks as if she is beginning to come back to us," the nurse said comfortingly. "Just talk to her, keep holding her hand as you are." He stroked her hand and talked again of the boys, of her gold dress and how beautiful she had looked, how stupid he had been to let her go, and how Jack and Jamie were coming soon.

*

She heard a scream and knew it was her. The helicopter was going down – the side of the Grand Canyon became closer and closer. The pain, the pain, the pain – her legs – her face, her head. Then nothing, nothing until this voice, the voice that was comfortingly familiar. Could she come back? It was dark here, she felt safe. The voice was persuasive, cajoling. Perhaps if she could just open her eyes. The lids felt heavy, but she wanted to now. She tried, she tried so hard. Philip felt her hand suddenly tighten on his. He could see the fast movement of her eyes under their fine lids. The nurse had fetched the doctor and he had his hand on her pulse. "Keep talking," he said to Philip.

233

Philip heard but was really aware of nothing except fingers clutching his. "Elizabeth, my dear sweet lovely Elizabeth. Please come back. I need you Elizabeth." His voice broke and he put his head down on her hand. It was a moment of utter despair. Then he heard, very faintly, a different sound. Head up, he looked at her. Her eyes were open. She was trying to say something. He put his head near her mouth to try and catch what she was trying to say.

*

She was finding it hard. She had left the dark place, now it was like being in a cloud – but the voice that kept calling her held her hand – she could feel the strength. She tried to see who it was, who called, and though the light was too bright and her eyes seemed not to be working properly, she saw a comforting, familiar shape. "Is that you Philip?" she finally managed the words.

He could hardly speak for the emotion that gripped him. He held her hand and bent his head to kiss it before looking up and into her eyes. "Yes Elizabeth, it's Philip and I am here to stay." With a smile, a contented smile, she closed her eyes and drifted off to sleep.

For a moment Philip was worried, the doctor sensing this, reassured him. "It's alright sir, she is having a natural sleep now." He encouraged Philip to leave for a rest but he was not to be persuaded. Elizabeth might wake while he was away and he did not want to risk her wakening to find him gone.

He looked at his watch. The boys were due to land about now. Judy had said she would meet them, in fact she had insisted, and although he felt bad about not being there, he knew on this occasion they would totally understand.

Judy recognised them immediately – the older boy was just

like a younger version of Philip and, almost, if not as, tall as his father. The younger boy Judy surmised must take after his mother, for he was as fair as his brother was dark. They were strikingly good-looking and as Judy walked with them to the waiting car she noticed the heads of a number of young women turning to look at them.

Jack and Jamie were surprised to be met at all, they had planned to take a cab directly to the hospital, knowing if their father wasn't at the airport that is where he would be. When Judy had stepped forward and introduced herself as an old school friend of Liz's they were pleased and assumed she would take them straight to the hospital. Judy quickly explained they were staying with her as their father was seldom at the hotel. After their initial disappointment, they could see the sense of staying with Liz's friends and after a quick wash and change of clothes, followed by a delicious hamburger cooked by Greg on the barbecue, they were all set to go.

Their body clocks told them it was around one a.m., but as it was six p.m. in Phoenix, it seemed good sense to adjust as quickly as possible. On the way, Jack pumped his host about Liz's condition. Not being aware that she had woken up that afternoon, Greg explained that she was still in a coma.

Jamie was very quiet and Jack hugged him and said, "She'll wake up Jamie, now we are here – I'm sure of it." Jamie looked at his older brother in gratitude, he so hoped he was right, he certainly couldn't bear the thought of losing Liz.

Greg took them up in the lift and left them outside Liz's door. He glanced through the small glass panel to make sure Philip was there, told the boys he would collect them in two hours and returned home.

As the door opened, Philip stood up. He didn't think he had ever been happier to see his sons and said in a very low tone. "She's sleeping."

"It's alright, Dad," Jack said in a normal voice. "Greg told us she is still in a coma."

Liz was having a lovely dream. She was in the sea with the horses, but the waves kept crashing overhead and suddenly, for the first time, she felt frightened of their power. The horses, perhaps sensing her fear, seemed fearful too. Then Philip seemed to be there, he took her in his arms and seemed to wade easily to the shore, the horses following.

She opened her eyes to see not just Philip, but Jack and Jamie too. "Hello," she said in a normal conversational tone. "What are you boys doing here? Shouldn't you be at school?" The family trio laughed delightedly. "We heard you were in a coma," Jamie said. Philip frowned and was about to shush his youngest son. "Was I?" came an interested voice from the bed. "Was I really in a coma? How long for?" she continued, feeling stronger with every word she spoke.

Philip sat down again on the bedside chair he had abruptly vacated. The boys went to the other side of the bed and both unhesitatingly kissed the patient. If Philip was surprised, which he was, he didn't show it. He knew there was something between the three of them and in due course he would find out the whys and wherefores, but for now he was content to see Liz's smiling and happy face and the relieved faces of his sons.

Jamie seemed particularly fascinated with all the tubes and drips and wanted to look at her legs under the cage. "Why not? I can't see them, I can't even feel them much," Liz said. Jamie lifted the sheet and saw a pair of badly burned legs with what looked like some patches of new skin in some places. "What a mess," he said in an interested voice, remembering the long, slim, perfect legs he had seen when she wore a bikini on the boat. He had been too young to appreciate them then, but now, seeing this, reminded him of how she had been.

"That's quite enough," Philip said. "You are being overly curious."

"No Dad really, I'm really interested…"

"Do you remember anything Liz?" Jack asked in his uncompromising way. A shadow passed over Liz's face. "Vivien," she said suddenly. "Vivien wouldn't jump. The pilot kept shouting at us. I managed to open the door, but she wouldn't jump. I waited and waited, then finally the ground got closer and closer. The helicopter burst into flames as I jumped and I remember my legs were – I was – on fire."

"You were," Philip said quietly.

"And Vivien?" she asked.

"Vivien never did jump," his tone was sombre. "She didn't survive, Elizabeth. You were the only survivor." Liz started to cry. Fortuitously Greg arrived a bit early and Philip insisted the boys went with him. They both kissed the weeping Liz who didn't even seem to notice their departure. It was a long while before she quietened. A nurse gave her an injection which seemed to calm her, and then once again she slept.

Philip had so much to think about. Liz's courage for one. Jumping out into the unknown, her bravery and non-complaining at her discomfort. He could tell she was in pain both now and when she had been in a coma by her very expressive face. Now he was thinking about Jack and Jamie, their closeness to Liz and when and how had it come about. The last time he had seen Jack with Liz he had been unbelievably angry at Jack. In hindsight, the situation had been almost comical – him naked, Liz hardly covered in bed and Jack standing in the doorway of the cabin, staring incredulously at the scene in front of him. He decided he must tackle the boys, he was happy they seemed so fond of Liz but his curiosity was awakened.

Liz was dreaming again, Philip could tell. She smiled and made contented little sounds, he wished he could be with her, sharing her happy thoughts. Liz wasn't completely asleep, she was in the twilight zone between consciousness and sleep. She had seen Philip again and could hardly believe her eyes when she first saw him sitting there beside her. The boys too – dear Jamie, dear Jack. Her thoughts as she lay there were that she must have been quite poorly for them all to be there.

Her mind tried to grasp what it all meant. She was riding Guinness, and Coco cantered alongside. At the far end of the beach, she turned towards the sea. Riding bareback meant she could take them into deep water. The horses swam side by side. She slipped into the sea and swam around them. Suddenly they had gone – she was alone – out of her depth.

The sea was cold, not the balmy warmth she was accustomed to. She tried to swim, but her legs hurt and she couldn't get any nearer to the shore. She felt herself sinking, once, twice, and knew that one more time and she would be finished. Just as she was about to give up, she felt strong arms around her. She opened her eyes. Philip had come from nowhere. "I heard you call," he said swimming to the shore, pulling her easily with him. The horses stood side by side. He lifted her tenderly on to Coco's back, leapt easily on to Guinness's and very slowly they walked back along the way she had come.

Philip was dozing. He found these "cat naps", when she slept, really useful and amazingly reviving. He woke with a start. She was moaning, she sounded frightened. Despite the tubes and drips he instinctively put his arms around her as gently as he could and held her tenderly, telling her she was safe and the nightmares would go away.

After a few more trembles she quietened, relaxed in his arms and, quite suddenly, opened her eyes. His face was close to hers, it seemed so natural to plant a loving kiss on her sensuous mouth. Contented, she kissed him back, then drifted off again, content to know he was by her side.

chapter 40

Philip and the boys had breakfast together the following morning. Greg had insisted Philip come to their home. "The boys need to talk to you," he said. "Jude and I will make ourselves scarce." As good as their word, and as soon as the five of them had consumed American pancakes with crispy bacon and maple syrup, with endless coffee for Philip and hot chocolate for the boys, Judy and Greg left the house. "I gather you have something to say," Philip said with a smile. It was so good to have their company, he hadn't realised how lonely these weeks had been. "It's not exactly that we have something to say," Jack began. "More we have something for you to read." Philip was intrigued.

"Actually," he said. "I rather wanted to talk to you about Elizabeth." He saw the boys exchange glances. Jamie got up and went to the room he and Jack were sharing. Jack's pile was smaller than his – but then he, Jamie, had been involved for longer.

He picked up the two bundles of letters from the dressing table and returned to the open-plan kitchen cum family room where breakfast had been laid out. "We want you to read these Dad, these first," Jamie said, pointing to his bundle. "Then

239

these," Jack added, pointing to the second bundle. "It will take a while so we are going for a swim in the community pool just down the road – you can come and find us if you want to."

Philip was alone in the house. Extracting a letter from the bundle Jamie had handed him, he noticed a discreet number one on the top left-hand corner of the envelope.

Dear Jamie, the letter began. He turned the sheet over, it was signed with a bold L. Where had he seen an L like that before? It didn't matter, he read letter after letter. The latest, more recent, letters were signed differently, *your loving A M L*. He went back to the first letter with the three initials to find a clue.

The clue was there, of course, in all the letters. *I was intrigued*, Liz had written, *by your code. I did as you told me and took the first letter of each line to make the words. Of course, darling Jamie*, Philip read, *I am honoured to be your adopted mother – just between us though – alright?*

"Adopted Mother Liz." Philip grinned at his younger son's games. He then started on Jack's letters. The first was relatively formal, referring to a teatime in Windsor, and how wonderful it had been at last to heal the rift. He read a few more letters, then skipped to the last, intrigued. She wrote of her impending American tour which would take her away for three months. She promised lots of postcards and a special meal in London when she returned.

Once again he found a reference to himself. *I hope your Father is keeping well and not missing the beautiful Jutta too much*. Philip nearly choked. The wretched boys kept nothing sacred! Then he noticed Jack's letters bore the same three initials, A M L.

He looked at his watch. He'd only read a selection of the letters, but he was moved that the woman he knew, beyond any shadow of a doubt, that he loved and wanted to spend the

240

rest of his life with, also seemed to love and be loved by his sons. He collected up the letters, put them in their appropriate bundles, and returned them to the boys' bedroom. Then, without a moment's hesitation, he left the house and walked across to the community pool.

The boys were sitting on the side of the pool, their legs dangling in the water. They were deep in conversation and Philip felt inordinately proud of them. They had helped get rid of the awful Jutta, and more importantly, they had kept faith with Liz, which was more than he had. Not for the first time he vowed inwardly he would stay with her forever, and his heart gladdened when he realised what a happy family they would be.

Jamie adored the hospital. He asked so many questions and seemed to easily absorb and remember what he was told, and he consistently fed information back to Liz and his father that they would rather know less about!

He was fascinated by the plastic surgery Liz had already had on her legs, and finally, the head plastic surgeon allowed him to watch some operations from the viewing gallery. If George Lloyds expected that it might "put off" the sixteen-year-old he was mistaken, and he found himself drawn to this enthusiastic youngster. "What are you going to do when you graduate from high school?" he asked one morning. Jamie did a quick translation – what would he do when he had completed his baccalaureate and what would he study at uni? "I am going to study medicine." He sounded so sure, so confident, that George Lloyds had no doubt this lad would achieve his dreams.

"Fine," he said with a smile. "When you are fully qualified let me know. Too many of our brightest grads are going into cosmetic surgery. We need the 'real stuff' done too, like on your mother." Jamie didn't correct the assumption. "But she will need cosmetic surgery too, on her face," Jamie said.

"That is not the cosmetic surgery that I object to young man, and when you are older and qualified you make sure you get in touch with me and we will talk further."

"Right," Jamie replied confidently. "I am sure now about what I want to do."

A few days later he told Philip and Liz. Philip was cautious. "You have two more years in school yet, Jamie. You may well change your mind several times between now and then." Jamie looked at Liz. "I won't you know 'AM'."

"I know," she answered quietly.

Liz was having physiotherapy. She was now in a wheelchair for several hours a day and feeling incredibly weak. She had despatched Philip to spend time with his sons and, once he realised she really wanted him to go, he drove his hired car to Greg and Judy's and tracked the boys down once again at the community pool. Although Judy and Greg had a pool it was really only a splash pool to go in and out of in the heat of the Arizona day. The community pool gave the boys a chance to talk and also they had already met other teenagers there who were very friendly towards the English "intruders".

When Philip arrived he noticed two silver-haired men in a somewhat heated conversation about golf and his sons equally deep in an earnest, though he was pleased to note a quiet, conversation. They didn't see their father until he was almost on them. "Can anyone join in?" he asked in a pleasant voice, taking his sandals off as he spoke and sitting down in the space they had made for him between them. Fortunately, he had Bermuda shorts on so, like his sons, he was able to enjoy the coolness of the water on his feet and lower legs.

Philip found Phoenix very hot. He had become used to the heat in India, but now after several years in Paris, the heat hit him like a sledgehammer! "I've read the letters," he said, by way of a preamble. Jack leaned forward and met Jamie's eyes but neither boy spoke. Only minutes before Philip had arrived they had agreed to listen to what he had to say, for after all they had reasoned, they had deceived him and supposed he might be angry about the "adopted mother" thing that had become important to them both.

"I am glad you like Elizabeth so much——" Philip began.

"We love her actually Dad," said Jamie in a very positive manner. Jack nodded in agreement, "Yes," he said. "We do."

"I will rephrase my statement," Philip said firmly, determined to have his say. "I am delighted you love her. For," he continued, "so do I, in fact, I am going to marry her. So she won't be your adopted mother any more, but your" – he hesitated, he didn't want to say stepmother – "your new mother," he said finally.

He put his arms around his sons and the three of them hugged and laughed. "Nice family that English lot," said the one elderly gentleman to the other.

"There is something about the British I can't help liking," said his friend in a pure southern drawl.

"I try not to like them – then you see something like that," he said, indicating Philip hugging and laughing with his sons, "and well, shucks Eddy. I like 'em."

They had moved to a bench and Philip borrowed a towel to dry himself off. "So when, Dad? When are you going to get married?" A frown crossed Philip's face.

"Well," he began. "I haven't actually asked her yet." Without a second thought, Jack and Jamie dragged their father the few feet to the pool and pushed him in. It was the deep end and Philip came up spluttering. "You little devils, look at me!"

"You'll soon dry in this heat, Dad," Jack said with a grin. Jamie was laughing so much – he hadn't had so much fun with his father for years.

Eddy and his friend looked on in amazement as the

dripping, fully clothed figure climbed out of the pool. "Mind you," he said, waving his arm in the direction of the trio. "As a race, I've always thought them a bit mad."

"I thought your family came from Ireland," his friend George responded.

"That ain't British," Eddy replied in a tone that brooked no argument!

Philip did dry quite quickly and he promised faithfully that he would ask Liz to marry him at the first appropriate moment, having made the boys swear not to breathe a word and threatening to dock their allowances if they betrayed him with even the slightest hint.

He borrowed some of Jack's clothes – not quite to his taste but, to his surprise, an excellent fit. The boy, now almost eighteen, was almost as tall as him, though leaner, Philip realised as he struggled to fasten the buttons at the waist of the shorts. He finally gave up, pulling the borrowed tee shirt over the top to hide the gap.

Liz had had a terrible morning. It was the first real physio and every part of her body felt inadequate. Her legs, still healing, but so slowly, seemed too weak for her to stand. The muscles seemed to have gone in her arms too, and squeezing soft rubber balls with her fingers seemed an almost impossible task.

She was at least on solid food now, but her poor throat was quite sore from the weeks of tubes. Chicken broth seemed to fill her right up and the thought of anything more substantial currently defeated her. She longed for home – she knew she would get better quicker there, but when she mentioned it to the doctor he said it was too soon to even contemplate the idea, particularly with such a long flight to India.

Finally, the physio left her. The massage of her back and neck had been fine, but trying to lift one leg at a time from the footrest of the wheelchair had been both painful and almost impossible. Once alone, she wept with frustration and for the first time in her life, she felt powerless to help herself.

The sound of cheery voices in the corridor made her realise Philip and the boys were returning. She hastily wiped her eyes and tried to get a grip on her emotions. They burst in, the trio laughing at something Philip had said. One look at her brave face, with the evidence of recent tears, made Philip realise how vulnerable she was.

The boys too sensed something – but it was Jamie to the rescue. He soon had her laughing when he described Philip being pushed into the pool. "I did wonder about those rather odd clothes," she was smiling now. "Odd," said Jack indignantly. "They are some of my favourites." Philip raised an eyebrow at Liz in mock despair. "But why did they push you in?" She saw a quick exchange of looks between the threesome and, despite much laughter, they wouldn't tell her.

Jack and Jamie only had one week left. Philip still hadn't asked Liz the "major" question and his sons were getting impatient. "Alright, alright," he agreed. "I will ask this evening when you have gone back to Greg and Judy's."

As usual Liz and Philip ate together in the evenings, it was thought that with Philip there she might be persuaded to eat a little more. She had looked in a mirror for the first time after her physio and was almost less shocked by the scar running from ear to jaw on the left side of her face and her cap of hair that was now looking quite pretty, than by the pallor and thinness of her face and body. She knew that she must get stronger and get out of this place. Philip would have to leave soon and she would be alone again.

There was a piece of poached salmon, some tiny buttered potatoes and a small bowl of green salad for dinner. Her broken right arm was now healing and was functioning better so she managed to eat with a fork at last. A few mouthfuls later, she had had enough and placed the fork on the plate. "No Elizabeth, that is not good enough," Philip said. She burst out laughing.

"You sound just like my father." Philip was not to be put off so easily. "I mean it, darling girl, we want you strong. I have something very important to say – but I won't say it until you have at least eaten the salmon." Liz felt her heart sink. He was leaving her, going back to Paris. She choked down some salmon because at least eating it stopped her crying.

She was so emotional these days – there seemed to be an unending well of tears that never dried up. "Well done, my darling." Philip took the tray and put it on a table on the other side of the room. He then returned to the chair and took hold of her hand – this was the moment. He smiled thinking of his sons sitting anxiously waiting for a phone call. Not many fathers had to report back to their sons about a proposal of marriage.

"Elizabeth, my sweet darling girl, I have a very straightforward and simple question to ask you. I hope you will answer straight away, but if you can't I will try and be patient. Elizabeth, will you marry me?" He looked deep into her eyes and saw them fill with tears. She could hardly speak. He waited, looking at her, stroking her hand and lifting it to his lips to gently kiss.

"Philip I can't," she finally blurted out. "I'm sorry, I can't."

He supposed it had been unreasonable to assume she would say yes. There might have been some hesitation, but this, this definite and positive no. "But I love you," he said.

"I know," she replied. She did not dare say she loved him too, he would never understand her refusal. But, how could she marry him? All she wanted was to go home to India. She couldn't see herself in Paris as the wife of the Ambassador. She couldn't expect him to give up his career for her so once again their paths were so close – but never quite together.

Philip returned to Judy's a defeated man. He could hardly bear to tell his sons, they had been so positive that soon she would officially become their mother. They had hoped for the past five years – at least Jamie had and Jack more recently – that the day would come.

Greg realised straight away that something was wrong. Usually Philip stayed with Liz until she fell asleep and lately Philip had been returning to the hotel and sleeping properly himself. So when Greg opened the door to him at eight p.m. he wondered briefly if Liz had collapsed or worse. He hadn't seen her in the last two weeks and didn't realise quite how much she had progressed despite Judy filling him in with progress reports.

He poured Philip a whisky. Gratefully Philip took several gulps. He was in no mood for finesse. "The boys?"

"In the yard with Judy, mucking about in the pond." The pool was small and Greg always referred to it in rather derogatory terms. Philip tried to smile, but couldn't. Whisky in hand, he left the cool air-conditioning and stepped out into the blast of warm air, even at this time in the evening.

The boys were chatting happily with Judy and looked expectantly at their father when he stepped outside. Philip shook his head. "You chickened out," Jack said in surprise.

"She turned me down," he replied shortly not liking personal matters aired in front of a third party.

"Oh Dad, you must have got it all wrong. We know she loves you. Don't we Jack?" Jamie appealed to his brother. "I honestly thought so Dad. I honestly did." He looked upset and Philip pulled, or tried to pull, himself together for his sons.

"I really don't want to interfere," Judy said carefully. "I think I know what you are talking about. If I am correct, perhaps I should find out what the problem is? You know another woman, sort of thing," she finished, hastily sensing

Philip's discomfort. Slowly he nodded. "Perhaps Judy. Just perhaps it might help, though she seemed so definite."

During dinner, which Greg and Judy had insisted Philip stay for, despite having had a little salmon at the hospital, he was sure whatever it was that Judy had prepared was delicious but he might as well have been eating sawdust. At ten-thirty he hugged his sons, thanked the couple for their hospitality and kindness and agreed Judy would visit Liz first thing in the morning. He would, he decided, arrive mid-morning after the two women would have had time for a heart to heart.

Liz had slept badly despite the sleeping draught they insisted she took. She had felt for a few nights now that she no longer needed it, and the one night she needed the oblivion of sleep it didn't "kick in" so she made up her mind that it was to be the last one she took.

She heard light steps along the corridor near her room and had a sense of disappointment that it was not Philip's firm step. He had usually arrived by now, perhaps after last night, he wouldn't visit her again. She felt a sense of total desolation.

With a light knock on the door, Judy walked in. Liz put on a bright smile and cheerful voice, at least she thought she did but Judy saw right through the pose. "It's no good Liz O'Malley I know you far too well for you to be all artificial smiles. I'm here to have a straight talk with you and find out why you turned down that beautiful man."

Liz was momentarily taken aback, then she remembered Judy had never been one to mince words – but this was personal and too direct. She tried to dissemble, but Judy stood up impatiently. "If you are going to give me a lot of blah I might as well leave now," and she made as if to leave. "Oh Judy, please don't go." It was such a quiet, unhappy voice that Judy walked to the wheelchair and hugged her. "Of course not you silly idiot – let's just talk Liz."

It took Liz a few minutes to compose herself trying to marshal her thoughts into some sort of cohesive pattern. "You see Judy," she began as if weighing every word carefully. "I love my home, the people, not just the people I see socially but the people who work in my home and garden, who help me to look after my horses." She broke off – the picture of her home was so vivid in her mind, her longing to be there so intense. "So, how could I marry Philip?"

"Go on," Judy spoke encouragingly.

"Well, how? He is the British Ambassador – he lives in France. I can't be an Ambassador's wife and live in another country – that would not be a marriage it would be a farce." Judy nodded. "You agree then? You see why I had to say no."

Judy nodded. "I understand why you said no – but I don't think you understand that Philip doesn't expect you to live in France." Judy thought back to the previous evening when he had told them in confidence about his conversation with Julia, the British Prime Minister. He had told them that there had been no question of him continuing in his role, that however persuasive she had been he had decided to tell her that his resignation held. "Did you realise that Philip had resigned his post?" Judy asked quietly.

Liz, who had been looking down at her hands, raised her eyes to Judy's face. "You mean it," she whispered. "He would do that for me?"

"That and more," Judy said briskly, standing suddenly and glancing at her watch. "Darling Liz I must dash, I have an appointment."

"But—" began Liz. She spoke to an empty space – Judy had already left. A little shiver of anticipation shook her body. Philip loved her that much. Still wrapped in thoughts of him, for once she did not hear his footsteps in the corridor.

chapter 41

The door opened and Liz glanced up automatically expecting to see Janet, her favourite nurse – the little cockney sparrow Philip always called her. Despite the fact that she had lived in the States for years she still had her bright cockney accent and a personality that matched it.

It was not Janet, it was Philip. He had been waiting anxiously for Judy at their rendezvous point near the nurses' desk. Her smile was enough to let him know the news was good. In seconds she explained why Liz had refused the proposal. "Now get up there Philip, she is one happy – if a rather stunned – lady."

Philip almost ran up the corridor, leaping the four steps up to her room. He took a deep breath to compose himself and walked in, in as nonchalant a manner as possible. He was nervous, more nervous than he could ever remember. Liz glanced up, their eyes met and held. "You would do that for me?" she said softly. "My darling I would walk to the ends of the earth for you, so your home being in India is a mere nothing." "But—" she began.

"There are no buts my darling Elizabeth. Whenever you smiled when you were in a coma I knew you were thinking of home. When I laid the pashmina over you and you clutched it so firmly – the first real sign that you were still 'in there'."

"You put the pashmina over me?" she questioned in a puzzled voice. "I thought it was Anjali."

"Perhaps you dreamed it was Anjali," he said thoughtfully. "Anyway, Elizabeth I shall try once more – but listen please to the end of what I have to say." She nodded with an amused and happy smile.

"I want to marry you. I want to take you home to Goa. I want to live with you in the lovely home I am sure you have created. I want my sons to be your sons. I shall be a lazy layabout. I have resigned – I am no longer an Ambassador and you will not be an Ambassador's wife. Now, Elizabeth O'Malley what do you say to all of that?"

"I say yes please, Mr ex-Ambassador!"

"Right, now I assume you want to get married from your home?" She nodded. "So, what you have to do is eat plenty, do lots of physio and be well enough so that we can travel home." It sounded wonderful. "But—" she began.

"I said no buts," he said sternly, softened by his smile. He felt he would never stop smiling again.

"Alright, not a 'but' – but I have an idea that's all," Liz said. They talked for hours, he liked her idea but wasn't sure how feasible it was.

He rang Judy and told her and Greg the good news. Jack and Jamie appeared with flowers and hugs and Liz told them she really could call them her boys now. It was such an exciting day and although Liz thought she would not be able to sleep, she refused a sleeping tablet and slept like the proverbial baby. Only one thing still puzzled her, she was so sure that Anjali had covered her with the pashmina, but of course, she must have been dreaming for Anjali was still in Goa.

Janet arrived at the hospital bright and early as usual. She loved being a nurse and when the recruitment agency in England had told her about this job she had thought it sounded like a wonderful opportunity and had never regretted it.

It had been pouring with rain she always remembered. It was November and the cold wind and rain had made her want to hibernate instead of going out, to wait at a bus stop, be rushed off her feet all day, only to make her way home in the dark, in the still wet and windy weather.

She was a cheerful girl, but in recent years, with her father having a heart attack only a year or so after her mother died of pre-senile dementia, even Janet had lost some of her bounce. Her only brother was several years older and had left home when their mother was first ill. Try as she could she couldn't find Tom for either funeral – it was as if he had never been. They had never been particularly close but it was not easy going through two funerals with just a few of her parents' friends for support. There had been no relatives as both her parents had been only children.

The recruitment agency snapped her up when she had first, somewhat cautiously, approached them and when she had arrived in Phoenix she felt immediately at home and was made to feel very welcome. The money was good, though accommodation was expensive but, through the hospital network, she soon found fellow nurses who wanted to share. She loved the climate. She loved the job and she had made a myriad of friends. Janet had never been happier.

Today she was popping in to see her favourite patient of the moment, Liz O'Malley. She had read several of Liz's books and was really hoping she would start to make good headway soon in her recovery so she would write some more! Her recovery since coming out of the coma had been slower than hoped. She was due for a bath, a ritual she knew Liz dreaded.

Normally Liz did dread the bath, but today she decided nothing would be too difficult. It was a case of mind over matter. With some difficulty, she manoeuvred the chair until she was triumphantly facing the door. "Oh, Liz, that's wonderful. You look wonderful too. Whatever has happened?" Janet said.

"So much dear Janet, so very much – and you – why you could be part of it."

The dreaded bath was over. Perhaps because she was so happy it didn't seem quite such an ordeal. Janet and a junior nurse were as kind and caring as ever, chatting away, distracting her, laughing with her in ways that she so much appreciated.

Once she was back in her cotton pyjamas – cotton that was almost as soft as silk, she had exclaimed when Janet, at her request, had brought in something more appealing than the hospital gowns she had worn during her "coma period" as she now referred to it. Today she wore yellow and the cheerful colour matched her mood.

"Janet, I need to talk to you," she said quietly as Sarah left the room with the bowl of used dressings.

"I'll slip back in my break, Liz, at about ten-thirty."

"Thank you," Liz responded with the most cheerful face Janet had ever seen on her. She was curious, Liz O'Malley had been a worry to them when she was in the coma – she seemed to have a series of highs and lows. The family visits, Philip and the boys, usually seemed to buoy her up, but two days ago when Philip Broderick – or Sir Philip, she mentally corrected herself – had left she had found Liz sobbing and inconsolable.

Gathering her scattered thoughts, she returned to the ward director for the daily briefing and set about her duties. As usual, the time sped by and it was not until her flatmate reminded her, that she realised it was time for her break. Grabbing a mug of coffee from the staff kitchen and a couple of much-needed biscuits (she was always starving at this point in the day), she walked as quickly as the coffee would allow without spilling it and arrived with Liz at ten-forty.

Liz was expecting her and, knowing Janet's penchant for biscuits, she had asked Philip to refill her small biscuit barrel. Philip had arrived with some freshly baked shortcake biscuits from Judy's kitchen. He had been with Liz for half an hour when Janet arrived. He kissed Liz lightly on the forehead and said he had some business to attend to.

Philip had a major shopping expedition in mind. Liz had talked and been encouraged by him to describe her home, her garden, the staff and, of course, the horses. Philip felt he had built up a mental picture of the home they would share. She had described how she loved to lie in the hammock and look up at the waving palm fronds, or at night, look up at the stars – crystal clear in the cloudless midnight blue where they were studded – it seemed like a magical roof to the world.

She told him how Ashok had, at her request, purchased the hammock and strung it from the trees. The cork-made hammock, with its individual corks threaded together, was not the most comfortable, but being Liz she had not wanted to hurt Ashok's feelings. Now Philip felt it was time for a new hammock, the perfect excuse being Liz's fragility.

Liz had mentioned that she had dreamed of home and swinging in a silken hammock with her horses standing nearby. Philip was determined that such a hammock would be there waiting for her return whenever that might be.

He drove to the mall and parked the hire car. It was such an enormous car park that he made a number of observations to enable him to locate his car again. He was amazed there were no row markings that he could see, and he thought in a distracted moment it would be all too easy to park, go straight into the mall and completely lose track of which of the many exits and entrances one had chosen.

Philip mentioned these thoughts to one of the friendly assistants in his chosen store. She laughed as she told him that customers regularly can't find their cars or trucks. "That's why our security people have a special vehicle to drive people around searching." Philip was bemused, in this most modern of countries, there was no system of numbering or lettering parking places!

He found the hammock he sought – it was made of durable but soft linen and the proportions were generous. He arranged to have it packed and sent c/o Anjali at Villa O'Mal. He gave the young woman who had attended to him so well a letter that must be attached clearly, so that when the package was opened the letter would be easily located. He had written:

Dear Anjali,

Please excuse me addressing you so informally but that is how your mistress always refers to you. It has been good talking to you on the phone and Elizabeth, as you know, continues to make good, but very slow, progress.

She wants so much to return home and as soon as we can persuade the doctors to "let her go", I shall bring her safely back to you. Meanwhile, I have bought a new hammock. Elizabeth has told me how much Nina loved the cork hammock, in fact, she knew that Nina sometimes enjoyed a secret swing in it! So will you please ask Ashok to take it down and give it to Nina. Please explain that Madame needs a very soft hammock and I am sending one to you because I know you will be able to arrange for it to be lined with padded silk.

You will know we are coming home as soon as we know, so you will know when the hammock should be ready and hung. Thank you for your help with this. I look forward to seeing you in Goa.

    Yours sincerely,
    Philip Broderick.

*

Anjali received quite a large parcel from America. She noticed it was addressed to her and wondered why Madame had not used her surname. Once opened she found the letter and read it through carefully, she recognised the name for Madame often spoke of Jack and Jamie Broderick, and Anjali knew she had met their father in Delhi. Now, he was writing as if he would be living with Madame. She remembered Alex with some horror. He had caused Madame to be so angry and upset everyone. This Philip Broderick did not seem like that, she hoped that was the case.

She read the instructions again very carefully, smiling when she read Nina could have the old hammock. That would make the girl very happy. She carefully opened the hammock out, it was wider than the cork one – almost double the width. She knew exactly what to do, it would be blissfully comfortable by the time it was finished.

Leaving it in her sitting room she went to find Ashok. Very carefully she explained that Madame would like Nina to have the hammock. Ashok looked both shocked and surprised. "But I chose it for Madame why should Nina have it now?"

"Madame has been hurt – many broken bones, she must lie on something soft, as soft as—" she hesitated. Looking up she noticed a rare, puffy cloud. "As soft as that cloud Ashok."

"I understand Anjali. My Nina will be happy. About the hammock," he added quickly. "Not Madame's pain, I mean, I will take it down this morning."

"Please do it later, Ashok. I need you to take me to the tailor with Madame's new hammock – sent all the way from America." Ashok looked astonished.

"All the way from America," he repeated. How Nina would love to hear that, and how she would love to swing in the cork hammock. He wished he could tell her straight away but instead he had to take Anjali and the new hammock to the tailor. It would be a nice surprise for Nina, he would tell her before the children arrived back from school.

A short while later Anjali and Ashok were in the car with the new hammock folded on the back seat. They had left the poles and rings behind at the villa. Ashok had to wait quite a long time while Anjali was with the tailor. Several times he went in but Anjali didn't notice him, she was so absorbed in the arrays of silk that the tailor was displaying.

Finally, finally, Anjali made up her mind, it had to be a restful colour for Madame would rest there until she grew stronger. She chose a green silk – the green of soft new shoots after the monsoon, and she explained to the tailor that the silk should be softly padded and ties should be placed on the hammock and the new silk-covered padding so it could be easily removed for cleaning and again during the monsoon.

The tailor knew exactly what she meant and produced some wondrous light padding that he kept to pad exotic garments for male clients who wanted to appear better endowed. "I shall make cushions," Anjali exclaimed. "Lots of different coloured silks and the wondrous padding." She chose gold, two different shades of blue, cream and magenta. They haggled over the price of the silk, the cost of the work and the padding, but finally they were both satisfied they had a bargain.

"It will be ready in four days – hand sewn of course," the tailor said.

"Of course," Anjali replied sweeping regally out of the small shop. She started sewing that evening. Meanwhile Ashok had taken down the cork hammock on their return from the tailors. Through the open window, Anjali could hear shrieks of laughter from Ashok and Nina's garden. She smiled to herself – Madame would be so happy for Nina. Madame though would need quiet and rest, she must remember to tell Ashok no noise like that again.

Her nimble fingers held a thin needle that went in and out of the fine silk, with every stitch she thought of her mistress and hoped it would not be too long before her head rested on one of these cushions.

*

Janet's break was nearly over. She was listening spellbound to what Liz O'Malley was saying. She felt excited, flattered, unsure. So many emotions. She loved her job, what was she giving up and what would she do when the contract ended?

Liz saw the gamut of emotions passing over Janet's face. "I really would love you to come, Janet, so would Philip. I could go back home so much sooner if you were there to help me. But of course, you must think it through very carefully." She then described the house, the staff, the gardens, the beach and even the horses. "I can't ride. I'm terrified of horses."

Liz laughed. "That won't be a requirement, Janet dear, I only mentioned it in case you rode!"

Janet wondered how long she would stay and the two women talked about Liz's rate of recovery, deciding that once she no longer had dressings that needed to be changed and could bathe herself that would be the natural break-off point. Liz explained that, as part of the contract, they would pay her airfare to wherever she wanted to go, back to England or the States or somewhere else.

"Can I think about it?"

"I would perhaps think less of you if you didn't. Just let me know when you can because I want to start working on these doctors. I know I shall make a quicker recovery once I'm home." Janet glanced at her watch and said, "I must fly. I'll see you before I leave – but I need to think about it overnight."

"Of course," Liz said with a smile, desperately wanting to put some pressure on but knowing she must not.

For Janet, the rest of the day was a bit of a blur. Her work didn't suffer despite the fact that her mind seemed to be somewhere else. She had a picture in her mind of Liz's home – it was appealing and different. Her first reaction had been to say yes, but some inner sense made her cautious and she knew that if she made the decision to go she must be very sure.

Her contract with the hospital was up for renewal and, strangely enough, although she was terrifically happy she had not yet signed on for another twelve months. So, legally, in one week she was free to walk away. Janet and her flatmate, Sarah, talked long into the night. Sarah tried to play a bit of a devil's advocate marshalling as many arguments against the proposal as she could.

One by one Janet demolished the arguments. "I suppose," said Sarah ruefully, "I shall have to find someone to share my apartment with. It's not everyone I'm prepared to share my bathroom with either, and you don't snore. My last flatmate snored so loudly that even with both bedroom doors shut I had to wear earplugs!"

"Oh Sarah, I shall miss you."

"You are going then?" Janet nodded.

"How can I lose? I like Liz O'Malley and Philip Broderick."

"Sir Philip to you," quipped Sarah with a wicked grin.

"Right, Sir Philip seems nice too. It's an opportunity to see part of the world I would probably never go to. I think Liz will need me for no more than about three months and, with any luck, the hospital will give me a new contract with a three-month break."

"Don't sign a contract here before you go," Sarah warned. "What happens if Liz is not ready to be left? Just tell them here, you hope to be back and as soon as you have a date you will email and renegotiate a contract."

It was sound advice and Janet decided to take it. Sarah raised the perhaps thorny subject of a contract with Liz. "Oh that's alright," Janet assured her. "Sir Philip is going to draw up something and I am only to sign if I am happy with it. Right?"

"Right," Sarah agreed but suggested she had sight of it as well.

Philip had, in fact, produced a letter for Janet which Liz gave her the following morning. The letter asked if she would like to travel with them to India and stay until she felt happy that Liz could cope. At that stage, the letter continued, they would purchase a ticket to whichever place or country she chose to go to. Whilst she was with them, Janet read, her salary would match that of the hospital. This all seemed very generous considering she was paying nothing for accommodation.

There were two copies of the letter and Philip and Liz had signed them both. An attached piece of paper suggested she keep one copy for herself and would she sign and date the other for them. Without hesitation, Janet did so, putting her copy in the back of her passport for safe keeping.

Liz was not very often cross, but the doctors were being obdurate in their refusal to let her travel. She was being equally obdurate but didn't seem to be getting through to them at all. Although Philip, half longing to get her away from the hospital, was also anxious about the proposed journey.

It was Janet who finally swung things. She had arrived as cheerfully as ever and walked into a maelstrom of massive proportion. "Our cockney sparrow came through for us, Liz," Philip said afterwards. Liz had cajoled, wept and been angry to no avail, but Janet calmly, more calmly than she felt, and with an unruffled air, talked to the medical staff assuring and reassuring. She finally got them to accept that if Liz could walk across the room unaided they would reconsider the possibility of her travelling.

Liz's legs were healing well now, her face too, although it was pointed out that at some time she might like cosmetic surgery to improve the appearance of the scar, now much less vivid but difficult to conceal with her shorter hair. She had got used to it now and felt that once her hair grew it would be quite well hidden. She could, she assured them, have plastic surgery at home if she wanted to.

She worked hard at her leg exercises, every day she added a step or two, and finally *the* day arrived and on sixteenth of September – a date forever cast in her brain – she walked slowly and carefully across the room.

If Philip was anxious he didn't let her see it. In turn, he had gently bullied, praised and scolded her, and now with Janet's ongoing help, she had walked slowly, very slowly, across the room. Once she stopped "thinking", her legs would begin to give way under her but, waving away help with her left arm, the right one still stiff from the multiple breaks (which, although healed, needed more time to re-learn how to function properly), she walked on, collapsing with relief into the wheelchair which Philip had pushed alongside her as she walked.

"You see," she triumphed. "I can walk – I can go home now." Smiling at her achievements her doctors agreed, albeit with reluctance. Liz O'Malley could be discharged with Nurse Janet Aiken in tow.

Philip produced a bottle of champagne and they all had a sip or two. The glasses, along with the champagne, had been carefully hidden in a bathroom cupboard – it was, of course, not chilled. However, even though doctors never drink on duty they informed their patient, "There has to be an exception to every rule", and they allowed themselves a sip or two.

chapter 42

Philip didn't rush at arranging the journey, as the travel plans were a shade complicated with a break in Delhi for a few days. Although Liz was walking a little further every day, she would be using a wheelchair for the journey. On the hospital's advice, they had purchased a fairly lightweight chair as it was anticipated that its use was finite, but it had also been chosen with comfort in mind.

Philip booked the flight and explained who would be travelling. As soon as they realised it was, as far as they were concerned, a current Ambassador plus a famous author, who was known to have had a serious accident whilst staying in their country, accompanied, of course, by a nurse, British Airways did all they could to make sure their Business Class seats were upgraded to First Class and that Liz would have particularly easy access to a toilet.

He contacted the embassy and arranged to stay overnight there. The newly appointed Ambassador and his wife were old friends and were delighted to have Philip, his fiancée and a nurse for as long as they wanted! They insisted the embassy limo would meet the flight, which would, of course, ease the chaos that seemed to prevail at airports in India.

Janet already had endeared herself to both of them and Philip's referring to her as a real cockney sparrow had stuck and now her nickname was, of course, Sparrow. Janet had never had a nickname in her life and had never liked her name anyway. She loved being addressed as Sparrow and she felt the nickname was a good omen.

She had finished work now, but arrived at the hospital every day to watch the physiotherapist at work. She, of course, watched with particular interest and it was not long before Shirley allowed her to "try her hand". "You are a natural, honey," the white-haired physio drawled and started teaching her movements that would help Liz as she progressed back to full health. Janet's nursing expertise was, of course, the important thing, but in conjunction with what she was learning she felt she could be more help to Liz than she had envisaged.

When Philip arrived on Friday evening he waved three airline tickets. "We are off on Sunday," he announced. "Oh my goodness," Janet clapped her hands in delight. "That will be luverly."

"Dear Sparrow – it will be perfect," Liz said happily. She was finally on her way home.

*

The monsoon was over, the gardens looked at their most lush. The buds on the frangipani and hibiscus were forming, ready to burst forth with their colour and perfume. The new hammock with its silk padding liner hung under the palms and, in Anjali's sitting room, seven beautifully made silk-covered cushions awaited their new owner.

Ashok cleaned the car inside and out every day. Not a speck of dust was to be seen. He was disappointed that he would not be driving Madame O'Mal home from the airport but he realised the limousine on loan from the Taj Hotel would provide a more comfortable and spacious journey.

Anjali had prepared the best guest room for Sir Philip. Madame's room was as always in perfect order. For the nurse, who Sir Philip said was travelling with them and would stay until Madame was totally fit again, she had prepared one of the top-floor bedrooms and an adjoining room that had at one time been a nursery would now be a sitting room. She would have to share a bathroom with Aarav but didn't think that would be a problem. Anjali mentioned it to Aarav who had shrugged good-naturedly. "It's only for a few weeks Anjali – what does it matter? She must be alright, the nurse, or Madame would not have brought her back."

"I am more worried about the man, Sir Philip Broderick," Anjali stated his name very formally. "He is the man Madame is to marry. I know what we think won't make any difference."

"He better not be like the last one that stayed here."

"He won't be," Anjali assured him with more confidence than she felt.

*

It was quite hard leaving the hospital – so many people who had cared for her during her protracted stay wanted to say goodbye. Sparrow's friends, who had discovered the nickname and liked it also, came to say goodbye to a friend who they hoped would be back with them in two to three months.

The lift carried the party downstairs to where a stretch limo was waiting at the kerbside. Very gently Philip helped Liz out of the chair and into the car. All the luggage, including a somewhat battered looking case of Sparrow's, was already loaded. They were on their way at last. Liz thought her face might crack she was smiling so much.

Once they were settled on the flight Liz wouldn't admit, even to herself, she felt exhausted from the mental as well as physical effort she had made so far. Sparrow was chattering away to the cabin crew – so excited that she thought she would burst. She had never dreamed in even her wildest imaginings that one day she would travel First Class.

With a sense of relief, Philip closed his eyes. Part one completed, he thought. Getting Liz out of hospital had taken patience, ingenuity and hard work on Liz's behalf. He allowed his mind to drift and thought back to the previous evening when he had spent a long time talking with the Prime Minister. Julia had finally agreed to accept Philip's resignation but only on one condition that he accepts another role. For a moment Philip was taken aback, but when he heard the proposal he agreed straight away.

"I can't even give you a date," he had said.

"When you can you will," she had answered pragmatically. Thoughtfully she asked about Jack and Jamie. "I shall look forward to seeing them again. Are they going to visit you again in India over Christmas?"

"I don't think I could keep them away if I tried," Philip had laughed. Now thinking back to the conversation, he thought how strange and how meaningful his phrase had been. It would be his and Elizabeth's first Christmas together. Christmas in India, he liked the sound of it, he thought as he drifted off into a light sleep.

They were met in Delhi as arranged. Sparrow was wonderful with Liz encouraging her – telling her how well she was doing; nevertheless, both she and Philip were a little anxious. Her pallor was noticeable, and she was very quiet, a sure sign, Philip knew, that she was exhausted.

Once at the embassy Liz went straight to bed – she didn't even feel guilty, just relieved to lie down between the cool sheets. She refused food and Sparrow decided sleep was the best thing for her. She left her with a glass of freshly squeezed lemonade and a small jug to refill her glass if she needed to.

That evening in the morning room, the room where Philip and Liz had eaten a quiet breakfast together so long ago, Sparrow sat with the new British Ambassador, his wife and Philip. She might have been daunted by the opulence, the grandeur – but Sparrow, being her usual chirpy self, kept them all amused with her questions and admiration of all she observed.

Paul and Cynthia Knightly listened with amazement when Philip told them he had resigned. He had waited to discuss personal matters until Sparrow was being taken on a guided tour of the embassy, followed by a drive through some of the busiest locations that it had been suggested she might enjoy seeing at night. She was accompanied by a young woman of much the same age who had been given the responsibility of keeping Sparrow company during the planned short stay in Delhi, and was a member of the secretariat at the embassy.

Philip would have been surprised had he heard the Knightlys talking as they lay in bed later that evening. They decided Philip was making a bad mistake. They had never met Liz and felt Philip had given up what had been a brilliant career for an invalid. "A bad mistake," Paul kept muttering as he undressed. "A bad mistake." Cynthia felt the same, but felt it was a heroic and romantic gesture and thought Liz O'Malley a lucky woman – even though she had been in such a terrible accident.

Sparrow crept in to see Liz before she herself went to bed. Liz looked serene lying asleep and she realised that once fully recovered Liz would be a beautiful woman again.

It was good not to have to fly for a few days and, by the next morning, Liz felt considerably stronger. With Sparrow's help, she dressed and was wheeled along the corridor to the lift. The wheelchair, at her insistence, was left outside the dining room and, with Sparrow hovering, she walked unaided into the room for breakfast.

Cynthia and Paul were surprised and delighted to see her so much recovered, and the four of them had a jolly breakfast with Paul regaling them with stories of his first weeks in post, when he found life in India more complex than he had imagined.

As breakfast progressed, Cynthia, always observant, saw looks exchanged between Philip and Liz and realised whatever they had gone through in the past and since the accident, they obviously had found happiness with each other. Several times during breakfast Liz found Philip looking at her with such intensity that she lowered her eyes. She saw so much there – love, passion, hope and she knew she must get well as quickly as she could. She longed for home and in two more days she would be there.

The plane landed at Goa. Excited and happy that she was finally almost home buoyed Liz so much that her exhaustion seemed to fade. Philip had used his influence and arranged for the plane to be met by the Taj limo at the foot of the gangplank. Within seconds of landing, they were whizzed across the compound to customs almost before anyone else had left the plane. Being an internal flight, security was minimal and before she knew it Liz was sitting in the comfortable Taj vehicle heading for home.

The noise of the airport with seemingly hundreds of porters touting for business had surrounded her. Traders plying their trade. Reunions of family members. Liz had almost forgotten the wonderful noise, the spices in the air and the organised chaos that somehow seemed to make everything go smoothly in the end.

"Stop the car," she said urgently, pressing the button to lower the electrically operated window as she spoke. "Ashok!" she called out the window. Ashok had just parked the car and was about to go and retrieve the luggage, feeling very important as he had a special pass enabling him to do so. The arrangement had been made to make sure Liz had minimal time waiting for the luggage to arrive.

Ashok came over to the window, his brown face beaming with delight. "Oh, Madame O'Mal welcome home – we have missed you. Welcome back to your home, we shall make you well again."

"Thank you Ashok – I shall soon get better now I am home."

Liz had seen, mirrored in his face, shock at her appearance. She had adjusted to how she looked these days with her thin face and figure and the scar, but she hadn't realised what a shock it would be for those whose last memory of her was when she left for the tour of the States.

Sparrow's eyes were on stalks. She was mesmerised and shocked by some of the sights she saw from the air-conditioned comfort of the limousine. She saw tented communities where there were dozens of tents, frequently made from rags and scavenged wood. Women crouching over smoky fires and small children running semi-naked through the dirt and rubble. How, she wondered, could Liz think this was beautiful and serene, the adjectives she had used to describe her home?

They passed a busy junction where brightly sari-clad women sold and bartered fruit and vegetables. A faded and slightly rusted sign swinging in the breeze declaiming "modern pharmacy" – everything medical. They passed countless little shops and stalls, several with "first-class tailor" signs written on white cards and proudly displayed. Dogs wandered freely across the road, seemingly impervious to speeding traffic on the narrow pot-holed surface. Cows and bullocks, leaner than she could have imagined, sucked at dried grasses. A few pigs, probably owned by someone, wandered aimlessly in piles of rubbish searching for food.

Sparrow had a sense of despair and, had she but known it, her thoughts were in part mirrored by Philip. He had lived in India for enough years to know its poverty, but after the elegance of Paris and the most modern of cities, Phoenix, it was a bit of a culture shock for him too.

He looked at Sparrow's face which reflected her thoughts. Feeling eyes on her, she turned her head and met Philip's gaze. He raised his eyebrows in an acknowledgement of her shock – she gave a slight grimace, followed by a smile which he found reassuring, then turned her gaze once more to the passing scene.

In the few seconds she had turned her gaze away, the car must have taken a turn off the "main road" for now the road, though still narrow, was lined with palm trees of varying sizes from the tall statuesque ones, to the smaller ones only four to five feet in height. Between the trees she noticed small thatched or tiled flat concrete-roofed houses, simple maybe, but to her relief looking like proper homes. Lines of washing were strung out between the trees and, every now and again, Sparrow noticed a house far back off the road. She saw an occasional glimpse of the sea and realised that, at last, they must be getting closer.

Liz found herself holding her breath. They passed Father Julian's church and the primary school that she had founded and continued to support. Bernadette and Shantaram's first home, and they had now opened a second one, managed by a like-minded couple who were happy to follow in their footsteps.

Finally, finally, she saw the gates and the sign Villa O'Mal. She was home – at last, she was home. The gates opened as the car drew near two of the garden boys who had been watching out. "Do not let Madame O'Mal wait," Ashok had warned them before he had left for the airport to collect the luggage.

Sparrow had the first glimpse of her new home. She began to realise why Liz had so badly wanted to return. The gardens were so beautiful and peaceful, and as the car finally drew to a stop near the flight of steps leading to the front door, Anjali, as if on cue, opened the door and stood for a moment, her hands clasped tightly together, trying hard to keep her emotions under control.

The chauffeur came round to open the door for Liz, but Philip was already out of the car, determined to carry her.

She put her hand on his arm. "No Philip, I shall walk up the steps of my home." With Philip on one side and Sparrow on the other, Liz slowly climbed the steps to the door. Triumphantly she arrived by Anjali. "I have come home, Anjali," she said softly. Anjali, the tears now falling uncontrollably from her eyes, put her arms around her mistress. "Yes, Madame dear, you have come home."

Liz looked beseechingly at Philip. Without a word he swung her up into his arms and she pointed to the stairs. "Please Philip, to my room." She was as light as a feather and he carried her effortlessly as directed.

Sparrow, for once a little unsure what to do, stood at the foot of the stairs. Liz needed her help but she also realised that she and Sir Philip needed to be alone for a while. The ever-perceptive Anjali took control. "Would you like to see your room or would you prefer a nice cup of tea? Madame will be having one in her room of course." A relieved Sparrow nodded. "A cuppa would be loverly," she said, her broad cockney accent sounding strange to Anjali's ear.

Sparrow followed the housekeeper to the breakfast room where she and Aarav ate their meals. "Come," Anjali said. "Meet Aarav." Sparrow dutifully followed Anjali into the kitchen where Aarav had already prepared a tray for Madame and her fiancée. A silver tea-pot and small milk jug. Some slices of fresh lemon – Madame liked her Earl Grey tea with lemon – and a small plate of freshly baked tiny shortbread biscuits.

Aarav glanced up as he adjusted the plate on the tray. He looked with interest at the young English girl who was going to live with them for a while. She was so pretty, was his first thought, though she had a strange haircut – a bit like a boy but a bit longer and fair, fair as the sunshine he thought.

Aarav loved the fair hair, probably because everyone he knew had dark hair and brown skin in various shades. Her skin looked almost as white as milk, he was enchanted. "Hello there, are you the cook?" she asked in her direct way, holding out her hand as she spoke. He took the neat square hand with the short square fingernails. He saw her eyes were vivid blue and he fell in love.

"What are you called?" he asked.

"My name is actually Janet, but now I am called Sparrow, and I like it best. I'm from London you see, born within the sound of Bow Bells so I'm, well I'm like a cockney sparrow, they say that back home. So they, your—" she hesitated. Anjali stepped into the breach.

"Madame O'Malley?"

"Yes, that's right. Your Madame and Sir Philip – they nicknamed me Sparrow. Like the bird," she added by way of explanation. "'Cos I'm always busy hopping about a bit and I sing as I go, so I guess I'm chirpy like a sparrow."

Aarav was bemused and bewitched, though he didn't really understand much of what she said. Perhaps because she felt more relaxed after the formality of the embassy, and travelling in the rather important company of Sir Philip and Liz O'Malley she now was chattering, her cockney accent becoming stronger by the minute.

"So," Anjali said. "Your real name is Janet." Sparrow nodded. "Then I shall call you Janet." Sparrow grinned. "You'll be the only one then," she said. "I like being called Sparrow." Anjali decided to say nothing she would wait and see what Madame O'Malley did, that would make her decision. To Aarav however she was Sparrow.

chapter 43

Philip carried Liz up the broad staircase and, following her directions, found her room. "On the bed?" he queried. "No, the chaise, please darling." He put her down so gently that she laughed a shade reproachfully. "Oh Philip, I'm not a china doll." He smiled but said nothing, looking at the peaceful and beautiful room, from whose windows he could glimpse the delightful views she had described so vividly.

"Isn't it beautiful here?" she almost whispered, partly telling herself and wanting confirmation from Philip. He turned away from the window, his face lit with a smile. "It certainly is, my darling!"

Anjali arrived with the tea tray and Aarav's home-baked cookies. Liz felt a peace and contentment and knew in her heart that now she would get strong again.

The household settled quickly into its new routine. Philip slept in the best guest room for the moment and Sparrow was happily ensconced on the top floor. Anjali, who had been shocked at her mistress's appearance, was happy to see a little colour returning to her wan face. Aarav was full of inventive ideas to tempt her with delicious morsels and, although she still struggled to regain her appetite, she was finding at last her pleasure in mealtimes returning.

Philip was up early every morning and having "met" Coco and Guinness, he decided he had no choice but to exercise them. He was unused to the saddle Liz had bought, but found on closer acquaintance he rather liked it. He soon resolved that he must find a horse of his own as he needed a horse more suited to his height. He and Liz talked it over and Liz decided she would like to buy him a horse as a wedding present. She was still overwhelmed by his constant concern for her – the hammock being a case in point.

The morning after they had arrived, and after her first proper night's sleep for weeks if not months, she wanted nothing more than to lie in the garden. Sparrow, who had settled into the household with amazing ease, helped her with her ablutions and re-dressed her legs.

When Liz confided that she would like to be in the garden on the hammock, but it would need something on it to make it more comfortable, Sparrow had gone to find Anjali. "You ask Sir Philip to carry Madame downstairs and into the garden, and she will see for herself the hammock needs nothing," Anjali had said. Sparrow repeated the conversation to Liz and Philip, who had just joined them, smiled and said nothing, but picked Liz up and carried her downstairs and outside. Sparrow followed, intrigued.

They made a small procession, Philip and Liz with Sparrow following and Anjali bringing up the rear. "Oh look, Philip, look at my lovely new hammock." Liz exclaimed. He laid her carefully on the silk-lined hammock with its colourful soft cushions. "What absolute bliss," she said, settling herself comfortably. "How did this come about?" she queried.

"Sir Philip," Anjali said quickly, "and Nina has the original one." Liz looked up at Philip gratefully.

"You spoil me," she said happily.

"I have a number of years to catch up with!"

So the daily routine began to take shape. Philip's early rides. Breakfast together in her bedroom, whilst Sparrow ate with Anjali and Aarav. Then Philip would disappear while Sparrow helped Liz. Liz would then be carried to the hammock. Philip would stay for a while, then go off on his mysterious trips. He was, he would say, looking for a horse or just finding his way around.

He visited Bernadette and Shantaram. He visited Father Julian and the school. The more he saw the more he understood Liz's feelings for the place. He talked with Ashok and met the enchanting Nina and the children. He admired the stables with their cooling fans. He started talking about an extension for his own horse. He acquired a dog who he had found on the beach in a pitiful condition. Lady had been a bony, flea-ridden bitch, whose body was heavily weighed down by numerous pregnancies and was dragging herself around with a prolapsed vagina.

His first thought was that he would take her to a vet and have her put out of her misery, but her soft brown beseeching eyes made him want to give her a chance of a happier life. Now, like a shadow, she followed him everywhere. An operation had dealt with the prolapse and neutering meant she would no longer have to contend with regular pregnancies. The flea problem no longer existed and, with regular food, for the first time in her life, her coat of dry, short brown hair took on a softer feel and gleamed with health.

She was shy except with Philip – with him she became a puppy again. It was as if the puppy in her had never had the opportunity to exist when she was one, and now she was recapturing what she should have enjoyed a few years earlier. She would roll over and pretend to bite his hand when he stroked her. She would lie by his feet if he was reading – or run with him on the beach when he was riding one of Liz's horses. Liz watched the pair with delight, wondering what Jack and Jamie would think of their relaxed father when they came home for Christmas.

She lay in the hammock one morning, feeling particularly happy and relaxed. She had walked to the hammock this morning, and perhaps even more exciting, had walked down the stairs. She could almost feel her body filling out again; her appetite which had been so poor had now returned and she found herself looking forward to mealtimes again instead of dreading them.

Philip was on one of his mysterious outings. He had bought a Mercedes as he said they needed two cars now, as there would be times when they might both need a car. Before he had purchased the car though, he had gone with Ashok to Anjuna, they had taken Sparrow too.

It was a welcome day off that Liz insisted she should have, and the market was somewhere she should visit. Philip had heard that on Wednesdays on the four-acre site everything could be found.

"Everything?" he questioned, when Ashok explained the market to him.

"Yes, sir."

"Even horses?" Ashok looked thoughtful for a moment or two.

"I have seen horses," he said slowly. Intrigued, Philip decided it would be an interesting experience for him and Sparrow and off they had gone, leaving Liz to enjoy a rest under the waving palms.

Liz lay looking upwards, watching the palm fronds move like great ostrich feathers. She had a feeling of deja vu. A rook cawed overhead and she looked expectantly towards the foot of the hammock, almost expecting to see her horses standing there, nodding their heads in unison.

As if on cue, Anjali came towards her, carrying a tray with two tall glasses of lemonade and over her arm she carried a blue pashmina. Liz almost pinched herself – this had happened before. She lay mesmerised as Anjali drew closer putting the tray on the small round table that stood near the hammock.

"Has someone come to visit?" Liz heard herself ask. She knew she had said this before.

"No Madame, if you don't mind, I thought we might share a glass of lemonade together."

"Oh, Anjali, as if I'd mind." There was silence, a restful silence, between the two women.

"Anjali—"

"Madame—" they both spoke, and laughed lightly at their speaking together. Anjali waited respectfully. Finally, Liz spoke in a slightly puzzled voice. "Have we done this before, Anjali, and did you put your pashmina over me when I was cold?" Anjali gave a deep sigh. "Only in my dreams, Madame O'Malley," she paused. "What do you mean?" Liz asked. As she asked the question Liz felt somewhere within her a stirring memory of grasping a hand – of Anjali being by her side.

"When you were ill, in a coma, and we all feared for your life, I sat here often by the old hammock, thinking of you and letting my mind travel to where you were. In my mind I saw the bed and the white sheet over you – I knew you were cold – so in my mind, I covered you with the pashmina you gave me. You held out your hand."

"Like this?" Liz said, stretching out her hand.

"Like that," repeated Anjali, taking it.

"I knew I was fortunate to have you as my friend," Liz said very slowly. Anjali held the warm hand in hers, so different from the cold one she had held in her head. The two women's eyes met in wonder. "How is this, how?" Liz began, then paused. Perhaps one should not question how it was – just

278

accept that it was, that it had been, that they, through deep affection, had connected many thousands of miles apart. They released hands, but knew as they did so, that neither would ever speak of this again; they knew that they had been together in some mysterious communication of their minds.

*

Philip, Sparrow and Ashok returned home in high spirits. Ashok driving Sparrow in the car and Philip driving an open-topped truck that barely looked roadworthy. Standing in the back, wearing an expression of bewilderment was a sight that Liz would never forget, was the tallest, gangliest-looking horse she had ever seen.

As Philip led him off the truck, down a hastily found plank, the horse seemed to be all uncontrollable limbs. At the sound of the vehicle, Liz had eased herself out of the hammock and leaning heavily on walking sticks, which she hated, made her way very slowly to the site of all the noise. Sparrow hastily fetched a small garden chair and, from this spot, Liz sat rocking with laughter – the tears pouring down her face.

The scene was like some carefully planned farce. First, the horse wouldn't move, then when he did, the plank moved and he slipped and wobbled with it, almost falling on Philip, who, despite Liz's laughter, seemed immensely serious and so completely engrossed that it set Liz off again.

Finally, the horse was known henceforth, Philip informed his semi-hysterical fiancée, as Black Beauty. The iconic name for such an emaciated creature set Liz off again. Philip attempted to be dignified about the whole affair, and appear aloof and untouched by her laughter.

At last Black Beauty was on terra firma – a tattered rope his only accompaniment. Ashok fetched a spare head collar from the stables, where two curious horses watched their new stablemate with apparently bored indifference.

"What—" Liz began, before laughter overcame her. "What are you proposing to do with 'that'?" She pointed her finger in the direction of the new acquisition. "That," Philip replied sternly. "That is my horse, Black Beauty, and I'll thank you to show him some respect!" This time Philip joined in the laughter too, and Sparrow who had disappeared into the house reappeared with Aarav.

The horse was still trembling and Liz started looking at him more carefully. Despite his very poor condition, he had a good shape. His legs were good and his back straight and firm looking. "How old?" she asked. "His teeth suggest seven to eight," Philip replied. "He will be a good ride one day, really, Elizabeth," he added, seeing her sceptical expression.

Liz and Black Beauty seemed to grow stronger together. The nervous animal was responding to kindness, food and, Liz discovered, conversation! Whenever Philip was out she would make her way slowly to the stables. A chair conveniently left there meant she could rest and talk quietly to the horse. She always talked to Coco and Guinness first who could wander freely out of their stable with a slight push on the hinged doors. They seemed not at all "put out" by their mistress's interest in their new stable companion and the more time she spent with all three horses the more she longed to ride again.

It was only a matter of weeks before Philip rode Black Beauty for the first time. It was, he explained, merely a gentle amble – but he sensed that Black Beauty also enjoyed walking in the sea, which to Sparrow's astonishment would, he told her, strengthen the horse's legs. "Of course Sir Philip," said Sparrow. "Why didn't I think of it earlier? We must get Liz in the water too!"

Sparrow was falling in love. It was all too much, and although she sensed feelings from him too, he neither indicated or encouraged. She wrote an outpouring letter to Sarah, her ex-flatmate in Phoenix, explaining that she didn't want to compromise her position with Liz, who, incidentally, was doing so well she would soon be fit enough to sit astride a horse for a quiet amble along the beach and go into the sea for a regular swim. Sparrow went into details about how she had watched Philip ride, or "Sir" as she referred to him in her letters, and was trying to pluck up the courage to ask him if he could teach her.

Before she had even received a reply from Sarah, she woke early one morning and, on a sudden impulse, pulled on a pair of cotton capris and a tee shirt, and arrived at the stables as Philip was putting a head collar on the ever sleeker, good-looking Black Beauty. "My goodness, Sparrow, it's even early for a sparrow!" They both laughed at his feeble joke.

"I wondered," she began hesitantly. "If I could learn to ride?" Philip looked at her, not surprised in any way, almost as if he had been expecting it. "Anyone who wants to learn can learn," he replied gently. "Is this morning too soon?" Sparrow felt her heart race. "No, I mean, yes, I mean I'd like that very much," she could hardly form her words her excitement was so great. "Hold this," Philip handed her the fine rope rein attached to Black Beauty's head collar. "I'll get Guinness, I think, yes," he continued, almost thinking aloud.

If Guinness was surprised, he also seemed pleased, in moments his head collar was in place as was a rope rein they used when taking the horses in the sea. "Are your clothes alright to get wet?" Sparrow nodded, barely able to speak with excitement. Philip gave her a leg up and there she was – sitting bareback on a beautiful horse in India about to walk on a beach and into the sea.

The two walked side by side down the sandy path to the beach. The sun was just coming up, the beach their own apart from the crows cawing and an occasional buzzard wheeling overhead too. They walked the horses for a while then Philip suggested a gentle canter. "Just relax," he said. "Feel the horse's body movements and try and move with him. If you feel nervous hold on to his mane."

After the first few seconds when she thought she was terrified she realised she was not! She imagined herself to be a young Red Indian bravely riding his pony across the American plains. After a few moments, she stopped clutching the mane and sat more upright, feeling the beautiful motion beneath her. She heard a laugh and realised she was laughing and crying for sheer joy.

Philip watched with some amazement. He had not expected this, she was a "natural". Without a word, he turned Black Beauty towards the beckoning waves that lapped the beach. Guinness followed and Sparrow felt the water creeping up her legs as the horse went in deeper and deeper. She screamed in sheer delight. Philip found himself laughing too, her youth and exuberance quite enchanting. If it hadn't been for Liz he could imagine himself falling for this little sparrow.

Now the horses, along with Coco who had decided to join them, were swimming, and Sparrow slipped off Guinness's back into the sea, holding onto his head collar from time to time. "Get back on now," she heard Sir Philip say and she slid easily onto her horse's back, and they turned towards the shore and were soon cantering in ankle-deep water as they made their way back along the beach.

They pulled up the horses to walk along the sandy path to the stables. For once, Sparrow was unusually quiet. Her feelings were overwhelming her. She didn't think, she knew, that she had just had the experience of a lifetime and, a bit like the first time she had had sex, she knew it was an experience that would stay with her. It was not the end of something but the beginning.

She slid off Guinness, her clothes already drying on her. "Can I do that again please?" she asked like a small child asking for another piece of cake. "You can, little Sparrow, and once you are really confident, or more confident even than this morning, then we shall both bring Liz out for a swim. Say a week from now?" Philip asked. Sparrow held out her hand.

"A week from now, Sir Philip." They shook hands to seal the bargain.

At breakfast with Anjali and Aarav, Sparrow could hardly contain herself. She described in some detail how she rode and swam and Philip's name occurred in every sentence. "He is so great with the horses"; "He told me exactly what to do"; "You should see him in the sea"; 'what a man".

Aarav was quiet and, finally, Sparrow seemed to realise. She looked into his eyes and saw a longing and an anguish and realised, for the first time, that her feelings for him were reciprocated, and he thought she fancied Sir Philip!

"Aarav," she said, gently reaching her hand across the table to him. "I wish you had been with me instead of Sir Philip – it would have been so much more special." If Anjali was surprised she didn't indicate it, just looked from one to the other. Aarav smiled, his white teeth gleaming against his dark skin. Sparrow thought he looked beautiful and longed to put her arms around him, but even holding hands across the table in front of Anjali was a statement of intent, almost like a public announcement.

"Come on, children," Anjali spoke more sharply than she meant to. "Let's clear away and get on with things." Automatically the two young people started clearing things away and, after a few moments, Anjali left them. They stood looking at each other. "I love you, Aarav," Sparrow said softly.

"I love you, Sparrow – I have since the moment I saw you." He put his hand on her face, his fingers moving over her lips, outlining them as if he wanted to memorise their shape. He cupped her face with his hands, the brown against her lightly tanned skin was warm and gentle. "We will talk this afternoon," he said finally. "When we are both free." Sparrow leaned forward to touch his mouth lightly with hers. "Until this afternoon," she said slowly, then turned and left the room, leaving a stunned Aarav amid an array of breakfast debris.

chapter 44

Philip was entertaining Liz with the story of Sparrow's first ride and swim. "She must be a natural," was Liz's reaction. "To ride bareback like that."

"We've made a pact," Philip continued. "This time next week it is you as well."

"I don't know about that," Liz demurred.

"No question my darling, it's in the sea for you. It will help strengthen your leg muscles no end." Liz looked dubious. "I'm not a horse Philip!"

"No sweetheart, but you have muscles as they do and both being on horseback and swimming in the sea could be just what the doctor ordered. In this case, I am the doctor and Sparrow the nurse."

*

Sparrow and Aarav spent the afternoon together. It was then she discovered that he had yearned for her as she had for him. "I want to marry you Sparrow, but I am nothing. My family is poor, I am only a cook and you are English and so beautiful."

Sparrow looked at him thoughtfully. "I have no family," she said. "I am only a nurse, but I knew, like you, almost from the first that I loved you. I want to marry you too." They clung together – a tenderness and sweetness filled her – she had never felt like this before. His smile, so gentle, made her smile – his touch, so caring, made her want to care for him the same. She didn't see the colour of his skin, it was Aarav – the man she had come across the world to find. The man she wanted to spend her life with.

They talked of past liaisons which seemed meaningless but important to air. They kissed tenderly at first but mounting passion made their kisses deeper and stronger. "I must marry you quickly," he said. "It will be difficult to wait now I know you care." She tried to tell him they didn't have to wait and found she had shocked him. "I want you to be my wife. I will respect you." He sounded so solemn and earnest that Sparrow had to try very hard not to laugh. "Then we must marry soon," she said smiling happily.

That evening as Sparrow ate dinner with Philip and Liz, Sparrow told them her news. "But that is wonderful, darling Sparrow, you won't leave us now," Liz said.

"Aarav is a lucky man," Philip said, remembering his brief thoughts when they were riding. He looked at Liz – his adorable, brave and beautiful Elizabeth and felt a pang of guilt that he had ever, however momentarily, had thoughts of another woman.

"Do ask Arrav and Anjali to come in and bring some champagne." Liz looked at Sparrow as she spoke. The girl sprang to her feet with alacrity and soon the four of them were sipping champagne and toasting the young couple.

Only Anjali had a frown that Liz was quick to notice. Drawing her aside she asked what the trouble was. "Where will they live Madame O'Malley? Arrav might leave us for a big hotel where they get accommodation." A shadow crossed Liz's face. "That would be awful. I know," she said, after a brief pause and smiling again. "We will knock two of the smaller rooms on the top floor together making them a bedroom and two others to make a sitting room. Arrav and Sparrow have a bathroom there already and there is still one tiny room which could be a nursery if one is needed!"

"Um," Anjali looked unconvinced. Liz clapped her hands for attention and then announced that the top floor would be converted into a self-contained flat for the young couple as a wedding present from Sir Philip and herself. Sparrow was thrilled. "With my own little kitchen too?" Liz hadn't thought of that, she looked at Philip who raised his eyebrows as if to say"this is your baby". "I didn't think of that." Liz looked worried and Philip wisely chose that moment to whisk her into his arms and carry a suddenly tired Liz up to her bedroom.

"Stay with me, Philip." It was as if the young had awoken her own longings.

"Are you sure? Are you ready? Are you strong enough?"

"I won't know if I don't try," she said, almost in a whisper. He helped her undress, she showered as he sat in her chair by the window. Once she was in bed he had a hasty shower himself and then slid between the sheets to lie close to the woman he loved.

At first, they just held each other. The warmth and feel of his arms around her comforted and strengthened her. He felt her still fragile body but sensed her indomitable inner strength. They lay, almost drifting off to sleep, then, as they relaxed, their longings grew and finally, tenderly, he loved her as she had never been loved before. She responded to his every touch – her body seeming to come alive as if by the sensitivity of his lovemaking. Finally, they relaxed again, kissing each other in loving appreciation. He left her and returned to his own room. His head buzzing. Now is the time, he thought, to make marriage plans.

A week had passed. Liz was on Coco, Sparrow on Guinness and Philip on Black Beauty. Sparrow's skills had come on apace and she longed to have Liz in the water swimming with the horses. The sand was still difficult for Liz to walk on, so the horses were the obvious way to the sea. It was pleasant in the early morning, the sun just rising as the three horses made their way slowly along the beach. No canters today – just a steady even pace before heading towards the sea.

This time it was Liz who screamed with delight as the water slowly moved up her body. Finally, she slipped into the sea and into Philip's arms. Together they moved their legs to keep afloat and, her smile, Philip thought, if it could be bottled, was pure gold.

Sparrow swam around to see if all was well and felt she had interrupted a lovers' idyll. They were so immersed in each other they seemed to have forgotten she was there too. She swam away and climbed on Guinness's back heading slowly for the shore.

Liz didn't need her anymore. She felt a pang of regret muted only by the knowledge that she had Aarav, but what was she to do with her life. She turned, Liz and Philip had remounted and were following her out of the sea, she sensed they were alone in their private world, and with her new confidence on horseback, pushed Guinness into a canter along the beach towards home, leaving the lovers on their own.

They talked about their wedding – Jack would be best man and Jamie would give the bride away. At least, Liz suggested, they should be asked if they would like to accept their proposed roles. Father Julian would take the ceremony. The guests would be limited to close family and local friends and staff. A marquee in the garden and an evening wedding.

Aarav would arrange a superb banquet. It was all perfectly straightforward and Christmas would be the ideal time.

*

A Christmas wedding, Aarav and Sparrow thought, would be perfect. By then the alterations on the top floor would be completed. Aarav was a Christian so he wanted Father Julian to take the service. Aarav's brother would be best man and just friends and staff would be invited. Sarah was to come over to be the bridesmaid. Yes a Christmas wedding would be perfect.

Later that evening, Sparrow asked Liz if she could talk to her privately. She began by saying she felt she was no longer needed in her nursing capacity at Villa O'Mal, but that she would try and find work at the local hospital. Meanwhile, she and Aarav wanted to get married at Christmas and she gave their reasons.

She was surprised and a bit taken aback when Liz laughed and clapped her hands in apparent glee. "It's so funny," she said, still laughing happily. "We, Sir Philip and I, have decided exactly the same thing. Why don't we have a double wedding?" Liz spoke without thinking. *What would Philip think?* her mind was saying, while the smile on her face became a little fixed. "Oh Liz, that would be wonderful – I'm sure Aarav will agree."

"Let's talk to our men and let them decide to agree," Liz suggested carefully. Sparrow nodded understandingly. "What a good idea," she answered. So that is how it was left.

Surprisingly, both men agreed, so wedding plans were at the forefront of every conversation. Meanwhile, Sparrow visited the hospital and had been welcomed with open arms. The pay compared with her current salary was a joke but she lived free and Aarav had a good wage and the accommodation of course.

Sparrow was impressed with her bank account, for the first time she had been able to save and she felt confident that she would be able to have a beautiful wedding gown and purchase some new things for "the flat" as it was already being called.

As it was to be a joint wedding Aarav would not be doing the catering, but instead, Liz's friends, the manager and his wife at the Taj Hotel, insisted the Taj would be honoured to do the catering.

Sarah had written to Sparrow, saying she would be thrilled to be the bridesmaid. Liz's sister and agent were coming. Kathy also said she insisted on being a bridesmaid. Ronnie and Tim were on the moderate guest list and Jack and Jamie apparently couldn't wait for Christmas. Jack had settled in well at Cambridge and Jamie would be leaving school before long.

Liz and Sparrow had numerous discussions and fittings with the tailor who had made Liz's dresses for the embassy functions which seemed a lifetime away, and both women loved their own and each other's choices. It was, after all, only two months away.

Invitations were sent out and, although the wedding was modest, Philip felt they should include one or two obligatory Foreign Office ones and, on the off chance, also sent one to Julia who was these days as much a friend as the Prime Minister. She had recently written to Philip requesting that he become a sort of roving Ambassador. Spending time in troubled spots – acting as a mediator to endeavour to prevent local situations of tension exploding into something more dangerous.

After some serious conversations with Liz, Philip decided to accept. He felt he needed the mental stimulation even though sometimes it would mean they would be apart. For her part, Liz thought it would provide her with the opportunity she needed to get on with her writing, which due to the accident had suffered somewhat of late.

Wedding gifts started to arrive and, after some serious debate, Liz and Philip decided on a generous cheque for Sparrow and Aarav, enough for them to buy their own home when, and if, they wanted to. As Liz said, they may well at some point have a family and the upstairs apartment would not be suitable in the long term.

Liz and Philip wanted for nothing, but the thoughtfulness of some of the gifts that came their way was touching. A new saddle and bridle for Black Beauty – who really lived up to his name these days. It was a gift from the management team at the Taj Hotel. The boys had clubbed together and commissioned Ashok to arrange for a beach shelter with chairs and table for when their father and Liz wanted to watch the sunsets and sunrises after they had ridden, or just to walk to at times for a peaceful "away from it all" venue.

Julia announced she was going "batty" trying to tie in attending their wedding with a visit to Pakistan to meet the new Premier.

Liz and Sparrow talked endlessly about fabrics and design and decided their dresses must complement each other. With very different figures their dresses would be personal to each of them but they decided they would both wear cream silk. The bridegrooms would wear lightweight dinner jackets and women guests would wear long summery gowns as there was to be dancing.

The boys arrived from England. Liz welcomed her soon to be sons with her usual affection and Philip, so relaxed these days, hugged them both warmly.

The wedding day finally arrived. The previous weeks had seen major changes to the top floor and now an attractive apartment with a luxuriously appointed kitchen and bathroom, a sitting/dining room and bedroom existed where once a series of rooms stood, for the most part unused.

To say that Sparrow and Aarav were surprised by the generosity of the cheque was an understatement and already Aarav was talking about building their own home in a few years, just as Liz had surmised.

Liz was getting steadier on her feet, hardly ever using her wheelchair. She was nervous about the walk down the aisle but she would have Jamie to lean on and was determined to walk to where Philip would be waiting. Father Julian had talked to both couples at length about the service and it was decided to do it in two parts – Sparrow and Aarav getting married first, followed by Liz and Philip. This would mean a shorter time at the altar steps and also give each bride the personal pleasure of walking down the aisle alone.

The day dawned, Liz had breakfast in bed, brought by a beaming Anjali. The day was to be spent being pampered. Both brides were to have a massage, pedicure and manicure. Their hair would be washed and arranged, and finally at five p.m. the dresses would be put on.

The men, for their part, were banished and rightly decided to go their own ways. Philip, Ronnie, Tim and the boys went to the golf club. After nine holes, Philip used the gym and had a massage. Then he sat with his sons and the other two, talking, eating a light lunch and then, finally, being taken to the Taj hotel, where he had been assigned a room so that there was no risk in him bumping into his bride.

He finally met his sons at the bar for a quick drink before Jamie shot off with Ashok, who had come to collect him and take him back to Villa O'Mal. Liz, supported by Anjali, walked carefully down the stairs. Jamie, waiting for her at the foot of the stairs, whistled as he saw her. "Oh, you look wonderful," he said, feeling very proud that he and Jack had helped to bring Liz into their father's life.

Her shining black hair had grown back and it hung, as

it always had, completely hiding the nearly faded scar. The cream dress skimmed her body – showing her slender frame. Several oleander flowers formed a small posy and, as she reached the foot of the stairs, Jamie leaned towards her and kissed her cheek. "Wow, Mother dear. I'd marry you myself if Dad would let me."

"How nice," said Liz with a happy smile.

The car, with Ashok driving carefully, trying hard to avoid the inevitable bumps, arrived only five minutes late at the church. Sparrow, already there and ready for her walk up the aisle, gave a relieved smile. "You are not going to believe it Liz – I was here early!"

"Are our men here?"

"Yes, bless them, looking a lot more nervous than us." Liz sank gratefully into a chair that had been placed strategically for her use.

The music began and Sparrow walked slowly and gracefully down the aisle with Ronnie acting as her escort. The ceremony began and finished, and a beamingly happy Sparrow, now accompanied by a proud and happy-looking Aarav, walked back down the aisle to where Liz still sat.

Now, it was her turn. Jamie could feel her trembling. He squeezed the arm that was resting on his. "Come on Liz, you can do it." Liz gave him a tremulous smile as the music began playing. Philip, waiting at the front of the church, watched a shade anxiously. She had walked this far and more, but today, with the added emotion, he felt his heart missed a beat knowing how hard she would be trying.

She walked slowly and carefully – looking ahead to the man she loved. He was willing her to walk to him. She couldn't, she couldn't – her legs began to weaken. Jamie felt her weight on his arm and released his arm so that he could put it around her waist. There was a pause, every eye seemed to be on her, willing her forward again. She took a deep breath, removed Jamie's arm, and started to move forward again. There was a collective breath of relief from the congregation of guests as she arrived at the altar steps. Philip smiled, he loved her so much and felt so proud of her. He held out his hand and she took it, squeezing it as she did.

"I did it," she said. "I am here to marry you at last."

I do hope you have enjoyed reading my fourth book *The Portuguese House*.

Please consider writing a review on Amazon and or Goodreads. Reviews are so important to authors and so much appreciated.

Thank you.

 Matador